2012: *The Eternal Night*

*To Danielle
Hope you enjoy it.*

by

Richard Jones

Grosvenor House
Publishing Limited

This book is published by
Grosvenor House Publishing Ltd
28-30 High Street, Guildford, Surrey, GU1 3HY.
www.grosvenorhousepublishing.co.uk

A CIP record for this book
is available from the British Library

ISBN 978-1-907652-67-7

ACKNOWLEDGEMENTS

This book would not be possible without the time and patience of my wife Jillian who encouraged me to write it and spent many long hours proof-reading and editing the final draft.

The artwork for the cover was by Richey Beckett
www.richeybeckett.com

Dedicated to the Memory of Mary Price

1934 to 2008

PROLOGUE

The Legend:

In the time before Columbus set sail for the New World an evil lay at the heart of the Americas. Human sacrifices gave souls for the armies of Hell; only Lucifer's plan was delayed when the altars were destroyed.

But his return is assured when the Morning Star shall rebel against the Light and darkness will rise from the centre of the heavens and descend upon the Earth.

*

The Truth:

On the 21st December 2012 at precisely 11.11 Coordinated Universal Time the Earth and the Sun form an alignment with the centre of our galaxy, in an area of the Milky Way known as The Dark Rift.

The Mayans and Aztecs called this area of darkness the Black Road, the point at which all souls passed on to the afterlife. Time ceases for them on the day of the galactic alignment.

In 2008, after sixteen years of observing this area of space, German astronomers confirmed the fact that existing at the galactic centre is a black hole many millions of times larger than our own Sun and around which the galaxy revolves.

Out of this specific – and imminent – date for the end of time has arisen a host of eschatological theories from a diverse section of human cultures and different historical periods. Science now confirms this day as the day when the Dark Rift and Earth face each other, perfectly aligned.

It is believed this day will herald Armageddon - the final battle between good and evil.

It will be the beginning of Apocalypse.

THE CALL

January 1275,
England:

Many times had he passed through this part of the forest, but this was the first time he felt fear. Somewhere among the trees evil followed him.

His pace quickened in time with his heartbeat until he broke into a run. The only noise he could hear, although he was hardly aware of it, was the snap of dead wood under his feet and the crunching of the thick morning frost as his feet thumped down onto the forest floor. There was a path, he knew, just ahead and he ran for all his worth toward it.

"Hey!" The old friar stepped aside as the young man burst out of the trees and onto the path.

He turned to face the friar, beads of sweat glistening on his brow despite the cold air of a January morning.

"Sorry Brother," he said looking back into the forest and wondering what sounds and shadows had terrified him so completely.

"Are you Graeme the Woodchopper?" asked the friar, his stooped emaciated frame shivered under the grey Franciscan habit.

"Yes," replied the young man, a puzzled expression crossing his face. "What do you want?"

"Is there somewhere a little warmer where we can speak?"

"Of course, we can speak in my hut."

It was a fairly short walk along the path before the two men entered a clearing. The Woodchopper was glad of the company as they walked back and the friar was glad to see Graeme's hut standing invitingly at the far end of the clearing.

"You go in and I'll get some logs," said the Woodchopper. "Once we've settled you can tell me why you've come out here to see me."

The friar entered the dim interior of the hut and eagerly began to clear the old ash from the hearth. It wasn't long before the crackling of the logs could be heard and Graeme set about warming up some oats.

The friar moved closer to the fire and as he held his hands toward the warmth of the flames he began to speak. "Have you heard of The Legend of the Eternal Night?"

✳

December 1273,
Rome:

Cardinal Caronni was lost in thought as he walked out of the papal gardens. He had expected words of reassurance from the Holy Father when he told him of his vision, but Pope Gregory only confirmed his fears.

"We do not publicly acknowledge the validity of the Legend of the Eternal Night, but we believe it to be true." Those were the words the Cardinal had not wanted to hear.

"You must follow your vision and find the Scroll of Explanation," the Holy Father had said. The Cardinal left for Cassino the following morning.

He had been celebrating Mass in Naples seven days earlier when he received a vision of a messenger; one who told him an ancient scroll would arrive at the Abbey at the top of the hill at Cassino during Advent. Leaving Naples at the earliest opportunity he did not stop at the Abbey, but hurried on to Rome and his meeting with the Pope.

✳

Two days after leaving Rome the Cardinal arrived at Monte Cassino with his attendant. From its high vantage point the abbey dominated the surrounding countryside. He knew this monastery was special. It was here St Benedict laid down the rules of monasticism.

From the window of his apartment the Abbot held a commanding view of the approach road to the monastery and it was through this window he saw the two figures approaching on horseback. He made his way down to the main gate to meet them.

It was not without some surprise he greeted his unexpected guests. "Your Eminence," he said bowing as the Cardinal removed his wide brimmed red hat. "I was not informed that we would be receiving such an esteemed visitor."

"There was no time to notify you of my intentions." The Cardinal spoke abruptly and with the assurance of one used to exercising his authority. "I am here to take possession of a package."

"I am unaware that we have anything that would be of use to you."

"I will know it when I see it," replied the Cardinal impatiently. "Please arrange for our horses to be fed and watered. Dusk will soon be upon us and they need to be bedded down."

"Of course you may take whatever you wish from here," said the Abbot signalling for one of the monks to attend to the animals.

The taller man turned toward his guest and held his arm out as an invitation for the Cardinal to walk with him. Both men were in their sixtieth decade, but the Abbot was of medium height and build with a slight stoop born of many years spent at study, which contrasted sharply with the Cardinal. He had a thick set powerful physique hidden under his cardinal's robes and carried himself with the upright stance of a military man rather than the bowed reverence of a man of God.

"You may have use of my rooms for your stay here your Eminence. I will show you the way." The two figures made their way toward the Abbot's apartments.

✻

Cardinal Caronni did not sleep well that night. In his dreams he was celebrating Mass and while consecrating the elements he suddenly found himself at a different altar. This altar was high atop a pyramid in a far away jungle. It was not a golden chalice or plate he held in his hand, but a knife and it was not the transubstantiated wine that flowed, but the blood of countless slaughtered innocents.

As he raised his hands to elevate the Host he awoke abruptly. Sitting upright in his bed, he realised that he was sweating profusely despite the cold December air. The image of the still beating heart of the sacrificed child remained vivid in his mind, the sticky warmth of the blood left a memory stain on his hands.

Caronni began to shiver as the perspiration dried against his skin. He rose and walked to the small table in the corner of the room and picking up a piece of cloth he began to dry himself. He felt around for an oil lamp and found one at the bedside table. Lighting the lamp he noticed a large piece of parchment on the floor at the side of the bed.

The reverberating beat of his heart quickened and resonated through his head as he realized that this parchment was not there when he went to bed – it was the Scroll of Explanation.

✳

At daybreak the Cardinal went to the refectory for breakfast. He ate sparingly and advised the Abbot he would be returning to his rooms for the rest of the day.

Opening out the scroll Caronni gazed in awe at the detailed ideograms laid out before him. The pictorial tale told of a mighty army being amassed in Hell, recruited from the souls of the slaughtered. This army would grow until two thousand and twelve years after the First Coming when, on the day of the Winter Solstice the Morning Star would rise and lead the army of the sacrificed out toward humanity. With the Seat of Light eclipsed, millions of screaming souls will pour out from the void unopposed and the Earth will be engulfed by the darkness.

Cardinal Caronni was jolted from his meditations on the scroll by a rap on the door. "What?" Exclaimed the Cardinal, irritated by the intrusion.

"I beg your pardon your Eminence, but there's someone here I think you should see."

Standing with the Abbot was a very large man, approximately twenty stone in weight, dressed in the habit of a Dominican. The Cardinal immediately recognised the friar standing before him. "Thomas it is good to see you."

"And you your Excellency."

"Come in. Come in."

Thomas followed the Cardinal into the sparsely furnished room. The two men walked toward a large oak table situated near the furthest wall.

"What brings you to Monte Cassino?" enquired the Cardinal.

"A few days ago I was celebrating the Mass of Saint Nicholas in Naples when such things were revealed that made me think that all I have written seems like straw now," replied Thomas. "There is no way that we, ignorant and sinful creatures that we are, can learn to understand God through our own faulty logic and limited powers of reason." Thomas Aquinas took a deep breath. "I have decided to write no more."

The Cardinal looked puzzled. "You have finished the Summa Theologica?"

"No," Thomas replied. "It will not be completed by me."

"But by who then, if not you?" The Cardinal spoke with some concern.

"What we do is of little importance when held up against the light of eternity, our lives no more than a flutter of a sparrow's wing in the infinite winds of the cosmos."

Placing his hands on the table, the Cardinal stared off into the distance. He sighed then began to speak once more. "Now is not the time to discuss these matters. I too have been subject to revelation and mystery."

As he spoke Caronni unravelled the scroll onto the tabletop. "It was also a divine revelation during Mass at Naples that brought me hurrying to this place. Last night further visions were granted to me in a dream. On awakening I found this scroll."

The Cardinal unfurled the scroll and placed it on the table, each man grabbing one end. The two men studied the faded parchment in silence for what seemed like an eternity. On finally breaking out of their private reflections, Thomas began to offer an interpretation.

"It is Lucifer. He must be the Morning Star. He is referred to in Sacred Scripture as the Son of the Morning." Thomas pointed at the sacrifice ideogram. "There must be somewhere here on Earth where this heathen, savage ritual is consigning souls to the armies of Hell."

"I did not recognise the landscape in my dream. I recall looking out over vast forests from the top of the sacrificial altar." The Cardinal shuddered as he recalled the throbbing heart he had held in his hand.

Thomas continued. "If this prophecy is fulfilled total darkness will reign; even Christ, the Light of the World, will be extinguished. However, these last few drawings offer hope. The temples of death are destroyed in this one and the cross of Christ replaces the altars of blood. Here a man with a woodcutter's axe stands at the gates of Hell."

"A woodchopper felling the armies of the damned," mused the Cardinal.

He walked to the window and looked out at the approach road to the monastery. "I have discussed my vision with the Holy Father and he too mentioned a man living in the forests of England who will be called to this battle."

Thomas ran a chubby finger along the parchment. "His name is Graeme, he is a woodchopper who works in a forest four days north of Canterbury."

"How do you know this?" asked the Cardinal.

"My vision also told me to come here to Monte Cassino today." Thomas joined the Cardinal at the window. "Did you know I began my studies here?" He didn't wait for the Cardinal to answer. "I was five years old."

"But how do you know of this Graeme the Woodchopper?"

"I heard the blowing of a horn as I was travelling here along the Appian Way," replied Thomas Aquinas. "I stopped and saw an old man with no hair and very little teeth. He was like no other man I have ever met. Despite his size and humble appearance he spoke with an authority and certainty greater even than the Holy Father."

Cardinal Caronni raised an eyebrow.

Thomas continued. "It was he who told me of the Woodchopper."

✳

Graeme the Woodchopper had spent fifteen winters living in the woods. He chopped up firewood and cut down timber for the people of the nearby settlement and supplemented this with the food he grew from a small vegetable garden at the back of his hut. There were plenty of wild animals to hunt in the woods too.

For the most part he enjoyed the solitude, but on the morning he met the friar he was thinking of the wife and children that might have been. The Woodchopper's life made it difficult to support a family, but by clearing more land he could raise some pigs and chickens, plant more crops. A melancholy look had come over his face as he considered these plans and it was then that fear overtook him.

"The Legend of the Eternal Night," repeated the friar. "Have you heard of it?"

The friar's question interrupted his thoughts and he turned to face the old man standing by the fire. "Yes." replied Graeme. "It is said that two thousand years after the birth of our Lord a darkness will rise from the centre of the heavens and descend upon us. The Morning Star will rebel against the daylight and the light shall be no more."

"That is right. In the deepest winter the gates of Hell itself will be thrown open and the forces of evil will overrun both Heaven and Earth."

"But isn't that supposed to happen hundreds of years from now?" asked the Woodchopper.

The friar changed the subject. "You looked as though you were running from something when we met this morning. Was something chasing you?"

"No. I was walking through the forest when I sensed something in the trees behind me."

"An animal?"

"I saw nothing, but my feeling of fear was so great I dared not look back." With an embarrassed look on his face Graeme continued. "I began to run."

A silence fell on the Woodchopper's hut and the friar withdrew into thought. "I feel the chill of a descending darkness," said the old man looking out into the foreboding outline of the forest. He turned back into the cabin and rested near to the fire. "Sit down. I have much to tell you," he said to the Woodchopper.

The crackling of the fire was the only sound besides the voice of the friar as he told his host the story of the Scroll of Explanation.

✳

The weak winter sunlight was disappearing fast as the old friar finished speaking. Graeme arose and walked to the small window at the front of the cabin. "I do not understand," he said.

"You have been called, my son," exclaimed the friar.

"Are you sure Aquinas meant me? Surely there are other forests? Other woodchoppers?"

"Not four days north of Cambridge." The friar walked over to Graeme and placed his hand reassuringly on the young man's shoulder. "And none with the name Graeme."

"What if I say no?"

"Who could blame you? If the scroll is correct you are on a journey to Hell."

Graeme picked up a log and walked to the fire. "But it is too soon, this army of the sacrificed will not march out of Hell for more than another seven hundred years."

"God must have His reasons and who are we to question them?" The friar sighed and then continued, "It is divine providence that has given you to us. The Cardinal and Friar Thomas travelled together to Rome after their meeting at Cassino. Thomas was summoned to the Second Council of Lyons, although he died before he could get there, but the Cardinal was given leave not to attend the Council; so he gathered together an entourage worthy of his standing, then made the long journey to Canterbury."

"The Cardinal is in Canterbury now?" Graeme knew that his days in these woods were over. He had been chosen by the Church, he could either do as they asked or he would have to flee for his life.

"His visions and dreams did not cease after he left Italy. They have now become so intense those closest to him fear for his sanity, some fear even for his life. He sent an aide to the nearby settlement and I happened to be there at the time. I was called to the man because he was taken with a fever. It was he who told me the story of the Scroll, and he who charged me with finding you. I must return to minister to him – you must come too."

After long reflection Graeme spoke. "We will leave in the morning."

✳

That night Graeme dreamt he was in a temple court. A man was teaching there when an angry crowd entered interrupting his lesson. A woman was brought in to him. Her captors accused her of adultery and demanded that she be stoned to death.

In the dream Graeme began to perspire under the desert heat. He looked over toward the teacher. The teacher drew shapes in the sand with his finger. Graeme moved forward to look at what was being written. He stepped back abruptly, ashen-faced. There upon the ground was a list of every sin he had ever committed. He looked up at a face of pure evil; the teacher's loving countenance was gone and Graeme remembered the terror he felt in the forest.

Evil spoke. "You are not worthy of this quest. Your sins consign you to Hell forever. Go there and you will not return."

✳

Somewhere beyond space and time golden wings began to unfold; "I will go to him." A jewelled hilt of a sword was slowly drawn away from the scabbard.

A gentle hand was placed tenderly on a shoulder and the movement was halted. "Not yet we must see how he responds."

❊

A ray of grey light gave some luminance to the room as Graeme awoke. He wrapped the blanket tightly around himself as he got up from the floor and walked over to the old friar asleep on the bed at the other side of the cabin. Graeme tapped him lightly on the shoulder. "I need to confess my sins before I sleep again."

❊

Within an hour the two men were travelling toward the settlement. Graeme had packed up what little belongings he had into a bundle - two tunics, some leggings, undergarments, and some provisions (salted meat and oats). He had a knife in his belt and the bundle was attached to the handle of his axe, which rested on his shoulder. The friar carried only a staff, given to him by Graeme to aid him on the journey.

By midday the settlement was in sight. The Woodchopper and the friar walked out of the wooded glade and into a cold light rain that had been falling steadily all morning. Although the woods offered some protection from the drizzle the two men were soaked to the skin.

At the centre of the settlement they could see a hut, slightly larger than the other dwellings in the village, with a large wooden cross on the roof. It was to this place of shelter that the friar led Graeme.

The church, if the hut could rightly be called that, was two and a half times longer than it was wide. There were some rows of benches either side of the centrally placed door and beyond the benches was a plain wooden altar with a large gold crucifix positioned in the middle. Beyond the altar there hung a large purple drape. The friar walked beyond the altar and held the heavy curtain aside for Graeme to pass through.

Lying on a narrow bunk was the Cardinal's assistant. Sitting on a small stool at his side was a priest, a thin man of medium height. He looked a lot older than his thirty-four years. The Woodchopper knew him to be the village priest, he had a reputation for goodness - a holy man - Graeme had received communion from the man a few times in the past.

The friar spoke first. "How is he Father?"

"His fever is much worse and he is suffering delusions. He ranted incoherently throughout the night and struggled with the strength of more than one man. I was forced to call upon the assistance of some of the men of the village to restrain him." His face contorted at the recollection. "The villagers have refused to come back here."

The Woodchopper moved a little closer to the comatose figure on the bed. "Is he possessed?"

"I fear he may be, but now he is close to death." The priest looked toward the friar. "I have given him the Last Rites."

"I will sit with him," offered the friar. "My companion here needs Absolution."

The priest walked to the other end of the church and bolted the door. He sat at the first bench on the right and beckoned Graeme to sit with him.

Graeme complied with the priest's request. Sitting down he began to speak, "Forgive me Father for I have sinned. It has been..."

In the dim, draughty ecclesiastical hut Graeme made peace with God while the friar watched the Cardinal's assistant pass on to his reward.

✻

That afternoon the priest dug a grave and performed the burial mass for the dead man. The Woodchopper and the friar were the only other persons present. In the evening they accepted the hospitality of the priest. They dried their garments by his fire and shared supper with him. They slept soundly on benches in front of the altar and awoke just after dawn. The priest added to their provisions from his alms, blessed them and wished them a safe journey. After a breakfast of bread and cheese they set out for Canterbury.

✻

It took the two men four days to reach Canterbury. They arrived late in the day, cold, tired and hungry. The Cathedral offered shelter from the elements, but the sight gave Graeme little comfort. The building was imposing and he was not used to such splendour. He looked at the large gothic tower with awe and some trepidation. Shivering he slowly entered the Cathedral; the high vaulted ceilings reached upward it seemed toward Heaven itself.

The Woodchopper sat at one of the pews, dumbstruck by the spiritual allure of the architecture and fearful of the unknown adventure that lay before him.

Out of the corner of his eye he could see the old friar talking to a monk. The monk approached him quietly and stood silently waiting for Graeme to face him. The

Woodchopper crossed himself before looking up at the hooded figure.

"Please, come with me," said the monk.

The two men walked out of the chapel and headed toward the Cardinal's rooms, Graeme looked back and saw the old friar leave. He waved and then continued to follow his guide.

The monk led him to one of the outbuildings. He pointed toward a large oak door and walked away. When Graeme knocked the Cardinal's door he was alone.

"Enter."

The voice from within sounded strained.

Graeme walked into a room, both spacious and elegantly furnished. He could see the Cardinal sitting at a large oak desk; his face looked gaunt and the red robes hung from his frame. His once-powerful physique was wasting under the strain of the incomprehensible mental and spiritual struggle he was undergoing.

"You must be Graeme the Woodchopper." This was a statement rather than a question. He beckoned for Graeme to sit on the chair opposite him at the table. Cardinal Caronni looked at him for a short while, and then spoke again. "The friar told you the tale of the scroll."

Again this was not a question, but Graeme answered anyway.

"Yes, he has told me everything. He also said your visions and nightmares continue."

Cardinal Caronni leaned forward, placing his forearms on the table as he spoke. "I have seen such horrors. I do not know whether God has shown me these things to strengthen my resolve, or if the Devil is trying to drive me out of my mind. I tell you I was witness to much killing and bloodshed in the Holy Land, but it does not compare."

He raised his forearms and placed his head in his hands with his elbows on the table.

"The hundred years before the Day of Darkness are the worse. They are truly terrible. There are wars that encompass the whole world; flying machines drop death from the skies, whole cities made into infernos hotter than hell itself. Corpse stacked upon corpse, countless millions of innocent people sent to their deaths, many millions more snuffed out before they are born; and the wars with Islam, they still continue.

I tell you even Satan himself must be surprised at how evil man becomes. Man alone will have the power to destroy all humanity. They will create weapons capable of destroying the Earth itself. They will not need God to turn their Sodoms and Gomorrahs into burning sulphur."

The Cardinal sat back in his chair, the strain and horror of remembering etched on his face.

Graeme walked across the room to a large window and stared out into the gardens below. He turned to the Cardinal and with more than a little fear in his voice said, "How do I stop all this from happening?"

"I do not know, but hidden in the horrors of the nightmares was a vision of an island. You must travel to the far west, to the lands of the Marcher Lordships because that is where you will find this island and from there you can depart to wherever this quest will take you."

"How will I know this island?"

"There is a Benedictine priory there and, by God's good grace, one of its brothers is in Canterbury at the moment."

The Cardinal rung a small bell placed at the side of the desk and a servant appeared. "Locate Brother Eulid and bring him to me."

✻

Two days later Graeme and the monk were outside the Cathedral ready to depart. There were horses and supplies for the journey and these were left in Brother Eulid's keeping as Graeme went inside for a final audience with the Cardinal.

He was surprised to find Cardinal Caronni with the Archbishop - both in full ceremonial robes - in front of the main altar.

The Cardinal gestured for Graeme to approach the altar and kneel.

The Archbishop laid his left hand on the Woodchopper's head and began to speak in Latin. "I entrust you to the care of Saint Michael to protect you, Saint Gabriel to strengthen you, Saint Raphael to heal you and may Almighty God bless you."

He raised his right hand and while making the sign of the cross he continued, "In the name of the Father and of the Son and of the Holy Spirit, Amen."

THE CROSSING

Five days out from Canterbury the two men broke camp just after dawn. They spent the night huddled under their blankets, close to a fire that had long since gone out. A cold, damp mist began to settle on the hillside as they emerged from beneath a rocky outcrop.

"If this fog gets any thicker we'll run a rope between us," said brother Eulid. "Just keep your eyes on the path. If it gets really thick then dismount, you'll be able to follow the trail better with your own feet."

The Woodchopper confirmed his compliance with a nod.

The monk led the way down toward the valley below. Slowly descending the hillside they rode into weak winter sunlight. Graeme smiled, but his pleasure was short-lived.

Brother Eulid pulled up his horse; turning toward the Woodchopper he pointed at the thick blanket of mist covering the valley. He took a rope out of his pack and tied it around his wrist. The Woodchopper did the same with the other end. Both men walked into the mist leading the horses as they went.

By the time they reached the valley floor the fog was so dense that the two travellers could barely make out the path in front of them. Graeme felt the reins tighten in his hand as his horse refused to go on. He felt the pull of the rope as his companion continued walking.

Suddenly the rope fell loose at his feet. "Brother Eulid!" he shouted. "Brother Eulid! Wait!"

The horse began to snort and stamp his feet. The oppressive fog closed in on the Woodchopper like a living presence threatening his personal space. He felt the fear rise in him, taking him back to the inexplicable terror he felt in the forest. His horse whinnied and rose up on his hind legs. Startled, the Woodchopper let go of the reins and the horse bolted into the mist; its silhouette disappeared almost instantly and the sound of the hooves fell silent soon after.

The Woodchopper walked quickly along the barely discernable path. He stopped. *"Was that a shape in the mist?"* he thought to himself. He shouted again after his companion. It felt to him like the mist itself was exuding an aura of evil and his fear forced him to quicken his pace even more. Monsters began to form in his mind.

An unearthly wail came out of the mist rooting the Woodchopper to the spot. His breathing became laboured, the shallow wheezing syncopated with the desperate rise of his thorax "Brother Eulid." His attempted cry was no more than a pitiful gasp.

"Was that another shadow in the swirling fog?" The mist moved, forming a dense black shape in front of him. His eyes formed large pools of fear on his face as they looked at the evil darkness in front of him.

"Graeme the Woodchopper."

His name had not been called. It felt like something had confirmed his existence. "I am here," he replied. He no longer felt afraid.

The mist began to rise and he saw Brother Eulid walking back toward him. The Woodchopper's legs went weak and he sat down onto the ground before he collapsed under his own trembling weight.

"Are you alright?" asked the monk. He knelt down by the Woodchopper's side.

"My horse, it bolted."

"No matter. We will rest here until the fog lifts then we will look for it."

✳

They found the carcass a few hundred yards away. The animal's head and legs were ripped from its body and the body itself had been torn to shreds. The monk heaved and spat the bile out of his mouth while the Woodchopper looked around nervously.

"We have to get out of this valley." He picked up his belongings from beside the mutilated horse. Tying the bundle to his axe he threw it across his shoulder and hurried off toward the path.

✳

Strong winds and driving rain at the time of their arrival made the final seaborne leg of the journey impossible. Not knowing how many days the storm would last Brother Eulid announced his intention to stay at the priest's house. "You are welcome to come too," he added.

"I'll look for a room elsewhere," answered the Woodchopper.

He decided to look for accommodation at one of the alehouses inside the fortified town. Taking his axe and bundle he set off alone.

The Woodchopper stooped as he walked through the door of the inn and down two steps into a low dark room. It was six yards wide and approximately ten yards to the furthest wall, although he could barely see that far in the gloom.

Tables and chairs were haphazardly arranged throughout the long narrow room. Each table had a candle, but only the ones on the occupied tables were lit.

As far as Graeme could tell, there were six people in the room including the innkeeper. Two men and a woman sat at one of the tables in the centre of the room, one man stood by the bar with the innkeeper and another man sat alone at a table at the furthest end of the bar. All stopped to look as Graeme entered the room.

"Good evening to you sir," said the innkeeper "we don't generally get visitors here at this time of year."

"I have business on the island." Replied Graeme.

"Are we thinking of taking up orders then?" There was a hint of mockery in the woman's voice. She was a short woman, a little overweight with a grubby frock that exposed an ample cleavage. "It would be a waste such a fine looking man as you giving yourself to the brothers."

The innkeeper and her two companions laughed.

"I have orders, but not of that sort – not that any of it is your business." There was a chill in the Woodchopper's reply.

"Don't take offence sir" the innkeeper's voice held no malice. "Megan there was only having some sport. Besides I try not to upset men who carry an axe on their shoulder."

"I need somewhere to stay until the weather breaks."

"Certainly sir, there's a room out back, Megan will show you the way. She can show you other things too if you're of a mind," answered the innkeeper.

"Just a room," replied Graeme curtly. "Will you serve me food as well?"

"Of course sir, come through when you're ready, I will be preparing some supper shortly."

The Woodchopper returned within the hour and sat down to eat his supper, a stew of potatoes, onions, cabbage and leeks served with some bread. Two more men had entered the inn during the time he was out of the room.

He finished his supper and was making his way to the bar to get some ale when he saw a figure at the table in a dark corner of the room. The candle was unlit at that table and he blamed this for not noticing the silhouette earlier.

An arm beckoned him from the shadow. He walked over slowly.

"Please sit." It was a woman's voice, speaking quietly, barely above a whisper. The timbre was hypnotic and the Woodchopper sat down as if compelled to comply.

"I have come to give you a choice," she said.

"A choice?"

The woman continued. "There is no need for you to continue. Evil follows you. I know you have seen it."

"How do you know this?" The Woodchopper's question revealed the anger of his response.

The woman ignored his question. "I can make it go away if you let me live with you in your forest. We can be safe from harm there."

"Who are you? What makes you think you can help me?"

The woman reached out to him. "Turn away from your quest and all will be well." Her voice reached deep into the Woodchopper and his commitment began to falter as he touched her hand.

"Let me see your face," he asked.

The candle ignited and its light surrounded the table. There was nothing outside of the illumination of the flame, all that existed was Graeme and the woman held captive in a prison of light.

She pulled back her hood to reveal a face of supernatural beauty, with hair the colour of an angel's wings and black unfathomable orbs that looked through Graeme, gazing into his very soul.

"What would you do in a woodcutter's cabin?" whispered Graeme, anxious not to break the bright bubble of serenity that enclosed them.

"Whatever you wish."

"Would we have children and a long happy life?" In his mind's eye the Woodchopper could see his family playing around the hut, sunlight pouring down into the clearing.

"Meet me on the quay as soon as you can," said the woman. She leaned forward and touched his cheek with her lips.

The light slowly faded as the dim darkness of the inn began to encroach. The Woodchopper realised that he was alone at the table and memories flooded his consciousness.

He remembered being taken to York as a child during the time of its fortification. He remembered going into the service of a nobleman and living in his house. The dream on the last night at his cabin came back vividly to him. He remembered the sins written on the ground, not just the little lies a man tells himself to get through the day, or the lustful thoughts at the sight of a woman, but also the mortal sins that threatened his immortal soul.

He remembered the time in his youth when he lived at the nobleman's court. It was here he learned to read and write. His future looked good as a favoured servant to the nobleman's son, he was even promised one of the servant girls as a wife. They had known each other for a few years and Graeme loved her very much.

Three weeks before they were due to be wed he accompanied his master's son, on a journey. When he got back Graeme rushed excitedly to the girl's room to find her in bed with the nobleman.

The girl looked away as he opened the door, her flushed face blushed even deeper at the sight of her betrothed.

"Leave us!" barked the lord as he nuzzled the girl's neck, his arms reached below the blanket. The girl giggled and leaned toward the man.

Graeme remembered losing his mind. He reached for the sword resting in its scabbard against the back of a chair. Engulfed with jealousy and rage he repeatedly plunged the sword into the nobleman and the girl.

✽

Graeme the Woodchopper walked through the wind and the rain toward the harbour. From the top of the hill he looked down on the quay. Docked there a single mast ship with a raised platform at the rear. A light burned out of the cabin fixed to the deck of the platform. He rushed down the hill as quickly as he could.

The ship appeared deserted. He walked up the gangplank and headed toward the light at the stern. The inside of the small wooden shelter was bathed in light.

"Our souls can sail through this storm, to the warmth of your woodman's hut." The familiar trance inducing tone of the woman's voice floated out toward the Woodchopper.

At the same time as he recognised the voice he felt the ship move away from the quay. He heard the timbers creek as the waves lashed against the overlapping outer planking on the hull. He walked into the wooden shelter and all became still. The raging storm did not reach this haven of dreams and desires. A bed appeared and Graeme approached it.

✻

Three winged demons flew alongside the ship. There was a demon supporting the ship on each side and one flying high above the stern. They were large winged muscular creatures, dark grey in colour; their hideous faces recognisable from church carvings and sculptures, but with a level of malevolence not apparent in architecture.

The demon at the rear let out a screech that could have come from the depth of Hell itself. The other two looked up to see a golden winged figure bathed in light descending toward them. In his right hand he held a mighty sword and in the left an oval shield.

The first demon flew straight at the heavenly messenger. Sharp talons disintegrated as they touched the shield. The demon let out a long scream of agony that shocked even the sound of the storm into silence. Before he could flee the sword sunk into him up to the jewelled hilt. The scream ceased as the winged monstrosity burst into flames and spiralled downward toward the tempest below.

The two remaining demons flew headlong into the storm, the ship held still within their grasp. The winged assailant turned, paused and then he pursued.

The starboard demon was struck first. The grotesque head was severed from the muscular neck with one swing of the sword. The portside demon skewered before the unsupported side of the ship could drop. The vessel followed the flaming figures as they fell into the sea below.

✻

The Woodchopper woke out of his reverie as he became aware of the ship lurching through the waves. The storm was throwing the craft about like a wood shaving in a waterfall. The shelter was in darkness and, as far as he could tell, he was alone. He held tight to the bed, but he could feel it sliding around. He felt a sharp pain in his left hand when the bed slammed against a wall. The ship was rising high on a wave – up and up it rose to a great height – then it plunged spectacularly into the swell.

The Woodchopper groaned as he was thrown from the bed and onto the floor. Seawater gushed in through the entrance. The sound of breaking timbers was the last thing the Woodchopper heard as he was washed out of the shelter and onto the deck; he collided with some rigging and lost consciousness.

✻

He opened his eyes, as he briefly regained his senses, and saw the face of a beautiful young man by his side.

The man looked at him and smiled. He felt safe and at peace as he drifted back into the blackness.

✳

The monk stared in disbelief at the soaking, bloodstained bundle at the gates of the monastery. He ran inside for help and came out with three other Brothers to carry the man inside. The Prior directed them to an unused cell.

"How did he get here?" asked one of the monks.

"It is a mystery indeed," responded the Prior, the concern evident in his voice.

✳

The Woodchopper's hand hurt and his head throbbed as he regained consciousness for a second time. He slowly opened his eyes and saw that he was in a small rectangular room. By the side of the bed there was a table and a chair, looking up he saw a crucifix.

The room spun as Graeme tried to lift his head off the bed. His body ached from head to foot. "Not a good idea," he said to himself.

The monk sitting in the corridor noticed him stir. "Careful, you have had quite a battering. Your body is covered in bruises and your left hand is swollen, though I do not think it is broken. There is a nasty swelling on your temple too."

"Where am I?" asked Graeme through gritted teeth; his head hurt so much he had to close his eyes.

"You are in the Priory. It seems you couldn't wait for Brother Eulid. He must still be waiting for the storm to subside before attempting a crossing."

"The ship?"

"There is no sign of any ship, or any wreckage for that matter. You were found in a heap at the monastery gates."

"Where is the young man I saw when I first awoke?"

"I am the only one who has attended to you since you were placed in this room. Four Brothers carried you here from the gate. What did he look like, this man?"

"I only saw his face." The Woodchopper paused before continuing. "There was a radiance about him."

The monk laughed. "We are all devout brethren here, but I do not think any of us actually glow with God's grace. Go back to sleep you need to get rest. The next time you wake up I will get you something to eat."

He could hear the monk's voice receding into the distance as fatigue overcame him. Soon he was sleeping.

*

The storm had subsided some time ago and the Woodchopper could see some faint winter sun shining down on the cloister outside as the monk opened the door to the cell.

"Good morning," said a rotund monk, with a jovial face walking into the room. Brother Simon is at prayer he will be back shortly. In the meantime I will get you something to eat if you are up to it."

"Yes, I would like that. Thank you," replied Graeme. He felt as though he hadn't eaten in weeks. "How long have I been here?"

"It's been three days since you were washed up at our gates. Although how you got here God only knows," said the monk.

After a hearty breakfast the Woodchopper felt much better. His hand was still a little sore and there was still evidence of bruising to his temple, but other than that he felt fine.

"May I come in?" Prior William was a large man with a long, thick grey beard that reached to the bottom of his chest.

"Of course." Graeme lifted himself up in the bed.

"I hear you are much improved."

"Yes, thanks to the kind ministering of your good Brothers."

"I spoke to Brother Eulid a little while ago and he has told me a little about you and the Cardinal at Canterbury. Unfortunately he knows very little other than it is at the Cardinal's bidding that you have come here."

The Woodchopper recited the tale of the Scroll of Explanation and the Legend of the Eternal Night. He spoke of the Cardinal's visions, and of the strange episode in the misty valley. He told the Prior about the meeting at the inn and setting out on the mysterious ship.

"Brother Eulid also spoke of the slaughter of the horse." The Prior made the sign of the cross as he spoke.

"Something infinitely evil is following me," replied the Woodchopper. "Of this I am convinced."

Finally, he advised the Prior of the Cardinal's pronouncement that this island was to be his place of departure.

Prior William looked intently at the fearful young man. "Wherever it is you are to go there are some very powerful forces that want to stop you. There also appears to be an even more powerful force looking out for you. It is the only explanation for your survival after the storm."

Graeme the Woodchopper looked away from the prior's gaze. "I accepted the Siren's call. I too could have been smashed against the rocks of deceit."

With a large chubby hand the monk stroked his beard thoughtfully. "You were undoubtedly deceived. Something delivered you here despite yourself and has protected you from grave danger, so I think we must wait to see what Heaven sends."

As he got up to leave the cell he looked back toward Graeme, "God be with you."

✻

The sky was clouding over by the time Graeme left the monastery grounds. He needed to stretch his legs. Pulling his cloak tightly around himself to protect against the keen wind, he walked up a small hill.

There was a little church ahead of him and he made his way to the door. The candle on the altar lit up the gold crucifix and drew Graeme to the front of the empty church. He knelt at a bench in front of the tabernacle and closed his eyes.

Time passed imperceptibly as he knelt in prayer. The little old man sitting on the bench beside him watched benignly.

The Woodchopper opened his eyes and jumped onto his feet at the sight of the old man. "I thought I was alone."

"None of us are ever really alone, otherwise you would have no one to talk to in your prayers?" said the old man.

"How long have you been there? I didn't hear you come in."

"I did not want to disturb you. But tell me; are those the questions you really want to ask? Why not enquire as to where you are expected to go from here, or how you are expected to get there. What are you supposed to do when you reach your destination?"

"Those are the questions I was just praying over," replied Graeme with a surprised look on his face.

The old man stood up. "Come with me."

The two men left the church and walked down toward the beach. The last of the daylight was beginning to fade into evening.

THE JOURNEY

There was a small rowing boat on the beach. The old man gestured toward it then pointed out to sea. Toward the horizon was a ship roughly twice the size of the one at the quay on the night of the storm.

"That ship will take you where you need to go."

"How do they know I am here?"

"I told them. They are expecting you."

Graeme the Woodchopper believed the old man, though he did not know why. He decided he was going to sail on that ship. "Where is it going?" he asked.

"West."

The Woodchopper remembered the Prior's words. *'Wait to see what Heaven sends,'* he had said. Heaven had sent a ship.

"We will meet again," said the old man as the Woodchopper pushed the rowing boat away from the shore.

The sea was calm and the short row to the vessel was easy. Graeme the Woodchopper looked back toward the shore, but the old man had disappeared. As he approached the ship one of the crew threw a rope over the side and he scaled it with little difficulty.

Waiting for him on the deck was a tall muscular man with an angular face. His main features were an aquiline nose and a jutting chin. He held himself with the poise of someone who had been giving orders all his life and expected them to be carried out.

"Welcome aboard the Harbinger, we've been expecting you."

The Woodchopper hauled himself onto the deck and looked around at the men working at various tasks. Two were raising the sails; another two were raising the anchor while one held the rudder on the raised platform at the rear of the ship. The other member of the crew stood next to the master of the vessel ready to retrieve the rope.

"Come back to the cabin and we can talk."

The two men entered the small cabin at the rear of the ship. The ship's Master gestured for his passenger to sit.

"We were told there would be someone requesting passage here. Where is it you intend to go? Ireland?"

"I do not know," answered the Woodchopper.

The Master looked at him with a puzzled frown. "Ireland is the only known destination between here and where I intend to sail."

"I was only told that you were heading west."

"That is right. I will tell you my story and then later I would like to hear your tale if you wish to tell it, for it is an interesting person that does not know his destination."

The Master got up onto his knees. "Before you begin I will get us some refreshments." He looked back at the Woodchopper. "I fear we may have quite a lot in common."

The Master of the vessel - his name was Hesper – had a grandfather called Madog. A long time ago Madog, a Welsh prince, had discovered a faraway land off to the west beyond the sunset. On returning after his discovery he provisioned ten ships and set sail to return there. None of the ships, including Hesper's grandfather's ship, came back. Ever since he first heard the story Hesper was driven by a desire to find this land, to see if his grandfather or any of the others had survived and settled there.

"So you do not really know your final destination either," stated the Woodchopper as the Master finished speaking.

"No. Now you must tell me your tale."

Graeme the Woodchopper recited his story for a second time that day and Hesper sat in rapt attention.

"I think your presence will prove to be a blessing," Hesper said after his passenger had finished. "The old man was very convincing when he asked me to allow you to travel with us. Especially when he said you had never been to sea before."

The Woodchopper looked puzzled. *'How did he know I had never been to sea before?'* he thought.

"Is something troubling you?"

"No, I was just thinking of something. Sorry, please continue."

"I had doubts when he said that your presence would ensure a successful passage," continued Hesper. "Your story has done much to reassure me."

The Woodchopper yawned. The day had been a long one. "It looks like we are both destined to follow in the wake of your grandfather," he said.

"You must be tired you can sleep in here tonight," said Hesper. "I will sleep on the deck with the crew."

The night was bitterly cold and a frost formed on the sails and on the blankets of the sleeping sailors. In the morning Hesper explained to his passenger that it was impossible to undertake a lengthy ocean voyage during the winter so they were sailing to Ireland, where they would wait until the days started to lengthen and the nights became warmer. They would stock up on provisions there.

Other than one heavy shower and a moderate wind the crossing was good. In no time at all, the Irish coast was in sight and the Harbinger pulled into a secluded bay.

For the next couple of months they sailed from bay to bay, stopping occasionally at a small harbour or port and storing provisions for the voyage. One bright morning in early spring the ship set sail from the bay of Coarha Beg on Valencia Island.

*

For the first few days the weather was good and with a strong wind behind them they made good headway. Sea conditions became rougher as they moved further away from land, although the weather remained fine. The crew settled into a daily pattern of working, eating, resting and sleeping. Hesper attempted to keep the ship on a westerly course, but the winds and currents took them southwest. They followed this course for two weeks.

"There's land ahead!" Murray - a short, slight man who looked younger and fitter than his thirty-nine years – was on the rudder when he spotted the island.

Hesper came out of the cabin and walked to the front of the ship. "Hold her steady we should make land in about two hours if this wind holds."

An excited buzz went through the crew as they considered the chances of finding a trace of Madog's crew. The Woodchopper also moved to the front of the ship to get a better view. He and Hesper peered toward the horizon shielding their eyes with their hands.

"I see smoke rising from above that far ridge!" Caddock, the oldest of the crew at forty-three, was of slim build and five feet eight inches tall. The others turned to look in the direction he was pointing.

The Woodchopper turned toward Hesper. "Fires from a settlement?" he asked.

"I don't know. It's a lot of smoke, but it seems to be coming from one source not several separate fires," Hesper replied. "Once we find somewhere to weigh anchor I'll take two men ashore with me and see what we can find."

Just over two hours later the Harbinger sailed into a sheltered inlet. Thick laurel forest grew down to the sea line on two sides of the inlet and there was a small shingle beach in front of them. The beach gave a welcome break to the oppressive green wall, before the humid subtropical forest closed in again.

The master of the vessel selected two of the younger members of the crew to pull in the rowing boat and prepare to land on the beach.

"I want to come with you," said the Woodchopper firmly.

"It's too dangerous, we don't know what we are going to find. Once we secure a landing area you can come ashore."

"I must insist," said the Woodchopper. "How else will I know if this is the place where my destiny lies?"

"As you wish," replied Hesper. "Take a sword and prepare to disembark."

*

Fighting their way through the thick undergrowth was hot, uncomfortable work in the subtropical climate. It wasn't long before all four men were drenched in sweat. Hesper led the way, swinging at the vegetation with his sword. The Woodchopper was behind him with the two young crewmen following closely. They had been fighting their way through the forest for about an hour when Hesper held his arm up and came to a halt.

"The vegetation is becoming thinner. I think we are nearing the edge of the forest," he whispered. "Wait here."

As Hesper disappeared out of sight the three men stood in silence. They became increasingly aware of the cacophony of sound coming from the birds and animals of the forest, although they had seen precious little of the indigenous wildlife so far. Soon they could here footsteps amid the jungle noise.

"Come forward! The forest opens out onto a ridge!" shouted Hesper.

The Woodchopper noticed a parrot take off from the treetops in response to Hesper's voice. He was struck by the vivid shades of yellow and green that made up the bird's plumage.

The air felt clear and fresh as they walked out from the heat and humidity of the jungle and into the slight breeze blowing across the ridge.

"Look," said Hesper pointing at a smoking, conical shaped mountain across the other side of a barren black plain.

"I have heard stories of mountains that spew out fire, I never thought I would see one though," said the crewman with black hair. Both crewmen were in

RICHARD JONES

their early twenties and roughly the same lean build although the ginger crewman carried a little more muscle.

"I thought it was just a myth," said the other crewman.

The Woodchopper could see little rivers of lava flowing over the top of the volcano. Every few minutes the cone threw some ash and dust into the air to accompany the billowing smoke rising high into the sky. "I don't think I like the look of this," he said.

"Let's get back to the ship," said Hesper.

The four men turned back into the forest each hacking at the undergrowth in their haste. The Woodchopper could see the three sailors in front of him as he stumbled over a piece of deadwood. He called as he got up off the ground, but his voice was lost in the complaining screech of the forest wildlife.

From the corner of his eye he thought he saw a dark shadow moving in behind him. He hurtled through the trees in his haste to catch up with the others, tearing his skin as he dashed headlong through the undergrowth. *'The evil presence is here too,'* he thought, fighting hard to keep the now familiar fear under control, *'and it is gaining on me'*. In the dank darkness of the forest the shadow stole silently forward.

✳

Graeme the Woodchopper burst out of the forest and onto the beach. The two young sailors were at the shoreline standing either side of the rowing boat and holding onto the sides.

"Have you seen the Master? He went back to look for you," said the ginger-haired sailor.

With that Hesper walked out of the forest. "Let's get back to the ship. I have a feeling this island could turn into a hell on earth some time soon."

Hesper and the Woodchopper jumped into the little boat. The two crewmen pushed it away from the shore and jumped in themselves. They picked up the oars and began rowing toward the Harbinger. Soon the four men were safely on board and raising the sails.

The Master and the Woodchopper looked toward the island as the ship made its way slowly west.

"I don't think Madog ever landed on that island," said the Woodchopper. "If he did he certainly didn't stay."

"No," replied Hesper.

The Woodchopper looked over at Hesper. "Did you see or feel anything on the way back through the forest?"

"Only the forest sounds. I saw the occasional bird fly off when we startled it."

"I felt as though something was following me. Something evil." The Woodchopper shivered despite the heat. "I thought I saw a shadow."

"It was probably just the trees," replied Hesper. "Your mind playing tricks on you." He stared intently into the Woodchopper's eyes.

"I suppose you're right." He felt uneasy under the Master's intense gaze as he peered back into the deep black pupils scrutinising him coldly.

✻

The Harbinger sailed on for two months without catching sight of land. She sailed through bright breezy days and through stormy seas. She drifted aimlessly during dead calm. The men fished when they could and watched their pile of provisions dwindle as the days passed by.

The monotony of the endless seascape and the uncertainty of finding land began to take its toll. Lack of fresh food and the cramped conditions were also having an effect. Two crewmen were complaining of aching joints and tiredness, even more so than the rest. Meirion, the youngest member of the crew, also had large purplish blotches on his legs and his gums were bleeding. The older sailors, Caddock and Murray, had seen this sort of thing before and they knew the situation was desperate. Caddock spoke to Hesper.

"We have been sailing westward long enough. The men think it is time to turn north or south...or even head east for home."

"You know as well as I, we don't have enough supplies to sail back east and if we start heading north or south we could sail around aimlessly until we all die. All the tales of Prince Madog's voyage say he sailed west with his brother Rhirid. He did it once with two ships and returned before he set sail for the final voyage. He was gone for one whole cycle of seasons before he returned. The winds and tides are taking us in a south westerly direction and I have no reason to doubt that they took my grandfather's ships in the same direction." Hesper raised his voice commandingly. "We need to sail on!"

He spoke with conviction and determination and this seemed to strengthen the crew's resolve. "Now, go and minister to Rhidian and Meirion."

✻

They sailed on for another week. The conditions were good with a fair breeze behind them and a clear sky overhead. However, the two sick crewmen were deteriorating. On Rhidian's legs dark purplish spots were forming and he was having constant nosebleeds. Merion was bleeding from the nose and mouth, his teeth were falling out and he had diarrhoea. Both looked as though their eyes had sunk into their heads. The Woodchopper also was feeling more listless than usual and he noticed his limbs were aching. The next day Meirion died, he would not see the end of his fifteenth year.

It was Murray who watched him die and it was Murray who told every one else. He had assumed the responsibility of looking after the sick sailors.

Hesper organised a makeshift funeral for the boy. Caddock and the two young men who had rowed to the island wrapped Meirion in a blanket and placed him on a plank at the end of the ship. Hesper walked forward and stood by the shrouded body.

"I commit the body of our ship mate Meirion ap Dafydd of Ynys Mon into the sea and into God's keeping. May God have mercy on his soul." He stepped back and nodded at Caddock. The three sailors lifted the plank and the body of Meirion slid off into the sea. The weights attached to it caused it to sink instantly.

There was a sombre mood on the ship for the rest of the day and The Woodchopper could sense that trouble was brewing. After darkness had fallen Caddock and the two young men held whispered conversations for about an hour. Then all went silent.

It was just after daybreak when he noticed Ionawr - the dark haired young man – holding another whispered conversation with Caddock. Rhidian's coughing drowned out the words, but the Woodchopper could see the older man signal to the other youngster and gesture toward the cabin.

The early morning sunlight glinted off the blade of the knife as the man made his way to the rear of the ship. The Woodchopper's mouth opened to let out a shout of warning, but before he could form the words he felt an explosion of pain somewhere at the back of his skull and he fell into a sea of blackness.

Caddock stood over the unconscious form of the Woodchopper and watched as the would-be assassin slowly pulled back the covering at the entrance to Hesper's shelter. He saw the tip of a sword suddenly appear between the young man's shoulder blades and watched as it travelled forward toward him. The force of the thrust caused the body to move backward then stop as the blade began to retract. The would-be assassin slumped to the floor. The Master up stood to his full height and stepped over the corpse. He leaned back slightly and drew the flat edges of the blade against the dead man's clothing.

The colour drained from Caddock's face as the Master emerged from the shelter. Ionawr stood frozen with fear. Murray awoke with a start at the sound of the body hitting the deck. He too was beginning to feel the effects of the illness.

"Now what have we here?" Hesper's voice was thick with bloodlust and menace.

He moved slowly past Murray in a circular movement always maintaining eye contact.

The Woodchopper began to stir.

Once he was out of Caddock's reach the Master turned to face Ionawr. The boy began to shake and the knife dropped out of his grasp to make a loud thud as it hit the wooden planks of the decking.

The sharp features of the Master broke into a smile as he bent down to pick up the knife with his left hand. As he rose he drove his sword up through a point just behind the young man's jawbone. The beginnings of a scream were curtailed. The sword twisted in the Master's hand whilst he pushed it further upward into Ionawr's brain. It stopped when it hit the top of his skull. Murray vomiting over the side of the ship broke the silence.

The Woodchopper's vision was blurred and his head was pounding, but he was lucid enough to be aware of the horror unfolding before him. He stood between Caddock and the advancing Hesper.

"That's enough!"

The Master's eyes narrowed imperceptibly.

"We need him or we are all going to die," said Graeme. "I am too weak to work, Rhidian is close to death and Murray is beginning to show the first symptoms of this plague. Kill Caddock and you are on your own."

There was a long uneasy silence before Hesper spoke. "Put him in irons."

The Woodchopper put manacles on the oldest of the sailors while Hesper and Murray threw the two bodies over board. Hesper returned to the cabin.

"I'll tie you to the rudder you can hold the ship steady on the current course." The Woodchopper said as he led the man to the stern of the ship.

✳

Later that same day Hesper sat eating a piece of salted meat as he took his turn at the tiller. He smiled as he watched a seagull come into view and land on the top of the mast.

Murray noticed it too. "Thank God," he said as he bathed Rhidian's sores.

"What does it mean?" asked The Woodchopper.

"It means we are not far from land," as he spoke Caddock leaned back as far as the manacles would allow so he could look at the bird.

Three days later they spotted land on the horizon.

✻

This was a large island indeed and Hesper felt confident he would find some trace of his grandfather.

The ship sailed around the southern tip until they found a secluded bay in the south east of the island surrounded by mountains. The Master gave the order to weigh anchor in the bay.

As soon as the ship was secured Hesper took the Woodchopper and Caddock ashore to get some supplies; Murray stayed aboard the Harbinger and attended to Rhidian.

After a couple of hours the rowing boat returned with a supply of oranges, lemons, some fruits that were unknown to them and a supply of drinking water. The crew stayed aboard the Harbinger that night, but Hesper decided they would set up camp on the mainland in the morning. The crew would take turns to keep a one-man presence on the ship, but Caddock was excluded. Hesper ordered that the old sailor be kept in manacles. The Woodchopper knew that once the Master decided Caddock was not needed any more he would kill him.

"Did you see any signs that the land is inhabited?" asked Murray.

The Woodchopper and Hesper were checking through what was left of the food store and throwing the bad food overboard.

"No, but we did not venture far into the mountains."

Hesper had become distant since he had thwarted the attempt on his life. He had not spoken to Caddock at all and only spoke to the others if they spoke first, or if he was giving an order.

"I tried to warn you when they attacked," said the Woodchopper in an attempt to stimulate conversation.

"I know," replied the Master. "I am grateful."

The Woodchopper did not sleep well that night. Men had already died and it was more than likely that others would too. He could not see a way of ever returning home to his hut and the thought of living the rest of his life stranded here with cutthroats, and surrounded by hostile natives filled him with dread. He dozed fitfully and dreamt of the Legend of the Eternal Night. The Woodchopper knew there would be no return.

✣

Early the next morning the Woodchopper went ashore again with Hesper and Caddock. The Master had decided to build a stockade to use as a base for exploring the mountains, and as a defence against any unfriendly natives.

"I'll chop down some trees," volunteered the Woodchopper. "You two can drag the wood to the camp."

The Master turned to look at him.

"Don't worry I was a woodchopper before I left on this quest." Grabbing an axe he headed for the forest.

The trees here were of a hardwood variety not known to him and he struggled to cut through them with the axe. He laboured all day chopping away and night was beginning to fall when Hesper dragged the manacled Caddock to a tree. He began to secure him to the trunk with some thick pieces of vine.

"What are you doing!" shouted Caddock.

"I'm leaving you here for the night."

"You can't do that," the Woodchopper said with concern in his voice. "We don't know what animals or people might be about in the forest or the mountains."

"I want to be able to sleep without worrying about getting my throat cut," said Hesper.

"I'll stay with him."

"As you wish."

The two men watched as the master pushed the boat away from the shore and began to row toward the ship.

The Woodchopper cut the other man free from the tree then lit a fire close by the pile of chopped logs and as near to the shoreline as possible. The two men sat close to the heat and protection of the flames.

"What made you come on this voyage?" he asked the older man as he watched the flames dance. "There couldn't have been any guarantees of riches or glory, Hesper was chasing a ghost."

"I needed to get away as soon as I could and this ship was going as far away as possible. If it had all worked out I could have carved a new start for myself with Madog's descendants where my past would not be known."

"What of your past?"

"It is of no concern of yours," said Caddock abruptly.

"What about the others do you know their reasons?"

"Murray has been a sailor all his life, to him it is just another voyage, but with the prospect of a better life at the end of it. The others all had relatives on Madog's ships." The older man stared into the fire for a while. "I could have killed you, you know."

"You needed me, just like Hesper needs you for the time being. I couldn't have allowed you to turn back though, I have to go on to realise my purpose."

"What is your purpose? I did not understand how Hesper picked you up in the first place. You're obviously no sailor and you're an extra mouth to feed. You're not even a subject of Prince Llewellyn."

"My purpose comes from a higher calling. You could say I'm here on the orders of the Church."

"That may well be, but Hesper will not trust you now. He will consider you my ally and will more than likely kill the two of us when we are no longer needed."

"You may be right," said the Woodchopper staring off into the darkness. "I'll take the first watch."

He slept fitfully during Caddock's watch. On one of his dozes he dreamt of his hut in the woods, it was a bright summer's day and he was sitting on a stump watching the sunlight shine through the trees. There was a golden eagle flying through the sky and the whooshing of the bird's wings made the Woodchopper look up. Instead of a beak and hawk eyes he saw the face of the little old man smiling down on him.

"We will meet again." The old man's words came back to him and he awoke reassured and strengthened.

In the morning Hesper brought Murray ashore with him.

"How is Rhidian?" The Woodchopper was a little surprised to see both men walking up the beach.

It was Murray that answered. "He's much improved, we can leave him on the boat for a day or two, then he should be able to come ashore."

Hesper turned to face the three men, "You carry on chopping the timber," he said pointing at the Woodchopper, "you two can carry the logs here and I will start to build the stockade."

✳

Within a week there was a sturdy rectangular shape about ten feet square on the beach, a canvas shelter covered about a third of it.

Each day Hesper set out, either on his own or with Murray or the Woodchopper. The mountains were covered at the bottom by forest, but after an initial climb they opened up into areas of grassland and some rocky outcrops higher up. From each peak they climbed the only view was of other peaks ranging into the distance. There was plenty of wildlife in the mountains and food was also plentiful, but in four weeks of exploring there had been no signs of Hesper's descendants or any indigenous people.

Hesper and the Woodchopper had just scaled another peak and were resting before the return to the beach when the Woodchopper decided to speak.

"We need to go further than we can travel from the stockade," he said. "Either we break camp and cross this range by foot, or we can set sail and continue westward."

Hesper looked thoughtfully into the distance, "We will sail around the shoreline for a while. If we find nothing then we sail on west."

The next morning they loaded the ship with provisions and set sail westward along the coast.

✳

"You need to come and look at these clouds," said Murray sticking his head into Hesper's cabin. The two men joined the others looking westward at the rolling mass of ominous, dark storm clouds engulfing the bright morning sky. Before long the rain started to thump down on the deck and splashes sprayed up from the sea as the deluge opened. The sky returned to the hours of darkness just past.

"Tie yourselves to something solid!" Murray shouted at the rest of the crew.

They all grabbed some rope and made for a sturdy fixture. Hesper strapped himself to the rudder and Rhidian moved down to the second mast where Murray was already attaching a rope. The Woodchopper tied himself off to the forward mast.

"Take these off me!" screamed Caddock wrestling with the manacles attached to a post at the front of the ship.

"There's no time! Try to..." the Woodchopper bellowed, but his voice was lost in the wind now howling across the deck before he could finish the sentence.

The sea became a tumultuous tide of rolling waves, the Harbinger tossed about on mountains of angry foam; the rain continued to hammer down. The sky itself appeared to have come alive with a deadly glee. Lightening drove down from the sky like innumerable demonic pitchforks being hurtled at the earth, the clouds a churning black mass of a satanic chorus.

He could barely make out Caddock's screams through the crescendo as the older man was tossed about by the storm, the manacles straining against his wrists. He turned to look back at the others, but all had merged in the blackness.

For a second the Woodchopper thought he saw a face toward the back of the ship illuminated by a lightening strike. It looked like Hesper - yet it did not - the angular features were more pronounced, the eyes were burning red orbs and it appeared to be squatting comfortably on the rudder, not strapped and struggling, as he should have been.

The storm raged on. Night came, but Graeme did not notice, he could no longer hear Caddock's screams, but could occasionally make out his shape rolling around by the post. He could sometimes see the silhouettes of the two men at the second mast during the lightening flashes. There were shadows out to sea as well, black wings riding on the foam crested ocean. The storm vented its fury, an evil entity damming all caught within.

Days and nights merged together, the ship hurtled uncontrollably through the turbulent black vortex, each man wishing for death to relieve the nightmare.

Finally Graeme the Woodchopper could take no more. His body exhausted from the battering and his mind close to insanity from the terror and pain, he passed into unconsciousness.

❉

The demons swarmed around the ship, their hideous forms hidden by the storm. They waited and watched as the first mast snapped and was taken by the winds; they saw parts of the outer planking at the sides of the hull peel away, and they saw Caddock swept from the deck and be taken by one of their kind far off into the darkness.

Two pairs of blood-red eyes watched with excited anticipation when the Woodchopper's binding finally snapped and he rolled around loosely on the deck. Another dark grey gargoyle flew in toward the ship to claim him.

The demon looked down upon the brow of the ship where Caddock had once stood and saw a figure standing rock steady against the torrent, its golden wings at rest behind its back, its sword and shield held poised. The demon's screech of frustration added to the terrible noise of the storm, but he knew better than to challenge this guardian.

Three more swept up beside him, but none approached the ship. They saw a second angelic figure glide onto the deck and take Graeme the Woodchopper in its arms. The angel at the brow of the ship unfurled his majestic wings to their full span and, with a downward sweep; led his companion up and out of the storm.

SHIPWRECKED

Graeme the Woodchopper felt the hot Caribbean sun on his face. He turned onto his side and opened his eyes. In front of him stretched the seemingly endless golden sands of a beach, broken here and there by palm trees. For the moment the memory of the terrible storm was hidden in the darker recesses of his mind. He stood up feeling disoriented, wondering where he was.

The Woodchopper sat against the nearest tree and tried to remember. He recalled again the feeling of safety and peace he had experienced during his time at the priory and a smile crossed his lips as he remembered the beautiful young man. This time he remembered the feeling of being safe in the young man's arms.

Other than a few cuts and bruises Graeme was remarkably unscathed from the ordeal. There was no sign of any wreckage or survivors on this stretch of the beach and so he decided to make a search later. First he needed to find some food and fresh water.

He headed inland and it wasn't long before he found an orange grove. With an arm full of oranges he sat down to peel them when a movement in the trees about thirty yards away caught his eye. He slowly put the oranges on the ground and sat very still focusing his whole being on the area around the trees.

The Woodchopper sat motionless, like a cat waiting to pounce on a passing mouse, when he heard a giggle.

"Who are you!" he shouted.

He heard another giggle and saw the undergrowth rustle. He caught a glimpse of a figure as it moved away. The Woodchopper gave chase, but could not keep up in the dense foliage. He slowed to a walk after running a few hundred yards.

The girl turned and began to walk back toward him. He saw her coming forward and stopped. They both gazed at each other over a distance of about twenty feet.

Graeme the Woodchopper saw standing before him a young girl with brown skin and long black hair reaching to her waist. She was about five feet seven inches tall, and of slim build. The cotton covering she wore was tight enough to reveal rounded, but not too wide, hips and small breasts. Her figure reflected a short and active life. She had a pretty oval shaped face, with a small nose and a mouth framed by full lips.

Graeme pointed to the earth and then sat cross-legged on the ground to show his intention not to harm her. She also sat down, but kept her distance.

He pointed repeatedly at himself, saying "Graeme."

The young girl looked confused initially, but then smiled and pointed at herself and said, "Centehua."

This pointing and naming of things went on for a while, after which Graeme returned to the place where he left the oranges and Centehua followed. He peeled an orange then gave it to her; she accepted.

"Ni-tlacua," she said smiling.

"Yes, that's right...you eat," Graeme smiled back.

As the girl ate the orange Graeme asked, "Have you seen others like me?" He was pointing at himself and toward the sea, but the girl did not understand. "I have to look for my shipmates."

Centehua's smooth forehead furrowed as Graeme walked toward the beach. She grabbed his arm to stop him. He turned to look at her and she pointed back toward the orange grove. "Moztla...moztla," she pointed at the sun, then pointed east.

Graeme looked at her quizzically, following her gestures. He smiled with realisation and said, "Tomorrow, you want me to come to the orange grove tomorrow."

The girl smiled back and then turned to leave.

For the rest of the day Graeme walked along the beach searching for signs of the Harbinger or for the men who had sailed on her. He returned to the orange grove at sunset without having seen any sign of a ship or its crew.

The search left Graeme exhausted. Lying down under an orange tree he thought about the possible fates of the Harbinger. The terror of the storm came back to him, the black skies, the lightening, also the foaming mass of ocean. He considered the most likely possibility was that the ship had broken up and the others drowned.

Of course, it could be that he was washed overboard and the others rode out the storm. Some or all of them could have been washed ashore here or on a nearby island. Eventually fatigue overcame him and he fell into a deep sleep. His last waking thought was of Centehua.

✳

Graeme saw a familiar face sitting next to his recumbent body.

"I told you we would meet again."

"But, how? .... Where?"

"Always questions with you," said the little old man with a laugh. "You have arrived in the land of your destiny. Here is where it begins."

Graeme looked at the old man incredulously. "Begins? I have been through Hell just to get here."

"Believe me you have been nowhere near Hell yet."

The despondency in Graeme's face was apparent.

"Do not worry. You will not be without assistance. How do you think you have got this far?"

"Where do I go from here then?" Graeme asked.

"Your path is already mapped out. Be careful not to stray from it or delay your journey along it, not for too long any way."

"How will I…"

Graeme felt the old man's hand on his face as the question began to form - or so he thought.

"Graeme, Graeme."

He opened his eyes and saw Centehua kneeling by his side. As he became fully awake he leapt to his feet.

Centehua was not alone; she had two companions with her. Both men wore little more than a loincloth. One had the sagging skin tone of an old man and the other the bronzed muscular frame of someone much younger.

"What is this?"

Centehua held out her hands toward Graeme. The two men stepped back. She approached Graeme slowly and he was won over by the openness in her face. He allowed her to take his hand and lead him away from the orange grove. The two men followed behind.

The four of them walked silently through grassland and past banana trees. Graeme noticed that they were walking uphill, almost imperceptibly at first, but after about an hour the gradient was steeper. He could also see the thicker tree line of a tropical forest and, rising up out of it in the distance toward the northwest was a mountain range. The younger man, who by now was walking on ahead, shouted something back to the others and pointed forward. Graeme saw the smoke plumes rising from about half a dozen fires.

Centehua turned to Graeme and smiled. "Nochan," she said as she pointed toward their destination.

Graeme smiled back guessing that she was trying to tell him she was home.

It was a small settlement of seven simple huts made of sticks with roofs thatched with palm. They were all single room dwellings, just big enough for a family to eat and sleep together. Centehua led the three men into one of the huts furthest from the fields. All the huts were laid out in a circle.

The smoke from the fire at the centre of the hut made Graeme squint his eyes as he entered. Through the haze and darkness he could make out three female shapes sitting close to the fire. Centehua spoke to them and the two younger women stood up to greet him. One was a few years older than Centehua the other one was in her late thirties. The older woman, who looked as though she had seen one winter too many, stayed seated at the fire.

"Xihuian," she said pointing to the two men stooping just inside the entrance. The two men turned and left.

The old woman gestured for Graeme to sit by the fire. He sat there while the four women entered into a lengthy discussion. One or all of them occasionally looked at him, sometimes they laughed and sometimes with more serious expressions. On times when they laughed Centehua would turn and look shyly down into the embers of the fire.

After some time, Centehua stood up and led Graeme out of the hut. They walked for a while until they arrived at the fields.

One of the men working there came over and spoke briefly with the girl; he then beckoned for Graeme to follow him. Centehua returned to the village and Graeme set about learning the tasks of tending the crops. He did not recognise some of the plants, but the majority of the fields were allocated to growing a type of corn.

Graeme counted twelve men working the fields. The man he worked with for most of that day he later found out was Centehua's father, his name was Manauia.

At dusk all the men headed back to the village. Graeme walked close to Manauia and the two men he met in the orange grove, they were Centehua's grandfather, Ueman and Yaotl her brother.

That night he was given food and ate with the family. They all chatted away amongst each other occasionally smiling at Graeme and trying to explain things.

Achcauhtli, the old woman gave him a blanket and he bedded down a discreet distance away from the rest. Each woman slept next to a man and Graeme guessed they were married, all except Centehua who also slept alone, but on the other side of the smouldering embers of the fire.

The next day everyone was woken by Chipahua, the wife of Manauia, the women fanned the fire back to life and prepared breakfast.

Centehua sat down next to Graeme. "Tlaxcalli," she said handing him a pancake-sized corn tortilla.

"Thanks," he replied, smiling at her.

✳

The daily routine of the village became Graeme's daily routine. There was a seductive familiarity about it that Graeme liked. He enjoyed the friendly company of the villagers and felt at home in the warmth of the communal hearth. Every morning he went to the fields to work and every evening he went back to the hut of Centehua's family.

The days turned into weeks and the weeks began to turn into months. Graeme was finding it much easier to communicate now and was quickly learning the villager's language.

The one part of the daily routine that Graeme stayed apart from was the offerings they made to their gods. Every morning Achcauhtli would encourage everyone to place copal or resin in a bowl in the sacred area of the hut and this was then burned to gain favour with the gods.

During this time Graeme took out a small cross he had fashioned from two sticks and knelt in front of it to pray.

Graeme recalled the words of the little old man while he prayed. "Do not delay your journey too long," was the warning he had given.

"What troubles you?" It was Yaotl who noticed Graeme's distracted uneasiness.

"I feel I may have stayed here too long," said Graeme echoing the old man's warning.

"You are part of us now there is no need to leave." It was Cualli, the wife of Yaotl who spoke.

"I have travelled so far, seen so much," Graeme said sadly. He thought of the woman at the alehouse and her promise of a home and family; he thought of the servant girl he had killed when he was little more than a child; and he thought of the woodchopper's hut to which he could never return.

Centehua put her arms around his neck. They had spent many hours together learning each other's languages and enjoying each other's company in the last three months. Graeme held her close.

It was Ueman who spoke next. "Do not come to the fields today, take the time to reflect."

✳

Graeme walked out of the village that morning and headed toward the forest. He wanted time alone to think. Centehua watched him leave with worry written across her young forehead.

The humidity of the jungle held little discomfort for him now. He wore little more than a pair of three quarter length britches and a pair of sandal-like shoes, cactli Centehua had called them when she gave them to him.

The forest grew dense as he pushed on so he decided to stop for a while. He placed his cross on the top of an old stump and began to ask God for guidance.

"You cannot stay here."

The Woodchopper stumbled to his left as the familiar voice startled him.

"How did you get here?" Graeme asked incredulously. "Who in God's name are you?"

"I am the wise old man who has guided people like you since man first walked the earth. I am the voice inside the mind of everyone that only a few ever heed."

Graeme's expression hardened, "My journey has led me to these people and I am going to stay."

"You would be very welcome among them, but there is an even bigger storm coming, bigger than the ones you have already sailed through."

"This place is everything I have ever wanted," said Graeme wistfully.

"Centehua is very pretty. She would give you strong, healthy children," said the old man.

"Maybe this is where I belong." There was conviction in Graeme's voice.

"You may have indeed come home." The old man looked at Graeme's cross. "Or will you listen to the voice that is calling you, calling you on? The choice is yours."

The Woodchopper and the old man walked over to a fallen tree and sat down. The old man listened to the sounds of the forest as Graeme came to a decision.

"My place is here. If I do not try to make a life for myself here then I may not have another chance."

The old man looked sad. "I am sorry," he said. There was no judgement in his voice only compassion. He looked at Graeme with pity in his eyes. "The storm will come."

"I will prepare..." He turned to face the old man, but there was no one there. He was alone in the forest.

Graeme felt a contentment and a sense of peace that he could not ever recall feeling in his life before. There was a spring in his step as he made his way back through the forest.

"Who's there?" He thought he saw a movement in the trees off to his right.

He stood completely still as he remembered the advice of the men from the village. "Be still and silent," they had said. "Wait for whatever stalks you to make the first move."

The Woodchopper watched and listened with every fibre of his being, not concentrating on any one spot, but letting his attention spread out over his field of vision.

"Yeeeargh!" An unearthly scream rose into the humid jungle air. It was soon joined by a host of other screeches and yells as the jungle wildlife took flight.

Graeme ran toward the noise. Through the trees he saw a large winged creature with grey skin drawn taught over its muscular frame. The creature looked at Graeme with red eyes that turned the Woodchopper's blood to ice.

Out of the jungle appeared another winged creature; it flew headlong toward the other with a raised sword in his hand. Before Graeme could grasp what was happening both creatures were gone.

He noticed an unmistakeable sulphurous smell that was soon replaced by the scent of roses. The Woodchopper looked around for the source of these aromas, but he did not see the figure moving away into the jungle. The little old man pulled his cloak about his shoulders, turned into the jungle and disappeared.

✶

The men ran back toward the village. They had heard the scream and feared for the safety of the women and children. Cualli and Chipahua held Centehua to stop her from running to the forest where she knew Graeme had gone earlier.

"There he is!" exclaimed Centenhua. She broke free from the clutches of her family and ran down the dirt track.

Graeme was walking slowly toward the village. They embraced, holding each other as if they would never let go.

"What happened?" asked Yaotl. He was the first villager to reach the couple.

"What animal could make a sound like that?" asked another man from the village.

Graeme and Centehua turned to meet the villagers; he kept his left arm on her shoulder, holding her tight to him, she kept her right arm wrapped tightly around his waist.

"It did not sound like any animal I have ever heard," said Manauia.

"It did not look like any animal I have ever seen either," said Graeme.

"Where is it now?" asked a man Graeme knew as Icnoyotl.

"I do not know, but I am sure it will not return."

"There may be others of its kind," said Manauia.

"I only saw the one today but, you are right, there may be more."

＊

The villagers lit a fire at the centre of the village and Graeme told them everything he could remember about his encounter with the demon. He did not mention the old man though; he posed no threat to the village and, in any case, Graeme wondered if his meetings with the guide were not all in his mind even though he recalled Hesper mentioning an old man of the same description.

At that moment the Woodchopper wished for the counsel of a priest. If only he could speak to Cardinal Caronni or the old friar, they may have heard of this creature from Hell, or even known of the little old man.

All the while Graeme was talking with the villagers Centehua remained at his side. She did not speak a word until the villagers finished the announcing of midnight by the ritual banging on kettles and drums, then she turned to look at him and said, "What of the reason you went to the forest?"

Graeme held her face in his hands, "I want to stay with you."

He pulled her face to his and kissed her. They held hands as they slowly made their way to the hut.

"Put your blanket next to mine tonight," Centehua said as she ducked into the entrance.

MOTHER AND GODDESS

The wedding was arranged after much consultation with the village soothsayer, an old man called Eleuia. He found the most auspicious days for the ceremonies to take place.

Once the days had been set Graeme moved out of the hut of Centehua's family and stayed with Icnoyotl and his family.

It was on a cool December morning that Graeme the Woodchopper found himself preparing for the wedding ceremony. Icnoyotl and his family were to act as the family of the groom for ceremonial reasons, but Graeme and Centehua were going to live in their own hut. Graeme and the men of the village had built another hut just behind Centehua's family's hut. It was in here that Graeme waited.

In the other hut feasting and drinking took place all day. At sunset Centehua was bathed and given her wedding dress – white cotton, with purple bands and white feathers around the hem.

Icnoyotl's family gave the bride her lecture on her duties as a wife and then they carried Centehua to Graeme's hut by torchlight. Once there she was led to a small stool on a mat where Graeme was waiting. Graeme's shirt and Centehua's dress were tied together and incense was burned on the hearth. Manauia's parents and two elders from Icnoyotl's family gave food to Graeme and Centehua before eating themselves.

The incense burned for four days, then another feast was held with much eating and drinking; finally the couple were married.

✳

Graeme's life with Centehua was everything he had ever dreamed of; he spent the days in the fields and nights at home with his wife. They often spent the evenings with Centehua's family, but always returned to their own hut.

The months began to turn into years and Graeme began to understand the daily and seasonal rituals; how they gave structure to village life and how they related to the growing cycle of the crops. He could not however, reconcile himself to the sacred calendar, neither could he understand the need for animal sacrifices to appease the gods of the villagers.

"It is not just animal blood that is spilt in this land." The familiar voice came to Graeme as he was walking home alone from the fields one evening. "Do you remember why you came here? Do you remember the Cardinal's visions?"

"The slaughter of countless innocents." There was no surprise in Graeme's voice just resignation.

"It is happening now in huge settlements along this coastline and beyond the mountains." The old man stood in front of Graeme forcing him to stand and listen.

"I was wondering when you would return," said Graeme.

"I have never been away," replied the old man. "You will follow your call sooner or later, but every day you refuse the Army of the Damned grows."

"You have been wrong about the storm. There have been terrible hurricanes and tempests, but none as bad as the one on the ship. Maybe you are wrong about the slaughter too."

"The maelstrom that will strike here has nothing to do with the weather." With great pleading and urgency in his voice the old man said, "Come with me now, before it is too late."

"This is my life now, my calling is here," said Graeme determinedly.

He walked on alone to the village.

*

"What is the matter?" Centehua saw the worry on her husband's face.

"I have been reminded of my past and I fear I may bring great harm to you and the village."

"Why don't you speak to the soothsayer," suggested Centehua.

"You know I have my own god and it is his prophesy I fear."

"Perhaps our gods will be kinder." Centehua took his hand, "Come, it is late. I have made supper." She led him into the hut.

Graeme did not sleep well that night; images from the Cardinal's visions played on his mind; the still beating heart held aloft, the millions snuffed out before they are even born, a large mushroom shaped cloud rising above a city destroyed in one flash.

He saw visions of his own, visions of the armies of Hell swarming through Heaven's gate. Angels lying dead and dying with charred and smouldering wings lying still on the ground; darkness spreading over the light of Heaven like the black impenetrable darkness of a starless night, and a little old man impaled on a stake his eyes witnessing a crucifixion from which there would be no resurrection.

Centehua pulled him close to her and held him tight. They both waited for dawn.

At first light Graeme kissed his wife and left for the fields. Centehua watched him walk out of the circle of huts and down the track; as she turned to go back into the hut she felt a wave of nausea flow over her, she turned to one side and vomited.

She spoke with Achcauhtli that day, Chipahua and Cualli too. When Graeme came home that evening she told him she was with child.

Graeme rode a tidal wave of emotions at the news, joy, worry, excitement, fear; Cardinal Caronni's vision came back to him and he felt terrified, he saw the heart of a child cut from its chest to appease the elemental gods of this land. He turned to Centehua and kissed her.

"I will give my life to make you and the child both happy and safe."

✳

A boy was born to Graeme and Chetehua and they called him Eztli. Centehua was a good mother and there was no shortage of helpers among the women of her family and the women of the village. Graeme liked to watch his wife breast-feed the baby when they were gathered around the fire and he enjoyed seeing the family bond strengthen. He thought that nothing could destroy that bond now.

*

Eztli had been with them for nearly two years and Graeme no longer thought of the warnings of the old man or the memories of the voyage; his life as a woodchopper were distant memories now and when he did think of those times it felt as though it was from another lifetime or another person.

"Strangers coming out of the woods!" It was Yaotl who shouted the warning.

The men grabbed hoes, scythes, knives or whatever was to hand to use as weapons. Ueman went back to the village as fast as he could to take the women and children into hiding.

The two bands of men approached each other slowly. There were twelve villagers including Graeme and fifteen strong, young warriors facing them. Each warrior carried a shield and a spear.

The warriors attacked. Two of the younger villagers fell, struck by blows from spears. Yeotl hurled himself at the warriors responsible. He lashed out with a scythe and one warrior fell his left leg cut through to the bone. Manauia was fending off blows from two spears with a hoe. Elsewhere villagers were slowly pulling back toward the village blows raining down on them from the advancing warriors.

Graeme could see the elder who officiated at his wedding lying prone on the floor; two attackers reached down and dragged him away toward the forest. Graeme swung his axe around his head and tried to move toward the men, but was struck a blow by a warrior of roughly the same size and build as himself.

Winded he fell to his knees, but managed to parry another blow aimed at his head. He rose with one foot and one knee on the ground and swung the axe low, the warrior fell to the ground with blood pouring from his left ankle at the spot where his foot used to be.

Graeme jumped up quickly and relieved the man of his spear and shield.

"Over here!" It was Manauia who called for help. He had been knocked to the ground and was wrestling with one of his assailants, the other stood waiting for a chance to strike again with his spear.

"AAAAARGH!!!" The Woodchopper charged with spear and shield in hand. The warrior turned at the sound of the battle cry and Graeme run him through with the spear.

The second warrior turned to flee as he saw Graeme put his foot on the body of the injured man and pull the spear out. The man's scream caused the other attackers to stop and look. They saw the Woodchopper launch the spear at the fleeing warrior and they saw the man drop to the floor with the spear sticking out of his back. As one they all ran back toward the forest taking their wounded with them.

"How many have we lost?" asked Manauia.

"Icnoyotl's father has been taken and one of the younger men," Graeme replied.

"We have to get back to the village," said Yaotl.

The village was deserted; the women and children had fled to the forest with Ueman, and there was no sign that any of the raiding party had been there.

"Icnoyotl, you go to the forest and find the women," ordered Manauia.

"We have to prepare, make weapons," said Graeme.

"You think they will come back?" It was Yaotl who spoke.

"Yes," he replied. "Do you know where they came from or why they attacked?"

The Soothsayer answered. "They have come from over the mountain. On the highlands over the ridge there is a settlement that is so big it cannot be walked around in one day." He put two fingers to his right temple; a lump was starting to rise through a bruise. "They take prisoners back there."

Graeme grabbed his arm. "Why. Why do they take prisoners back there?" There was a sense of urgency in his voice that startled the Soothsayer and caused concerned looks from everyone else.

"It is said that the prisoners are sacrificed to the warriors' gods."

Graeme stood rooted to the spot; the Cardinal's visions and the Legend of the Eternal Night became a waking nightmare in his memories.

"The women are coming!" shouted the lookout.

Graeme broke out of his reflections and ran toward the approaching group. His wife was walking in the centre of the group alongside Cualli and Chipahua. She held Eztli's hand as he toddled unsteadily along by her side.

That night the villagers gathered at the centre of the village. Three men were positioned to watch the darkness for attackers.

"We have to leave here," said Graeme.

"Where would we go?" asked Ueman.

70

"I do not know, but if they come back we will all die."

"We can fight them, we beat them today we will beat them again." Yaotl's voice carried the strength of his convictions.

"If we flee they may find us again," said Manauia. "We need to prepare, to find safe refuge for the women and children and build strong defences for the village."

"We must make weapons also," said Yaotl.

"No, you don't understand, I have been told of visions, there are many horrors to come," said Graeme desperately. "We must leave here, flee and go far away."

"We cannot," said Achcauhtli "this is our home." The old woman left the group and walked slowly to her hut.

That night Graeme pleaded desperately with Centehua to leave with him, to take their son and the three of them disappear into the woods.

"I can hunt and fish and pick berries," he said. "We will be safe, no one will know where we are; no one will find us."

"I cannot," she replied sadly "I cannot leave my family."

Graeme sat outside the hut that night, partly because he was worried that the warriors would return, but mostly because he wanted to be alone. He held his little wooden cross in his hand and prayed that his family be spared from the horrors he had been told would come.

✳

Shortly before dawn Graeme was dozing when a bright light in his eyes awoke him and a voice called his name.

"Who's there?" he said sleepily.

Standing over him he saw a woman in a white dress that reached from her neck to the floor, she also wore a white shawl and white head covering.

"You will undergo much hardship and pain before you complete your quest, but let it be known that those who turn to me for help will not be left unaided. For I am the Mother of all and I will hear their cries."

Graeme rubbed his eyes against the radiant light, but as he focused on the light it faded rapidly; the apparition was gone.

*

The villagers prepared a place in a particularly dense area of the forest where they could hide. Provisions and weapons were stored there and all the children were shown the route as soon as they were old enough to leave the village on their own.

As time went on Graeme was more and more to be found walking the forest and climbing the mountains. The old man's warning of what was to come drove him to keep lonely vigils for weeks on end.

"Your son is growing up and you will regret not being here," Centehua said to her husband when he had returned from yet another stay in the forest.

"I must be able to warn you when they come."

"Eztli is nearly three now and they have not returned, they may never come back."

Graeme sighed, "They will return. I know."

"Your god has prophesied this you say, but the Soothsayer sees no danger at the moment. Stay home for a week. You never work in the fields any more and my father and brother have to provide for us."

"I have to keep watch."

Manauia came into the hut with a grave expression on his face. "It is nearly time for Achcauhtli to make the crossing."

Centehua followed her father to the family hut, with Graeme walking behind and holding his son's hand.

Chipahua looked at Centehua as the younger woman ducked through the entrance to the hut. She shook her head as Centehua gave her a pleading look.

The old lady was lying on her blanket, Cualli and Ueman kneeling by her side. Ueman held Achcauhtli's hand with his two hands; a tear traced its way slowly down his cheek.

Graeme came in last with his son in his arms; he could see the shallow and infrequent rise and fall of the old lady's chest. He knew she did not have long to live.

Yaotl returned from the field and the seven adults sat with the old lady in silence. Eztli slept.

Night fell as the evening slipped away. The kettles and drums were not banged in the village that midnight.

About an hour before dawn Eztli awoke and Graeme took him back to his own hut to get him something to eat. He was peeling a banana when Centehua came in.

"She has gone."

Graeme put his arms around her; their son toddled over and tapped his mother's leg. She bent down and picked him up. Graeme ran his fingers through the child's hair; then wiped the tears from his wife's face.

❋

The mourning lasted for ten days, during which time Achcauhtli was prepared for her crossing over into Mictlan, that part of the underworld where those who died of old age were to go.

The old lady was cremated, her ashes placed in an urn and Ueman buried them inside the hut.

Centehua persuaded Graeme to return to the fields after her grandmother's funeral and, for a while the three of them lived a settled life. The feelings of foreboding were never far away for Graeme the Woodchopper however, and he started to occasionally wander into the mountains and jungle again.

*

One morning in summer, Graeme rose before dawn and walked out into the forest. He never took provisions on his patrols only a bow, some arrows and an obsidian knife.

The temperature was already rising as he left the village and a very humid dawn saw him arrive at the edge of the forest. The familiar forest sounds stroked his eardrums reassuringly as he walked on, following routes he had travelled many times.

Just before nightfall he heard a voice speak in a language he had not heard for a long time.

"Tell them to keep together and keep them quiet."

Graeme saw the men through the undergrowth and followed them at a discreet distance. His heart raced as he heard the voice; he did not know what to do.

Murray was turning around and speaking to a man with a scarred face. Graeme recognised Rhidian. They were not alone, Graeme the Woodchopper reckoned on about thirty warriors accompanying his former shipmates.

He knew these warriors were heading for his village, but he could not understand why Murray and Rhididan were leading them. He thought about approaching them and explaining to them that he lived in the village. *"Of course they would understand,"* he thought to himself; *"I will go onto them and explain."*

"They may let you live, but they will take the villagers."

Graeme turned to look at the old man.

The old man put an index finger to his lips. "Do not answer me. They will hear you. Only you can hear me."

He pointed toward the gang of men, "They are not the storm; you can save the villagers this time."

Graeme looked on as the warriors stopped to make camp. He turned back toward the old man, but he had gone.

Silently, but with great haste Graeme moved through the forest and back to the village.

"Quickly, we must hide." He woke Centehua with a shake. "The warriors are returning."

He ran into Manauia's hut to warn those inside and within minutes the whole village was preparing to go into hiding. They followed a plan they had rehearsed many times, taking what was needed they made their way to the hiding place.

All stayed in the den except Graeme and Icnoyotl; the two men circled the hiding place at a distance on the look out for danger.

✻

The warriors found the village by early afternoon the following day.

"It has been abandon," said Rhidian.

"No, they have gone into hiding. There were people here up until at least yesterday." Murray turned over the ash of a fire. "Some embers are still warm."

"They must be close by then, I'll take some men and go look for them."

"There's no rush we will stay here for the night, there's shelter and fresh food." He walked over to Manauia's hut. "Tomorrow we will destroy the crops and burn the village, then we will go look for them."

*

Graeme could see the smoke rising into the morning sky and he knew that the village had been razed to the ground. His face flushed with anger as he thought of the men eating their food and sleeping in their huts before carrying out the acts of wanton destruction.

Icnoyotl saw the smoke too. "We must go back closer to our people they will come to look for us now."

The two men made their way back to the villagers hidden in the deepest part of the forest. A number of foxholes had been dug and camouflaged coverings made. At the first sign of danger, people could lie in the holes, invisible to the enemy once the coverings were in place. There were also a number of hollow trees in the area, big enough to hide a person. Manauia and some others hid in these ready to defend the position if anyone was discovered.

Icnoyotl and Graeme moved back closer and closer to the hideaway as Rhidian led a group of ten warriors through the forest toward them. All the villagers were hidden and Manauia and his men waited with bated breath. They could hear the sound of the men approaching.

Graeme and Icnoyotl disappeared into the forest canopy above the hideaway.

"You three into that thicket!" Rhidian pointed toward the hideaway as he barked the order at the three warriors nearest to him. He pushed their backs with his right hand as they filed past him.

Graeme's hand tightened around the handle of his knife, his heart was beating so hard he was afraid one of the warriors would hear it.

The men beat at the undergrowth with their spears as they made their way slowly through the area of the hideaway. One of the men turned suddenly.

Graeme couldn't be sure, but he thought he heard the muffled cough of a child. The other two stopped and held their spears poised to strike. Suddenly, one of the villagers broke cover from his hiding place in a tree toward the edge of the thicket. He loosed off two arrows before running out of the thicket and north toward the mountains.

One warrior fell with an arrow shaft protruding from his right shoulder, the other arrow disappeared into the undergrowth.

"Over there! Quickly!" shouted one of the warriors. Both men ran in pursuit.

Rhidian shouted into the thicket, "What's happening?"

The wounded man groaned.

"Follow me!" the sailor shouted and led a charge into the hideaway.

Two men stopped by the wounded man sitting on the floor with his back against a tree.

"Which way!" shouted Rhidian. The man pointed north and the rest of the men gave chase.

The villagers remained still and silent.

"Come on," said one of the men, "let's get him out of the forest."

They put an arm each around their necks and dragged him out of the thicket, the arrow still extending in front of him.

After a little while Graeme could hear the warriors walking back from the chase. They did not enter the thicket, but travelled past it toward the east. They travelled in silence, which made him think they had failed to catch up with the villager.

It was just after midday when Graeme and Icnoyotl ventured out of their hiding places and moved toward the village. Icnoyotl circled around to the north while Graeme headed due west.

Moving slowly through the trees the smell of smoke started to assault their nostrils. Leaving the forest behind they crouched down low in the grass and edged forward. In the distance they could see the raiding party travelling northeast and away from the village.

"I will follow them in case they return this way," said Graeme softly. "Go and tell the others to spend another night in the forest. It should be safe to return tomorrow."

The Woodchopper trailed the band of men for two days. He watched them ascend the mountains and head west along the plateau. Then he turned for home.

✱

The village was nearly rebuilt in the few days he had been away.

"Manauia! Graeme approaches!" Eleuia shouted.

"I should have known you would see him coming," joked Centehua. She walked to the edge of the village to greet her husband.

Graeme noticed the huts all in a circle as before. "I will build a hut for us, I'll start it in the morning."

"There is no need, we have discussed it as a family and Manauia has decided it will be best if we live in their hut. He has rebuilt it a little bigger than before."

"What are you trying to say?"

"You spend so much time away from the village that it will be safer for me and the child if we have company to look out for us when we sleep."

"But we would have all died if I had not been out there." Graeme was saddened at Centehua's wish to move back with her family.

"I know," said his wife, "you must be out there watching over us." She laid a hand on his cheek. She thought to herself how haunted his expression had become, how drawn were his cheeks. "I will be here waiting with Eztli for the times when you do come home." She reached up and kissed him.

They sat alone outside the circle of huts, Graeme and Centehua; looking at the ashes of their old home. Eztli slept in the family hut.

"I wish this nightmare would end," said Graeme mournfully.

"Wherever we go we could be found, you know that don't you," stated Centehua. "Share the burden with the other men. I am sure they would all take turns in patrolling the forest."

"I vowed I would keep you happy and safe, but I don't think I can do both unless we leave."

They sat together in silence for a while. "Can you tell me of your visions?" she asked.

On that warm summer's night, he told her about the Cardinal's visions of the sacrifices and the Soothsayer's stories of human offerings. Graeme told her of the old man and the prophesy of the woodchopper freeing all the sacrificed souls; he told her he was that woodchopper.

"I wish we could go and live in your woodman's hut."

Graeme smiled, "you would find it very cold in the woods." He pulled out his little wooden cross. "The only flesh and blood sacrificed there though is the body and blood of God Himself."

"How can that be?" asked Centehua with a puzzled look on her face.

"He died for our sins and perpetually offers Himself for our atonement."

"What is sin?" she asked innocently.

"In the case of your people..."

"Our people now," she interjected with a smile.

Graeme took a hold of her hand and smiled back.

"Here it would be something we did to make the gods angry, something that would cause them to stop the sun from rising, or the crops from growing."

"Or send men to come and take us away?"

"I think those men are guided by Lucifer, the Morning Star of the Eternal Night legend."

"Then we are not being punished for our sins?"

"No we are caught up in a war between good and evil and I do not think we have any control over it."

"So your god sends punishment down on the just and unjust alike?"

"No, we just have to do what we think is best according to his Word, He will judge us after we die."

"I see. He will judge you on how you have lived, how you have followed his precepts and handled his trials."

"More or less, yes."

"I think I like my gods better, they are simpler. We give them offerings, they give us sunlight and rain to make our crops grow."

"But your gods have been usurped for evil purposes."

Centehua did not answer straight away; she looked off into the night toward the forest and the mountains, their outline was visible, lit by the stars of the summer sky.

"If my gods have been corrupted then you must follow your god. He will not judge you well if you do not follow His quest."

Centehua took a deep breath before carrying on. "Leaving us may be the one chance you have of saving us. If you can end the sacrifices and free the souls of the slaughtered then maybe you will be able to return to us and we can live in peace; the two of us will be able to watch Eztli grow up together."

Graeme held her close. He pulled his head back and looked into her eyes. "I remember a temptress telling me I could have all that I wanted, a home a family, by foregoing the quest." He smiled at Centehua. "Now you tell me I can only have it by completing it." He kissed her and held her in his arms for a long time.

"Come," Centehua said as she led him into the hut. They both climbed under Centehua's blanket.

Centehua took Graeme's breakfast to him outside the hut the following morning. "It is Eztli's birthday in a few days," she said handing him the Tlaxcalli, "will you wait until then before you leave?"

"Yes. I must speak to your father to tell him of our decision."

"Tell me of what decision?" Manauia asked stooping as he came out of the hut.

"We have decided I must take up my quest."

"Yes," said Centehua. "If he is successful it's the only way he could possibly make it safe for us here and the only way for him to be at peace with himself."

Graeme looked at Centehua's father, he had come to admire and respect Manauia over these last few years. His strength and patience were attributes Graeme attempted to emulate. His devotion and loyalty to his family and to the village were character traits that Graeme wished he could explore more fully, but always there was the Call. He knew if he did not answer it now then eventually they would all die.

"I will leave the day after my son's birthday."

✻

Graeme spent every waking moment with his family for the next few days. After the early morning meal he spent an hour playing ball with Eztli, then each morning, Centehua would join them and they went bathing in a nearby stream; one morning they even took Eztli back to the beach and the orange grove where they met.

They walked the tracks to the fields and talked with the men. Graeme worked for a few hours in the early afternoon before walking back with his wife and child. They spent the last two evenings with the family around the hearth. Everyone talked of crops and the weather and Eztli's birthday celebration, but no one spoke of Graeme's leaving.

"You will have to pick out a costume to wear during the dance," said Centehua.

Graeme smiled, "You've been trying to get me into one of those costumes since I first arrived here."

"Well Eztli is too young to dance for his own birthday so I thought you could do it for him."

"It will please our gods," Chipahua said from the other side of the fire.

"I will make a costume for Eztli to match yours," said Cualli.

"If it will please my wife then I will do it." Graeme walked over to where his son slept. He sat beside him and very gently stroked the boy's forehead.

By the time Graeme arose the following morning the preparations for Eztli's birthday celebration had already begun. The whole village celebrated with much eating and drinking and everyone put on costumes and danced. Graeme and Eztli both wore costumes with feathered wings. Eztli followed his father around all day, even trying to copy the dances.

When Graeme was watching others dance Manauia came up and stood beside him. "This celebration isn't only for your son, you know that don't you?"

Graeme put his hand on the older man's shoulder. "I know my friend, I wish I did not have to go."

Yaotl and Icnoyotl approached the two men.

"You have been good friends; and I have a family too, something I thought I would never be a part of."

"Come back to us," said Yaotl. He placed a beautifully carved wooden cross in Graeme's hand, it was styled with a circle linking the top cross section in the Celtic style. The cross was six inches high with a very small base that allowed it to be placed standing up on a flat surface.

Graeme looked down at the gift.

"I have seen you praying to those two bits of stick and I remember you telling me what it meant. I made this from the description of the cross you told me about, the one you saw on the island when you met the old man."

"Thank you," said Graeme his voice thick with emotion. He embraced each man in turn.

"This is your home you must return." Manauia released himself from Graeme's embrace and walked back toward the celebrations.

That night Graeme and Centehua slept with Eztli between them under the blanket. Graeme's day had been filled with strong emotions and he knew he would never ever be happier than he was living with these people.

Dawn broke and Graeme and Centehua stood at the edge of the village holding Eztli's hands.

"You have to come back to me." Centehua was speaking with tears running down her face.

"I promise I will do all I can to return to you." He handed his cross, made of two sticks to his wife. "Keep this for me until I get back, I have another one now."

They held each other tight, until Graeme let go and bent down to pick up his son. Cenetehua put her arms around the two of them.

"I have to go," said Graeme finally. With a heavy heart and tears in his eyes he kissed them both and walked away from the village toward the forest.

Just before he entered the forest, Graeme the Woodchopper took a final glance back toward the village. He was surprised to see a figure hurrying toward him. He stopped to take a closer look and saw Eleuia the Soothsayer approaching.

"What? Is there a problem?" Graeme's concern was evident in his voice.

"No," answered the Soothsayer. "I have to come to tell you about Quetzalcoatl."

"I do not know that name."

"You never really showed a great deal of interest in our gods, but I think you need to know about this one."

The two men sat down under the shade of a large laurel tree and the Soothsayer began his story.

"Quetzalcoatl is the god who gave us maize to eat, he is also the protector of the sun when it passes through the dark place during the night. He is the god we give burnt offerings to every day before dawn so that he will allow the sun to come and nourish our crops and give us light. We live in the time of the Fifth Sun and it was Quetzalcoatl that created this time."

"What happened to the time of the other four suns?"

"During the time of the First Sun, giants lived upon the earth, but they were eaten by jaguars."

The old man coughed to clear his throat.

"The time of the Second Sun was ended by great winds and the Third Sun rained fire down upon the land and it was destroyed."

The old man paused again; he looked as if he did not want to speak of the Fourth Sun.

"What of the fourth?' asked Graeme impatiently.

"The time of the Fourth Sun ended in a flood."

"In my sacred scriptures it tells of a flood that destroyed the world."

"I know, you told me once when I asked you about your god."

"My Holy Scriptures tell of a good man who was warned by God about the coming rain and he and his family were spared. They also saved all the animals in the world by building a huge boat." Graeme gazed thoughtfully into the forest, then he asked, "Does your story talk of the end of the Fifth Sun?"

"It will end, but not for at least seven hundred cycles."

"Do you know during which season?" Graeme knew this was very close to the time given in the Legend of the Eternal Night and revealed to Cardinal Caronni in the Scroll of Explanation.

"It will end on a winter solstice that is all I know."

Graeme wished he could speak to the Cardinal now. He thought too of Thomas Aquinas, he could have helped him make sense of all this.

"You should go back; it will take you a while to make the return journey."

"Wait I haven't finished the story yet. I heard you tell Centehua of the Morning Star, you called him by a name."

"Lucifer."

"I think Lucifer and Quetzalcoatl are the same. Both are likened to the Morning Star."

The old man looked intently at Graeme. "I want to come with you I need to know if my god is evil like you say."

"You cannot, it is a long and hard journey. There will be many dangers and you will probably die."

"I am stronger than I look, besides you will need me to assist you. There will be many things that you will not understand and I can explain them to you. My knowledge may even save your life."

"We are heading to almost certain death," said the Woodchopper.

"I am going to die sooner rather than later anyway. If I die a worthwhile death, a warrior's death, then my journey into the afterlife will be a good one and the gods will smile upon me."

Graeme picked up the old man's bundle and passed it to him.

"Come we have a great distance to travel," he said smiling at the old man.

The Soothsayer threw the bag over his shoulder and followed Graeme the Woodchopper into the forest.

THE TEMPLE

The two men travelled through the forest by day. They killed small animals for meat and supplemented this by picking berries and fruit, camping down at sunset and rising with the dawn.

"We'll make a fire tonight," said the Woodchopper. "You can cook the rabbit I killed earlier."

Eleuia the Soothsayer gathered some wood and lit a fire while Graeme skinned the rabbit.

"How many more days until we leave the forest?" asked the Soothsayer.

"There's a lake not far from here and just beyond that we will start to climb the mountain ridge. It should be our last day in the forest tomorrow."

Graeme watched the old man skewer the rabbit and place it over the flames. Before long the smell of the meat cooking wafted into their nostrils and enticed their taste buds. The two men sat in silence their faces illuminated by the glow from the fire; the only sounds were the sounds of the jungle and the crackling of burning wood, there was hissing every now and again as fat dripped from the rabbit onto the flames.

After a while the old man said, "I think the meat is ready now."

He leaned over and removed the rabbit from the fire, cut a large strip of meat off and handed it to the Woodchopper.

"Tell me, how did you become a soothsayer?"

"My grandfather was a soothsayer and he taught me how to read the stars and enter into trances."

"Do you have a spirit guide?"

"Yes, it is the spirit of a coyote he guides me in my visions."

"Have you asked him about my quest?"

"Yes." The Soothsayer cut off another strip of meat and started to eat. "It was my spirit guide that told me to accompany you," he said through a mouthful of rabbit.

"Do you think we will be successful?" asked Graeme pensively.

"I do not know."

The Soothsayer gazed into the fire for a long while then spoke again. "I had a wife once. We lived in a town on the plateau over this mountain ridge. When the warriors came to the village it brought it all back to me. I want to stop it happening again if I can."

"What happened to her?"

"Warriors came to our town; there were a great number of them. They took many of my people including my wife to use for their sacrifices. I was captured and tortured after trying to free my wife. They left me for dead. When I came around I hid in this forest until my wounds healed. I wandered here for many days after in my grief and eventually I was taken in and accepted by the villagers. They are good people, I hope no harm will come to them."

"You never found another wife?"

"No. In the place where we lived it was not unusual for men to have more than one wife, but I never wanted anyone else and there was no one who could replace her once she was gone."

The Soothsayer turned and climbed under his blanket, lost in his memories. Graeme took out his cross and began to pray silently in the darkness.

❊

They reached the lake about noon. The day was hot and the water looked cool. Graeme glanced up at the cloudless sky.

"We may as well camp here, I'll go and see if I can kill something to eat, you can make a fire."

It wasn't long before he spotted a small deer in the forest making its way toward the watering hole. Very slowly and without making a sound the Woodchopper placed an arrow in his bow and aimed. The deer dropped its head to chew on some grass; he shot off an arrow hitting the deer in the neck. The animal jumped into the air and started to run through the trees, Graeme loosed off another arrow then gave chase. The second arrow hit just below the first strike, the deer stumbled down on its front legs, it tried to get up, but Graeme was on it, he pulled the animal's head back and slit its throat. It fell to the ground, life oozing out of it as the bloodstain spread out across the grass.

Graeme carried the deer out of the woods to the camp on his shoulders. He could see the Soothsayer bathing in the lake.

When he saw Graeme approaching the old man got out of the lake and walked toward the fire to put his clothes on. This was the first time the Woodchopper had seen the Soothsayer without a garment covering his upper body. Unlike the other males in the village he always kept his torso covered, but now Graeme could see the marks left by the torture.

His entire upper body was covered in the scars left by numerous deep cuts, even his nipples had at some point been sliced off. By the time Graeme reached the campfire the old man was covered up.

The two companions spent the afternoon preparing and cooking the deer. Graeme bathed in the lake while the deer roasted over the fire.

"One of us will need to keep a watch at all times from now on," said Graeme. "There will be precious little cover now and we will be more likely to meet people once we are beyond the ridge."

"Yes," agreed the Soothsayer. "I'll take the first watch tonight. I'll wake you when the moon is half way across the night sky."

✼

It was a beautiful, balmy starlit night and the old man was looking out toward the mountain ridge when he thought he heard something in the trees. He turned slowly, reaching for his bow and arrows resting on the ground beside him. In the trees he thought he saw two blood red orbs staring back at him. Silently he placed an arrow in the bow.

"Graeme," he called softly to the Woodchopper.

The Woodchopper opened his eyes and saw his companion kneeling facing the forest with the bow and arrow in his hands. He reached for the knife at his side.

"What is it?" he whispered.

"There, look, there's something in there."

"I've seen this before," the Woodchopper said as he saw the two red orbs move toward them.

The demon walked slowly out of the trees and into the light of the starry night.

"By the gods what is it?" the Soothsayer's voice betrayed the fear in his heart.

A sharp rustling sound ran through the quiet of the night as the demon flexed his wings slightly.

The Woodchopper heard the quiet hiss of displaced air as the arrow flew toward the demon. He heard the demon's blood curdling shriek when the arrow pierced the grey muscular torso.

"Run!" he shouted when he saw the demon pull the arrow from his chest and unfurl his wings. It was too late; the demon landed in front of the Soothsayer before he could flee.

Graeme dived at him with his knife in his hand; the demon turned and struck him with a downward blow, one of its talons cutting across his bare chest before the demon's hand struck his temple. The smell of sulphur filled Graeme's nostrils as he lost consciousness.

✳

In the dream he was drifting across a large black river, he could see no sky and wondered if the river was in a cave. The stench from the water was overpowering.

On the far bank he saw a figure wearing a big black hat; he could hear it calling him on, it was calling him by name. He wanted to go toward the man, but he could see Centehua standing on the other side of the river holding Eztli's hand. He tried to put his hands in the water to guide the boat back to his wife and child, but the water burned his hands and the boat drifted on toward the man in black.

He thought he had woken, but he didn't know for sure. The face of the beautiful young man was once again smiling reassuringly at him and he was bathed in light. A profound sense of peace overcame him and he drifted back into the darkness.

The man in black was there again, but Graeme was no longer on a boat the man was pulling his hand; Graeme felt as if he couldn't breathe, everywhere there was a choking grey dust.

The dust was gone now and Graeme opened his eyes; about six feet above him he could see the domed rock roof of a cave. For a moment he was expecting to see the man in black again, but this felt different the air seemed fresher. He felt alive.

"I thought you'd never wake up," said the Soothsayer.

"Where are we?" said Graeme turning toward him.

"We are in a cave at the foot of the mountain ridge, just above the tree line."

"What happened to the demon?"

"I'm not really sure, I saw you fall and the demon turn toward me; then I was blinded by a brilliant white light and the next thing I knew we were both in this cave."

"How long have we been here?"

"I have seen seven sunsets. I don't know how long I was unconscious before that though."

"Is there food here?"

"Yes, whatever brought us here brought the deer as well, there are berries and fruits just down below in the jungle and there is fresh water running through the back of the cave there."

Graeme hadn't been aware of it before, but now he could hear the trickle of water. He looked around in the dim half-light and saw that he was in a cave approximately six feet high by about nine feet wide; it extended back ten feet to where the water ran through a crack in the rock, the cave narrowed to about four feet in height at the rear.

The Soothsayer cut up some meat and gave it to Graeme. He watched him devour it ravenously.

"Are you well enough to get up?"

"I think so."

"Well you've certainly got your appetite back," the Soothsayer said as he gave the Woodchopper a hand to get to his feet.

It took him a few minutes, but Graeme eventually managed to stand unaided. He felt a burning sensation across his chest as he made his way slowly to the entrance of the cave.

Across his chest were three parallel cuts that had not fully healed. The Woodchopper ran the middle finger of his right hand across the cut at the top of his chest and remembered the searing pain he felt just before the demon knocked him out.

Standing just outside the cave, Graeme could see that he was just above the tree line. Below him stretched the green canopy of the forest. He could see the trail made by the Soothsayer in his forages into the forest to pick fruit and berries. There was no clear path above him to the top of the ridge.

'It's not too steep,' he thought 'we should be able to climb it from here.'

Graeme sat down outside the cave, he felt a little disorientated after looking up at the ridge.

"Are you ok?"

"I just need to rest a little more."

Eleuia the Soothsayer passed him some water.

"Thanks." The Woodchopper took a sip. "We'll stay here for a day or two before we move on."

*

It was the afternoon of the second day after Graeme had regained consciousness and he was feeling strong enough to go foraging with the old man, but as they were about to leave both men stopped and looked at each other. There was a commotion going on down on the forest floor.

It was the Soothsayer who spoke first. "Something has disturbed the animals."

"We're visible on this ridge," said Graeme, "get down on the ground."

Both men lay down and peered intently toward the thick green jungle. The trees parted about four hundred yards south of them and warriors started to file out of the forest.

It was a large party, Graeme counted fifty warriors and in the middle of the line there were eight figures tied together.

"They've got prisoners," whispered the Soothsayer.

"Do you recognise any of them?"

"I can't make them out from here."

"It looks like three people and five children." Graeme gazed down intently trying to make out some features of the captives.

The warriors marched on relentlessly, one child fell and a warrior poked him with his spear before one of the older prisoners bent down to pick him up.

"We have to get closer," said Graeme.

"If we follow them they will lead us to the temples of sacrifice," said the Soothsayer.

94

"Do you think they are from the same tribe as the ones who raided the village?"

"Yes," said the old man. His voice betrayed the depth of concern he was experiencing.

"We will have to get close to them tonight, once they get up onto the plateau it will be difficult to stay close to them without being spotted." Graeme slouched back toward the cave, being careful not to get sky-lined. "Quick, let's gather some provisions for the journey."

Graeme could barely contain himself in his hurry to get close to the raiding party. He was desperate to know if the captives were from their village and he knew he had to do it tonight.

"Do not worry," said the Soothsayer, "they will be easy to track." The old man began putting food in a leather pouch he retrieved from his bundle. "Get some rest until sunset we will set out then."

✳

Just before dusk the two men left the cave and headed south. They soon picked up the raiding party's trail and after a few hours they saw the smoke from the campfires rising into the starry sky. Before long they could see the light of the flames casting shadows through the trees.

"Wait here while I try to get in closer," whispered Graeme the Woodchopper.

He moved slowly through the grass on his hands and knees, when he could hear the voices of the men he dropped down onto his stomach. He knew that the captives were all tied together in the middle of the camp, but if he could get to a spot between the guards he thought he might be able to see the faces of the prisoners from the light of the campfires.

Slowly he slithered forward on his stomach, he was no more than ten yards away from one guard now. He heard the man cough then saw him turn to look toward the prisoners. Another warrior approached.

"Here," said the warrior as he handed the guard an avocado.

"Thanks."

"The pale skins are in a hurry to get back to the city."

"Yes," said the guard. "They do not like it in the forest."

Graeme guessed they were talking about his old shipmates. He felt his heart rate quicken and panic rising as he wondered if they had been back to the village.

❊

"They will slow up a bit now we are coming out into the grassland," said the warrior turning and walking back to the centre of the camp.

Graeme crawled in a few yards closer and slowly lifted his head to look at the captives. He dropped down quickly, killing a cry of anguish in his throat before it could escape. He had watched his wife pull his son toward her in a gesture of protection as the warrior walked past them.

"The captives are from our village," whispered Graeme to the Soothsayer when he crept back. "I just saw Centehua and Eztli."

The Soothsayer put his hand on Graeme's shoulder.

❊

It was difficult trailing the warriors through the grassland; there was very little cover and Graeme and the Soothsayer had to drop quite a distance behind to remain unseen. The two men soon adopted a pattern of breaking camp just before noon and following the trail well into the night.

"We can only be a few days travel from the city now," said the old man. "We should start to see some outlying farms and settlements shortly."

"That's going to make it difficult to remain unnoticed," replied Graeme.

The two men picked up their bundles ready to move on.

"I am going to try to free the captives tonight," said Graeme decidedly.

✳

There were two guards circling the camp. The three adult prisoners were separated from the children and tied to a stake driven into the ground about twenty yards from the edge of the encampment. Three fires lit the camp, forming a triangle and equally spaced from each other. The warriors were bedded down as an outer ring around the fires and the five children were tethered together a few yards from the other prisoners.

Both guards died simultaneously and silently as Graeme and the Soothsayer shot off an arrow each. Graeme moved quickly into the camp. He drove his knife through the eye of a warrior and stepped over the body; he rushed up to the captives and cut through the restraining rope with the bloodstained obsidian blade.

Although the fires were dying his silhouette was plainly visible by the light of the burning embers. Any warrior could have spotted him if he woke up. He quickly freed the children's bonds. Grabbing his son and waving to his wife to follow he ran out of the camp.

"Quickly, they're escaping!"

Graeme recognised Murray's voice as he ran into the dark night.

He heard the whoosh of arrows flying past him as the Soothsayer let fly. Warriors began to fall under the steady stream of arrows. Three children were recaptured quickly and one captive lay bleeding on the ground after being felled by a blow from a lance, seven warriors took off in pursuit.

"Form a defence," commanded Murray. He turned to Rhidian. "Take those men with you and look for the others."

Rhidian took four men with him and joined the other seven in pursuit.

Graeme ran as fast as he could with his son in his arms. He looked around frantically for signs of Centehua, but she had disappeared into the night.

The noise of the warriors chasing them was getting louder. He heard the whoosh of arrows again, but this time they were aimed at him. Two of the pursuers were nearly on him now and he knew he would have to put down his son and fight.

"Run!" he shouted to his son as he put him down.

Before he could turn he felt two arms around his shoulders and the force of a collision as one of the warriors tackled him. He reached for his knife, but he lost his balance; spinning as he fell he thrust the weapon into the man's side between two of his ribs. The man yelled with pain and loosened his grip.

Graeme leapt to his feet and thrust out into the darkness, the tip of the knife connected with the second assailant's collarbone. The warrior put his arm up to the wound as he let out a yell; the Woodchopper pulled the knife back and thrust it into the assailant's neck. He fell to the floor with blood spurting from a punctured artery.

"Stop," the other warrior commanded. "I have the child."

Graeme turned to see his son's petrified face held high in front of the man's chest; there was a knife at his neck.

"Put your knife down and lay on the floor or I cut his throat."

Graeme did as he was told.

"Over here!" the warrior attracted the attention of his companions.

"Well done." Graeme recognised the voice as Rhidian's. "We have the others too."

The rest of the chasing group arrived.

"You two help him back to camp." Rhidian pointed at the injured man. He knelt down to look at the other warrior. "This one is already dead." He gestured toward the captives. "Take the prisoners back." He walked on ahead without recognising his former shipmate.

✻

"Well, what have we here?" Murray was watching Graeme and his son being led into camp, the Woodchopper's hands were tied behind his back. "I never thought I'd see you again."

"What do you want with these people?" asked Graeme.

"I was going to ask you the same thing." Murray squatted down to look at Eztli. "You risked almost certain death to free these people." He reached out to touch the boy's face.

Graeme lurched forward, but was held by a warrior.

"Interesting." Murray slapped the boy hard against his cheek; the boy spun around and fell to the floor.

Graeme let out a yell and struggled violently against his captor. The captor struck him with the handle of his own knife and he fell dazed to the ground. Centehua broke from the clutches of her captor and ran toward the two fallen bodies.

"I see," said Murray with a smile on his lips. "Tie the three of them together and watch them closely." He turned and looked at Graeme as he walked back to his blanket. "We'll talk in the morning."

"What happened? Did they return?" Graeme asked his wife.

"A few days after you left they came back to the village," replied Centehua.

"The others?"

"Yaotl is dead," Centehua's eyes brimmed with tears, "I saw him fall."

"Your father?"

"I don't know."

The three of them pulled closer together with Eztli wedged in between his mother and father.

"Ueman led some of the women and children into the forest."

"They must be safe then," said Graeme hopefully.

They both watched the sun come up over the plateau in front of them while Eztli slept fitfully.

Graeme could see Murray striding toward them with two warriors at his side.

"Cut him free and put the other two with the rest of the prisoners." Murray ordered.

One man cut Graeme free from the other two and re-tied his hands behind his back. The other man led

Centehua and Eztli away toward the other captives. Eztli reached for his father, but Centehua swept him up in her arms.

Murray offered Graeme a bowl of atole. He turned away.

"You may as well eat it, you're going to be hungry by the end of the day."

Graeme accepted the bowl and started to eat the porridge-like substance.

"I should be angry with you," said Murray. "You have killed four of my men and left several seriously injured."

'He hasn't found the Soothsayer' thought Graeme.

"But seeing you with your family," he looked at Graeme intently. "They are your wife and child I take it?"

Graeme did not look up from his porridge.

Murray grabbed Graeme's hair and jerked his head back. "I'll take that as a yes," he said with anger in his voice.

Graeme the Woodchopper looked back into his eyes without expression.

"Aren't you wondering why we are in charge of these people?"

"Right now I'm more concerned with what you're going to do to us."

"You're all going to die."

The Woodchopper thought to himself how hard Murray had become. On the ship he was a good sailor who kept himself to himself. Now he was brutal and sadistic.

"So what turned you into a cold-blooded killer and murderer of innocent women and children."

Murray let out a harsh laugh with no humour in it only malice.

"Rhidian, Hesper and myself grounded with the ship, or what was left of it a long way north of here and wandered inland through the jungle for days on end. Eventually we were discovered by some local tribesmen." Murray paused. "From then on our fortunes improved. The natives mistook Hesper for one of their gods come back to life."

"Which god?"

"I don't know, Quitlcottle or something."

"Quetzalcoatl," corrected Graeme.

"That's the one." Murray took a long drink of water from a round leather container. "The thing is they treat us like Christ resurrected, all we have to do is go along with the sacrifices they make to Hesper every week."

"Human sacrifices," said Graeme dejectedly.

"Yes, they're particularly fond of..."

"Children," Graeme said interrupting his captor.

"Do you know why I came on this journey?" he asked Murray.

"I heard you mention some sort of quest."

"Did you hear me speak of the Legend of the Eternal Night?"

"Yes."

"Well the main goal of the quest is to stop the recruitment of souls for the armies of Hell."

Murray laughed. "It won't be long before you are in Hell yourself."

"That may be, but I have to defeat the Morning Star in the process."

"And where do you expect to find this Morning Star?" asked Murray sardonically.

"We know him as Lucifer." Graeme gazed deeply and intently into Murray's eyes, his face carved with conviction. "The people here call him Quetzalcoatl."

Murray turned from the Woodchopper's gaze, "Wait until we get to the city before you make any plans." Looking back as he began to walk away he said, "Then you will see what you're up against."

✳

Murray kept Graeme apart from the rest of the captives for the remainder of the journey. He only caught fleeting glimpses of his wife and child, usually at night as they were bedding down. He had seen no sign of the Soothsayer since the night of his capture, but he felt sure that the old man was out there somewhere biding his time.

With each day they passed more and more signs of human life. At first they began to pass isolated farms and houses. Soon they were passing villages. These were always very quiet, as if the people did not want to be noticed by the raiding party as it passed through.

Then, late one afternoon they climbed up on to a hill overlooking a huge basin and on this plateau, as far as the eye could see, were buildings of all shapes and sizes. He could also see roads, public squares and huge stone aqueducts that supplied the city with water. Graeme had seen nothing like this before.

Facing them, on the other side of the valley was a temple; the sun caught the stone altar at the top and it glistened red in the sunlight. In the distance behind the temple was a great conical shaped mountain dominating the skyline. The party wove its way down a well-worn track toward the bustling metropolis.

People stopped to look at them as they made their way through the city streets; occasionally there was a cheer from bystanders and curious children ran up to touch the captives.

Graeme managed to get a glimpse of his wife and child and noticed the look of fear on Eztli's face. He saw Centehua try to comfort his son. What surprised the Woodchopper was the lack of malice or even indifference. Every one they saw looked pleased to see them.

"Come with us." Two guards led Graeme away from the rest of the captives onto a wide street at the bottom of which was a large plaza.

He looked back and saw the others being led in the direction of the temple. Beads of sweat began to break out on his forehead and his stomach churned, bile rose in his throat. He fought an inner battle to regain control as the image of a beating heart held high filled his consciousness.

"Quickly, the Master awaits." A prod from the second guard's spear served to bring him back to the moment. He looked around in vain for a glimpse of the Soothsayer.

The two guards and their captive crossed the plaza and stood at a set of mighty gates. Another guard opened the gates and led them into a magnificent courtyard defined by its symmetrical lines and the perfect geometry of the walls and buildings within.

In the centre of the courtyard was a statue of a man that reached up sixteen feet dominating the courtyard; it had an elaborately ornamented skirt and on its head was carved a huge feather headdress.

Graeme the Woodchopper gasped as he recognised the bird-like, angular facial features of Hesper; and yet the statue showed the weathering of great age, he thought to himself.

The three men continued on until they stood at the door of the largest most spectacular building of all.

After entering the group walked down a corridor that seemed to go on and on, until they finally arrived at a throne room.

✻

The throne was about two hundred yards away from the entrance and in an elevated position on a platform with pillars at each corner. The walls of the room were highly decorated with murals of gods and goddesses, battles and sacrifices; the mythology of the people played out in paint and plaster.

"We wondered what had happened to you," said Hesper. He was sitting on the step at the front of the platform wearing a loose white cotton gown, open at the neck and reaching down to his calves. His hair was pulled back in a ponytail. "The others thought you might have drowned, but I just knew we would meet again."

The Master stood up and beckoned to Graeme to approach him. "Let's get you cleaned up."

He clapped his hands twice and two young, tall, slim female attendants with straight dark shoulder-length hair entered from a room off to the right of the throne platform. They wore garments similar in style to Hesper's.

Graeme the Woodchopper followed them through to a large square room with a sunken bath in the middle of the floor. One attendant helped him out of his leggings while the other added aromatic oils to the bath.

Graeme immersed himself in the water and, despite his worries, he found himself relaxing into the warmth of the water.

After a few minutes the two women returned with garments for him. One of them handed him a towel and watched as he dried himself. The other handed him a blue breechcloth similar in style to the Maxtlatl worn by the peasants, only of a finer quality. While he was putting this on the other women fetched a long blue heavily decorated cape that reached down to the bottom of Graeme's calves.

"I find Maxtlatl a little too revealing for me, but I thought you wouldn't mind." Hesper entered the room carrying two drinks. "I hear you've entered fully into the customs of this land."

"My wife and child were taken toward the temple." The magnitude of his concern expressed in his tone of voice.

"They are safe for now," said Hesper as he handed him a drink.

The Master led Graeme into the throne room. "Allow me to show you around some of my palace. You know, I could do with some stimulating company. I always found you more interesting than the others."

The two men walked down endless corridors stopping occasionally to look inside magnificently ornate rooms. Finally they came to a wing where the rooms were of a smaller, but still luxurious, scale.

"All this could be yours." Hesper waved his arm around in a semi-circle in front of his torso. "What do you think?"

"It is all very impressive."

Hesper led Graeme into a large white-walled room. There was a bed at the far end of the room and in the centre were three wooden chairs and a table. Down one side of the room was a large assortment of cushions. Graeme was struck by how much it reminded him of large stately rooms he had seen in England.

The Master walked to the table and picked up a bundle of items wrapped in a blanket. There was another one of similar size on the table.

"I believe this is yours." He walked over to the bed and unfurled the blanket leaving its contents open to display. Graeme the Woodchopper moved forward to look at the opened bundle.

"Did you carve this yourself?" The Master picked up a wooden cross, carved in the Celtic fashion. He gazed intently at it.

The Woodchopper looked over at the cross and noticed it was beginning to smoulder. He shifted his gaze to the Master who was lost in his own thoughts.

Graeme remembered the bloodlust and menace in Hesper's eyes after he had killed the men on the boat, but what he saw now was much deeper. He couldn't be sure, but he thought he saw red flames deep within the Master's eyes. What he was sure of was the hatred apparent on the hard angular features of Hesper's face. The depth of hatred emanating from the Master was unfathomable to Graeme and he looked away disconcertedly. The hatred seemed to reach back in time, spanning millennia.

The cross eventually burst into flames. The Master dropped it, turned away and walked back to the table.

The Woodchopper bent down to touch the cross and was surprised to find that it felt cold. He stood up and looked at it; it was unmarked.

"Come, let us talk about your family," said Hesper gesturing for Graeme to join him at the table.

"Can I see them?"

"Yes, I will take you to the temple tomorrow."

"Thank you," he said with a certain amount of deference in his voice. He did not know why, but he feared the Master now in a way he never had before; in a way that he had never feared another human being before.

"Rest tonight and reflect upon my offer." The Master stood up to leave. "You can live here in the lap of luxury for the rest of your days." He stopped at the door. "Your wife and child can be with you also, safe from the slaughter at the temple," and with that he left the room and closed the door behind him.

Graeme the Woodchopper picked up the bundle on the table and placed it on the floor, very carefully he positioned the cross at the centre of the table and began to pray.

He asked God to protect his family, to save them from the holocaust at the temple. He asked God to guide his actions and to show him his path. He also asked for the strength and courage to follow that path.

"You know where your destiny lies."

"What happened to the Soothsayer?" asked Graeme as he opened his eyes. The Woodchopper showed no surprise at the old man's appearance.

"He followed you to the city and has avoided capture," said the little old man sitting opposite Graeme.

"You must tell him to leave this place."

"My work is with you."

"Then tell me how to rescue my family and destroy the temple."

"You are narrowing your field of vision to this existence, this time."

The old man leaned forward and picked up the cross. "Do you remember the dream in which the Holy Mother came to you?"

"Yes."

"Well no matter what happens here to your family, they will be placed within the enclosed garden of her Immaculate Heart."

"Are you telling me that they have to die?" Graeme's voice was rising in anger.

The little old man handed him the cross. He looked at the cross in his hand and noticed it had changed. It was now a crucifix, showing the figure of the crucified Christ.

"How did you…?"

"Remember the true message of the cross," interrupted the old man. "Through suffering there is hope, but most of all death is not the end."

The little old man stood up and walked over to the Woodchopper, he placed his hand on his shoulder. "You have to kill Hesper for he has now truly become the Master of Evil."

"He has changed," Graeme said. "I felt fear down to the depth of my soul in his company earlier."

"He is possessed," said the old man. "The Morning Star rises in his soul. Lucifer, Quetzalcoatl or whatever you want to call him is attempting to increase the harvest of souls. He knows someone is here to stop him, and he knows it is you."

Graeme the Woodchopper put his head in his hands and looked down at the table. His despair was a tangible presence in the room. The little old man removed his hand from Graeme's shoulder. When the Woodchopper eventually lifted his head up he was alone.

Graeme lay down on the bed and dozed fitfully. His sleep was disturbed by the faces of Centehua and of Eztli, by visions of carnage atop the temple and by the deep timeless hatred etched in the face of Hesper when he looked at the cross.

*

"Did you sleep well?" Murray entered the room with a tray of tortillas and a drink. "I've brought you something to eat." He lay the tray down on the table. "I prefer to eat later in the day myself, but I know you've settled into the local customs."

He grinned as he looked over at Graeme. "That wife of yours is quite something, I hope nothing happens to her."

"If she is harmed in any way I will kill you," said the Woodchopper in a matter of fact manner.

"Enjoy your food, you will be going to the temple soon."

An hour later Murray returned with four guards.

"It's time to worship their gods." He put his face up close to Graeme's and looked into his eyes, "or should I say your gods?"

The Woodchopper remained silent.

*

Murray led the four, armed guards through the city and up the hill toward the temple; Graeme walked in the middle of the guards. He looked up and saw a large crowd of people gathered around the sacrificial altar at the top. The temple was shaped like a pyramid, only with the point cut away. There was a series of steps leading up to a large flat area at the top. At the centre of this space was a large stone altar. The nearer they got to the place of carnage the redder everything became. At the top of the temple the altar stone, the platform, everything was dyed a deep red from the blood of the sacrificed.

The Woodchopper noticed the Master sitting on a huge wooden throne off to the side of the altar surrounded by a host of armed warriors. It was toward this vantage point that Murray led the group.

The throng parted to allow the small party to make its way to the Master. "Come sit up here," he said to Graeme, "we've been waiting for you." He turned to Murray. "You can go now."

The Woodchopper climbed up onto the raised platform.

"Sit here." The Master pointed to a wooden chair just in front and to the side of his own elaborate throne.

From his vantage point he could see a row of people all standing in single file at the other side of the altar. This line of humanity reached back to the end of the sacrificial area and he noticed that it continued down the steps at the rear of the pyramid, the side hidden from the city.

There were five priests standing by the altar, one held a large flint knife in his hand.

The first in line was a woman of forty, two guards stripped her of her clothing and handed her to the four unarmed priests. They placed her on the cold stone altar slab and the fifth priest quickly cut through her abdomen and pulled the knife up through her diaphragm. He reached inside and ripped out her still-beating heart.

The Woodchopper was amazed at the speed of the operation; it was all over in a second or so. The priest held the beating heart aloft and then it was placed in a basin held by a statue of a god known as Huitzilopochtli. The other four priests threw the body down the steps of the temple; the Woodchopper could see warriors taking it away.

"That is the statue of the god that is being worshipped today," said the Master.

Graeme couldn't answer because he was trying to keep down the bile rising into his throat.

"You look a little pale, here have a drink." The Master passed him a container of water. "Didn't your village offer sacrifices to the gods?"

"Only animal sacrifices." He looked back toward the altar and could see another victim, a man in his early twenties, being led to the slab. Graeme turned his head away.

The Master gestured to two nearby guards to restrain the Woodchopper. They grabbed him and turned his head toward the altar.

"If he doesn't watch kill him." A knife was held at his throat.

All morning the killing went on until finally there was no one left in line to kill.

"Tomorrow we worship the water gods." The Master stood up to leave. "They prefer children."

Graeme the Woodchopper was led down off the platform with the Master.

"They particularly like to see the children's tears first so we have to pull their fingernails out before they are sacrificed to make them cry."

Graeme and the Master walked down the steps of the temple until at the bottom they came to a door. One of the Master's entourage pressed a stone near to the door and it swung open. Inside was a dark corridor; the

Master entered first, followed by Graeme and two guards. The rest of the group remained outside.

The corridor was cold and damp and the two guards held flaming torches that gave some light for them to walk by. They walked on until they came to another door, a large wooden one. The Master knocked twice and another guard opened the door. Behind it lay another corridor, but this one was better lit. Graeme could see that the corridor ran on for quite some distance and either side there were doorways with bars running vertically down them. The bars were too close to let anyone pass through and as they walked on Graeme could see people behind them.

"Is my wife down here?" he asked.

"No I have sent her back to your room, you can see her later."

"Then why have you brought me here?"

Just then they came to a large room at the end of the corridor. Graeme figured that they must have by now walked the entire length of the base of the temple. This room was bigger than the others. Graeme looked in and saw that it was full of children.

"We don't normally separate them from their families, but this room is for the following day's sacrifices. And tomorrow it is the turn of the children."

One child broke suddenly from the mass of children huddled away from the gate.

Graeme recognised his son. He knelt down and put his arms through the bars. Eztli ran into his father's arms and Graeme held him tight to the gate.

"I want you to go back to your room and discuss your possible future here with your wife."

The two guards pulled Graeme away from the child who began crying and sobbing uncontrollably.

"He should save the tears for tomorrow, it will save us having to rip his fingernails out."

The Woodchopper lunged for the Master, but was held firm by the two guards.

Laughing the Master said, "I think you need to discuss this with your wife."

The Master signalled to the two men to lead Graeme back down the corridor. The two men struggled with their prisoner as he resisted their attempts to move him.

"Tatli! Tatli!" Eztli shouted as Graeme tried to free himself.

"Walk with me or I will kill the boy now." The Master's voice was heavy with malice.

Graeme felt again the fear rising in him as he recognised pure evil emanating from the Master; he saw again the red flame flickering deep within his eyes. Graeme stopped struggling and the Master nodded at the two guards to let him go and the four men walked on down the corridor.

"Do you remember our conversation on the Harbinger when we first met?" The Master talked as they walked through the temple corridors and out into the daylight.

"I told you of the circumstances that led me to you." Graeme squinted at the sunlight as he spoke.

"Yes, your quest." The Master looked up at the bright sunlight. The day was well into the afternoon now and it was very hot. "You are to prevent the Eternal Night."

Graeme could feel his fear of the Master engulfing his whole being now and the Master recognised it too. It lay heavily in the air around them.

"Do you think you can stop the Morning Star from rebelling against the sunlight? The Master's eyes flashed red. "What chance do you think you have of stopping this consignment of souls to Hell?"

The Woodchopper flinched under the onslaught of the Master's words, each accusing question stabbing at his soul.

They walked in silence for the rest of the way to the palace.

"I will leave you now to decide," the Master said as they passed through the palace gates. "I am offering you a chance to join me here, your wife and child as well."

"And if I refuse?" The Woodchopper's voice wavered nervously.

"I will see you in the temple tomorrow."

The Master walked off toward a separate section of the palace while one of the guards led Graeme back toward his apartments.

❊

Centehua rushed to greet him as he walked through the door. They hugged each other then Centehua lifted her face and they kissed.

"They still have Eztli in the temple," said Centehua worriedly.

"I have seen him," Graeme said. "He is alright for now."

"What are we to do?"

"The Master has told me we can be safe here for the rest of our lives if I abandon my quest."

"If you do not?"

"Eztli will be sacrificed with all the other children tomorrow."

Centehua sat down on the bed. "And will you?"

Graeme knelt down in front of her and put his hands around hers. "My guide has told me I must kill the Master."

"Did your guide tell you what would happen to us?" Cenetehua's voice was steady, but Graeme could see a tear run down her cheek.

"If I forsake the quest then we will be safe here, the Master knows I have come to stop him."

Graeme sat up on the bed next to his wife and put his arm around her. "We would have to watch the slaughter every day knowing I could have stopped it."

"This is the way it is here," said Centehua. "We have always appeased the gods with animal and human sacrifices." She looked pleadingly at Graeme.

"It has to stop."

"And you are prepared to destroy your family for this?" she asked angrily.

"Look how many families are being destroyed and will continue to be."

Centehua sobbed and Graeme held her close.

"Let's rest for a while we will talk later," he said.

They lay down side by side on the bed in a face-to-face embrace. After a while Graeme spoke. "Maybe I can think of a way to kill the Master after getting you and Eztli away from this place."

❊

Graeme the Woodchopper rose in the middle of the night. He could see Centehua's eyelids moving rapidly and guessed her dreams were not pleasant. He walked into one of the rooms next to the bedroom holding the crucifix in his hand. There was a windowsill just through the door and he placed the wooden cross on the sill. He knelt down before it and began to pray out loud.

"I ask that my family be placed within the enclosed garden of the Immaculate Heart of Mary our Mother."

The Woodchopper felt a hand on his shoulder. He opened his eyes and saw the Master by his side.

"You disappoint me," he said.

Graeme was petrified as he looked up at the sharp evil features standing over him.

The tall man looked at the crucifix. "Did you do that yourself?" He said, pointing at the figure of Christ on the cross.

The Woodchopper did not know what to say, he sat back onto to his heels and his shoulders slumped forward.

"Does your wife know you are handing her over to a strange god?"

"Send me up to the altar, let my wife and child return to the village." Graeme pleaded.

"It's tempting, Murray seems quite taken with her, perhaps he could look after her, you know satisfy her needs once you are gone."

The Master walked over to the window and began to inspect the crucifix. Graeme noticed that he made no attempt to pick it up.

"I don't know how much use he would have for your child though."

He was kneeling down in front of the sill now, his face six inches from the carved figure of Christ.

"Maybe Rhidian could look after him for you, he doesn't seem to have much time for girls and he does particularly enjoy the sacrifices to the water gods."

The Master stood up and turned his back to the crucifix.

"You shouldn't have set that up here." He nodded his head in the direction of the makeshift altar. "I have to accept that as your decision."

"Wait!" The Woodchopper shouted as the Master walked toward the door.

The Master turned around angrily. "You were prepared to sacrifice your family, you were praying for them to be accepted into some fantasy of a loving mother's heart." He pulled the Woodchopper down onto his knees by his hair.

"What is the difference between me sacrificing them to the Son of the Morning and you sacrificing them to the Son of Man? Either way they die."

He let the Woodchopper go and walked out of the room.

Graeme the Woodchopper jumped up and ran into the bedroom. He wept as he fell onto the empty bed. His wife was gone.

"Quickly, you do not have much time."

The Woodchopper jumped up off the bed. Before him stood the little old man, and he was holding the crucifix in his hand.

"What can I do?" asked Graeme. "It is hopeless."

The little old man offered the crucifix to him. He reached out to take it.

"You must wear this at all times."

The little old man had altered the crucifix; the small base was gone and there was a leather thong attached to it. The Woodchopper put it over his head, allowing it to hang freely on his chest.

"You may want to cover it up for the time being." The little old man looked at the Woodchopper. "Put some breeches on and wear a jerkin. Tomorrow the Master will take you to the temple to watch the slaughter of the innocents, it is then you have to find a way to kill him."

"My family?"

"They are in God's hands now, all we can hope for is that they can be kept out of Hell."

The little old man put his hands on Graeme the Woodchopper as he sat on the bed. "Now sleep my friend, you will need all of your strength in the morning."

✳

The Woodchopper slept deeply that night and in his sleep he dreamt of an Eternal Mother who would look after his wife and child, someone who could comfort them after their release from the valley of tears.

"Do not be afraid," the woman in white said to him. "They will come to me and I will lead them home."

"Home?" asked the Woodchopper.

The vision vanished as quickly as it came.

✳

The Woodchopper watched Murray, Rhidian and six guards enter the room.

"It's time to go to the temple," said Murray.

Graeme stood up and walked toward them, against his chest he could feel the warm wood of the crucifix. "I am ready."

He made the journey to the temple for a second time. He could see the Master sitting on his wooden throne at the other side of the altar and the crowd of children stretching out and down the steps. There were warriors with spears everywhere and lining the top step all around the altar area were men armed with bows, their arrows poised.

Graeme the Woodchopper took his seat at the foot of the Master's throne. The Master leaned forward and tapped him on the shoulder. He looked at the direction in which the Master pointed and he could see Centehua tied to a pole behind the area where the five priests were preparing to begin the sacrifice.

"I thought I would give her a good view," he said.

The first young boy was brought forward. Two priests held him while a third ripped out his fingernails one by one. The Woodchopper felt sick to the stomach as the child screamed in agony.

From her vantage point Centehua could see the priest place an instrument onto the nail of the child and pull it out quickly with one swift yank. She saw the terror and pain on the child's face.

Centehua looked over toward her husband and screamed, "End it!"

The Master smiled and waved a hand at the priest with the knife. The priest walked over to her and drew the knife casually across her throat.

"No!" Graeme screamed as he watched the blood spurt out and his wife's head slump forward onto her chest, in an instant he remembered the times when he had lain his head on her chest. She hung from the restraints now like a child's toy; all life drained from her.

Without thinking the Woodchopper reached under his shirt and pulled out the crucifix; simultaneously he launched himself at the Master.

Before the guards realised what was happening Graeme drove the crucifix straight into the Master's neck the blunt instrument tearing at muscle and sinew. The injured man let out a rasping gargle as the Woodchopper twisted and pushed the crucifix further into his larynx. A warrior lunged at his Master's assailant with a knife held in front of him and the Woodchopper spun around placing his victim in between himself and his attacker. The warrior's knife pierced the Master's heart and the Woodchopper could hear his death rattle and final sigh.

Graeme the Woodchopper was soon overwhelmed by the weight of the warriors overpowering him then everything went black.

*

Graeme heard someone calling and he felt the ash in his throat; two pairs of hands took a hold of him and pulled him through the dark and the dust. Beams of light shyly made their way through the grey cloud and then he returned to the darkness.

*

"He's waking."

The Woodchopper could hear the voice in the distance.

"Throw some water on him."

He recognised Murray's voice and then he felt the cold water hit him in the face. He tried to move, but could only feel the burn of the ropes against his ankles and wrists. He opened his eyes.

"Sit him up!" Murray ordered.

The Woodchopper could see that he was still on the platform on top of the temple. Two warriors lifted him and placed him on his chair.

"We had to delay the sacrifices for a short while because of the untimely end of Hesper," Murray said.

"You've missed some, but we've saved the best until you were well enough to appreciate it."

Murray nodded toward the warriors guarding the children; one of them walked in amongst them and came out leading Eztli.

Graeme the Woodchopper struggled against his restraints with all his might. Blood started to run from cuts on both ankles and both wrists as the guard gave the boy to two priests. Graeme's son shrieked with pain as his fingernails were pulled out one by one.

"Eztli!" Graeme screamed.

The boy was placed on the altar his little, still beating heart held aloft before Graeme's scream had subsided.

The Woodchopper's mind broke and a veil of darkness descended over his face. The sacrifices and the screams continued for hours and he watched expressionless, the horrors not penetrating his dark, unblinking, fathomless stare.

"Take him inside!" Murray ordered.

Rhidian and the guards led the Woodchopper down the steps and into the interior of the temple; at the centre was a small cell with a wooden door, the guards threw him through and Rhidian slammed the door shut.

He lay in the cell oblivious to his surroundings, not knowing or caring whether it was day or night and hearing neither the sounds of captives brought in, or the sounds of those chosen for sacrifice, leaving.

As night followed day the only thoughts in his mind were of his wife and child; remembering the last few days together at the village, playing games with Eztli, the first time he saw Centehua at the orange grove, but always returning to the pictures of his son's beating heart and his wife's slumped lifeless body.

THE RESCUE

After the demise of the Master, The Soothsayer waited until the sacrifices had ceased and the crowds dissipated and walked up to the raised platform. He saw the men pick up the lifeless body and noticed one of them pull out the crucifix and throw it down on the floor. The Soothsayer picked it up and was surprised to see that there were no bloodstains on it. He tied the two pieces of the broken leather thong together and placed it around his neck, he pushed it down inside his shirt.

Eleuia the Soothsayer had managed to live in the city unnoticed. He slept in the parks and lived off what scraps he could find. He was in the crowd during Eztli's death and saw the Woodchopper kill the Master, what he did not understand was why the sacrifices continued if the Master was dead.

Eleuia realised that the people considered this man to be Quetzalcoatl, he saw with his own eyes his likeness to the ancient statues. Indeed when he first saw Hesper he was afraid for Graeme's life, but now he knew he had to free him from the temple to finish the work. If only he could find a way in.

*

Graeme the Woodchopper languished in the cell for three weeks. On the night of the full moon they came to take him up to the high altar.

"You have killed their god, these people fear you now." Murray sat on the step leading to the raised platform. "So long as I have you I can keep control of them otherwise you and me both would have our hearts cut out on the altar."

The Woodchopper did not respond to the man's words, he stared straight ahead with unfeeling eyes.

*

The Soothsayer waited at the entrance to the temple that night knowing that Graeme was due to appear at the ceremony. He was shocked at the sight of his friend; his once muscular frame was reduced to little more than skin and bone and his face little more than a skull.

Graeme was escorted up the steps and the Soothsayer followed close behind. He got himself close enough to hear Murray speak to the Woodchopper, but he couldn't understand the language and it was with some surprise he watched the guards sit Graeme on the throne. He asked someone nearby what was happening.

"Where have you been?" said the man at his side. "He killed Quetzalcoatl."

"But he is only a man," said the Soothsayer.

"Can't you see? He is loosing his human form as the priests said he would. By the next full moon we will know what god we must worship."

"Because he will have transformed?"

"Yes"

Further up on the platform the Soothsayer noticed Rhidian glance over at Murray and caught the glint of envy in his eyes.

*

For the next two weeks the Soothsayer started prophesising in the plazas and the market places. He held up the crucifix and declared that the figure on the cross would be the god to arrive on the next full moon.

"Who is this fortune teller?" Asked Murray.

"I don't know, but it is a crucifix he uses and it is Christ he says will come on the full moon," replied Rhidian.

"Where did he get it?"

"It is the one the Woodchopper used to kill Hesper."

"Bring him to me," Murray ordered.

"He is developing quite a following," warned Rhidian.

"Then bring him to me without anyone noticing," said Murray impatiently.

A look of disdain crossed the younger man's face as he turned and left the room.

Rhidian found the Soothsayer sitting under a tree on one of the smaller plazas enjoying some Atole given to him by an old woman. The old man recognised the pale-skinned one and smiled to himself.

"I have been expecting you," said the Soothsayer.

"Come, I have to take you to the palace."

The Soothsayer stood up and the two men made their way slowly to the palace.

"I am sorry, but my legs are not as young as they used to be, quick movement is a thing of the past."

Rhidian slowed down to the old man's pace and walked beside him.

"You are the other pale skin, second only in importance to the older one," said Eleuia the Soothsayer with a slightly mocking tone to his voice.

"Take care old man, I may hold more power one day."

"You are here at his bidding?"

"It was me who first noticed you."

"Then maybe you should be doing the bidding."

Rhidian looked smugly at the Soothsayer. "What do you see for me fortune teller?"

"I can see you relieve your friend of power." The Soothsayer observed Rhidian carefully and noticed his interest rising. "I can help you."

"How?"

"The other pale skin's power comes from his control over Graeme. If you remove the Woodchopper he will be weakened."

"What about the priests? It is they who hold the true power."

"Only because of their relationship to the gods. The Master held power because they thought he was a god and now your friend exercises power because he controls the man who killed their god."

"You threaten all that because you say you know when the true god will come," said Rhidian accusingly. "That is why he sent me to fetch you."

"Take me to him. I will put him to sleep and then we must free Graeme."

"What good will that do?" said Rhidian suspiciously.

"If I prophesise the disappearance of Graeme as a sign then his claim to power will be undermined."

❋

The palace gates were visible as they turned a corner. The Soothsayer spoke faster. "You need to convince the priests of my prophecy and then allow Graeme and myself to disappear into the night."

Rhidian did not answer and they walked into the palace in silence.

"Here is the fortune teller," said Rhidian as they entered the throne room.

Murray was leaning to his left, with one elbow resting against the throne. "So you are the one who talks of a foreign god," he said.

"It is your god," replied the Soothsayer.

"Do you really think he will return on the next full moon?"

"Of course I have seen him resurrected."

"Then you must not be allowed to live," stated Murray calmly.

"Wait." The Soothsayer moved closer to the throne platform and pointed to Rhidian. "Send him out of the room and I will show you what I have seen."

Murray looked closely at the Soothsayer, scrutinising his face for signs of falsehood and trickery.

"Leave us!" Rhidian walked out of the door and waited in the corridor.

The Soothsayer reached into a pouch fixed to the cord around his waist and took out some berries. "We must take these and then the vision will appear."

Murray took a handful of the berries offered to him.

"You first," he said handing half of the berries back to the old man.

The Soothsayer reached into Murray's palm and took the berries; he put his hand to his mouth and popped them in.

Murray watched him swallow the berries, then put the rest into his own mouth. He sat on the throne and waited for the vision to take form.

"Close your eyes and I will lead you into it," said the Soothsayer.

Murray did as he was directed.

"Picture yourself in a forest, you are walking along a narrow path."

The old man's voice took on a hypnotic drone. "You can see a wooden gate and a high wall at the end of the path, keep on walking toward it."

Murray let out a sigh.

"Behind the door is your true nature." As he spoke the Soothsayer took a potion from his pouch.

In his mind Murray reached the door. The Soothsayer paused and drank the potion - an antidote to the berries.

"Now open the door."

Murray screamed as the jaguar leapt through the door, he felt the animal's jaws fasten around his throat and the teeth sink into his neck.

The Soothsayer watched Murray slump forward his head falling onto his chest. He walked over and lifted his head by the hair. Murray's face was the ashen grey colour of a death mask.

The old man walked to the door and let Rhidian in. He looked at the figure slumped on the throne and then turned to the old man. "Let us go to the temple."

"You must go to the priests and convince them first. I will prophesise Graeme's disappearance and then we will go to the temple."

"There is no time we must go to the temple now. Murray is dead and we must act before he is discovered."

"No," insisted the Soothsayer

"Do as I say," instructed Rhidian firmly.

*

The old man followed him out of the palace and across the city. Rhidian signalled to the guards at the temple and they opened the door. The two men hurried down the corridor to the Woodchopper's cell. Rhidian took the guard to one side and muttered something to him that the Soothsayer could not hear.

"I have dismissed him," Rhidian said as he unlocked the door to the cell.

The two men lifted Graeme the Woodchopper up onto his feet and helped him through the door.

"We need to go this way," said Rhidian pointing further into the temple. "There is a secret passage down here."

Rhidian and the old man dragged the emaciated figure down the corridor.

"Here we are." Rhidian bent down and lifted a trap door to reveal a stairway leading down into the earth. As Rhidian closed the hatch behind them the world turned black.

"Just follow the stairs we will eventually come to a passage and it will lead us outside."

The two men felt their way down the stairs carrying the Woodchopper in between them; they stumbled along a passage and eventually the Soothsayer noticed a dim light in the distance. He walked out first into the moonlight and fell instantly to the ground as an arrow pierced his chest.

"Come out!" Shouted a priest.

Rhidian dropped the Woodchopper to the ground and walked out slowly into the night with his arms held high.

"Where is the Holy One?" asked the second priest.

"He is just in there as I promised, but he is too weak to stand unaided.

A blinding light suddenly emanated from the entrance and all three men covered their eyes.

Out of the tunnel stepped an angel in a purple robe. In his arms he held the Woodchopper.

Rhidian and the priests staggered back from the light as the angel with the beautiful face walked past them toward the mountain.

*

The Woodchopper felt himself gaining strength as he floated above the ground, the angel effortlessly ascending the mountain. He opened his eyes and saw the familiar angelic face; he remembered the feelings of peace and safety he felt in their previous encounters. A smile played across his mouth as he looked into the angel's eyes. The angel smiled back and the Woodchopper drifted off to a contented sleep.

*

When Graeme the Woodchopper awoke he was in a very large cave, much larger than the one he had shared with the Soothsayer. The first thing he noticed was the warmth emanating from a large fire in the centre of the cave.

"Did you sleep well?"

He recognised the voice of the little old man.

"Where have you brought me?"

"Actually I have not brought you anywhere, it was my friend Raphael who brought you here. He is very good at healing people."

The Woodchopper looked down at himself; he was no longer the skeletal figure from the temple, he was restored to his formerly healthy state.

"I am here to strengthen and prepare you."

"You never have told me your name." There was no questioning in the Woodchopper's voice; he was just stating a fact.

"My name is Gabriel."

"Sanctus Gabriel fulcio vos," muttered the Woodchopper.

"You remember the prayer of the Archbishop."

"Sanctus Raphael sono vos," he continued.

"Saint Gabriel to strengthen you and Saint Raphael to heal you," the little old man translated.

"Where's Saint Michael?"

"He has been protecting you along the way."

The Woodchopper became very sad. "Why did you not protect my wife and child?" there was deep anger in his voice.

"It was not God's will, you were warned not to stray from the path, but you chose to ignore the warnings."

"Can you bring them back?"

"Where they are now they would not want to leave."

"Take me there."

"You have work here and it begins with some elucidation from me."

"Do angels eat?"

"I am sorry I forgot about your need for sustenance, I will get you some food."

Gabriel turned to the fire then back to the Woodchopper with a steaming bowl of stew.

"I hope you don't mind me saying but you don't look very angelic."

"This is the form I thought would be acceptable to you."

"So you don't really look like that?" asked the Woodchopper.

Gabriel chose to ignore the question. "I have to go, I will return shortly."

The Woodchopper, who had been gazing into the flames of the fire, looked up. He was alone.

There was no discernable way out of the cave that he could see; he also noticed that the fire did not give off any smoke.

After a while the Woodchopper began to yawn. He gave up his search for the cave exit and gave in to his body's need for sleep. He slept well and was awoken sometime later by the smell of pancakes.

"I thought you might be hungry again," said the old man.

"Thanks." The Woodchopper sat up and took the pancakes.

"Is there a way out of here?" He enquired.

The old man walked over to one of the cave walls and an entrance appeared. "You are not a prisoner here," he said.

The Woodchopper stood up and walked over to the exit. He found himself looking over a vast range of mountains with peaks as far as the eye could see. The mouth of the cave seemed to be a part of a sheer cliff face.

"The only thing that could get out of here would be an eagle."

"Just ask and you will be taken away." The little old man stood next to him. "But remember you have work to do first."

"Can you take me to see my wife and child?"

"Sleep well tonight for your dreams hold some reality and you may get some answers, but first we need to talk."

The cave exit closed as they turned and walked back towards the fire. The two men sat side by side and Gabriel began to speak.

"You have already seen that things are not always what they seem in this cave; the fire never diminishes, openings appear where once there were only walls."

"And close again," interjected the Woodchopper.

"Just as space is handled differently here so is time."

The Woodchopper stared intently at Gabriel as the angel continued. "God exists outside space and time and therefore sees things in an eternal present."

A baffled frown drew across the Woodchopper's forehead. Gabriel continued with the explanation. "If you are walking down a path for instance, you see the section of the path and the surrounding countryside that you are on in any given moment of time."

"Yes," agreed the Woodchopper.

"God however sees all of the road as if He is looking down from above. He sees the start of your journey, He sees you at any given point on that journey and at the journey's end. All those points are now to Him. All things that exist do not only exist spatially, they also exist through time, but you only experience the time you are in. God experiences through the extra dimension of time."

"So all time is present to Him and He sees everything through all time just as he can see the whole world," suggested the Woodchopper.

"Yes, He sees all that is, all that ever was and all that is to come in an eternal present."

Gabriel stared at the fire for a while before continuing. "And there is a part of that in this cave. You are moving through time quicker than you are aware of, yet it is not affecting you physically."

Gabriel spoke to the Woodchopper for a long time. He explained that although the Master was dead the slaughter was continuing. "Although not on the same scale," he explained. "It is not yet time for you to return to the city, now you must rest," said the angel.

The Woodchopper settled down close to the fire. Before very long he was sound asleep.

He found himself in a brilliant white world. Whichever way he turned there was nothing but white, above, below and on all sides. "I am dreaming," he thought to himself. He knew he was dreaming yet he was conscious of the brilliance as a reality that he could not explain. Out of the light walked a woman even more radiant than the white world that they both now inhabited.

"I have listened to your prayers and your family are safe and happy now."

"May I see them?"

"For now just be glad that they are beyond harm."

With that the figure disappeared back into the brilliant whiteness.

The Woodchopper felt a warmth in his heart that he had not felt since he left the village. The brilliance began to dim and he felt himself falling back into a very deep, peaceful sleep.

*

When the Woodchopper woke up he felt as though he had slept for a very long time. He was still alone in the cave and the fire had lost none of its warmth and brightness, but his stomach rumbled as he sat up realising how hungry he was. Looking at the fire he could see a large bowl of porridge at the side; he picked it up and ate as if he had never eaten before.

"It is time for us to leave this place." The little old man was standing at the exit to the cave.

The Woodchopper finished off his porridge and walked toward the opening. He gasped in amazement as he watched the little old man turn into a tall powerful winged creature, with a beauty to rival that of Raphael. "Now you look like an angel!" he exclaimed.

Gabriel smiled as he lifted the Woodchopper up into his arms and flew out of the cave.

They soared high above the clouds. The Woodchopper's fear soon turned to exhilaration as he felt the wind in his face and saw the mountains below turn into plateau.

"There is the city," said Gabriel.

The Woodchopper looked down and for the first time really appreciated how big the city was. He could make out the temple where Centehua and Eztli were murdered, and the palace from where Hesper had reigned.

They flew on to the mountain ridge and down toward the forest. The angel came down among the trees and placed the Woodchopper gently on the ground.

"There is a hut just through those trees, you must go there and wait."

"Wait for what?" he asked.

"More of your kind are coming you must convince them to end the sacrifices."

"But how?"

"There will be many more of them, enough to eventually rule this land."

The Woodchopper looked over to Gabriel who was back in the form of the little old man.

"Do not worry I will be with you this time."

✻

The two companions stayed at the hut for a few days; the Woodchopper did some hunting and in the evenings Gabriel explained to him how the city was now one of many cities.

"The sacrifices are increasing again and the people think that Quetzalcoatl is due to return," explained the little old man.

"Then surely it will all be repeated again." The Woodchopper's concern evident in his voice.

"Your kind bring friars and priests with them, this time Lucifer cannot lead them into the darkness as easily."

*

It was mid afternoon the following day and the Woodchopper had been fetching water.

"I smell smoke," he said as he walked into the hut.

"There are ships burning down at the coast," replied Gabriel.

"Ships? How many ships?"

"Eleven."

"Eleven!" The Woodchopper said with surprise in his voice.

"I told you there are many of your people not far from this land now. Six hundred of them were on those boats."

"They do not make ships that big."

"They do now. When you meet these people there will be much about them that you will not understand."

The younger man looked puzzled.

"It has been over two hundred years since I took you to the cave in the mountains."

Graeme the Woodchopper sank down onto the floor. "Two hundred years," he whispered to himself in disbelief.

Gabriel sat down beside him. "I know it is difficult for you to understand."

"All the people from the village, Manauia, Ueman they are long gone."

"Their time here was always going to be limited."

"I need some time to think," said the Woodchopper as he walked out of the hut.

He stepped outside and sniffed the air; the smell of burning wood was unmistakeable. He thought about time and what the Archangel had said; he knew he would leave everything behind to follow this quest and his wife and child were already dead before he went to the mountain. *'Maybe once it's finished I can go back to a happier time,'* he thought.

"Maybe," said the little old man, "but it might not be the time you are thinking of."

"You should not read my thoughts."

"Sorry, but you have to appreciate Centehua and Eztli are with God now; you should be concerned with keeping them there."

Gabriel looked at him and smiled. "No matter how much you fly back and forth through time, eventually you too will die and you can be with them forever, but only if your quest is successful."

"They will be marching inland shortly."

"Yes we need to go to the city you can meet them there."

"You know most places have names and yet I do not know the name of the place where my family were killed."

"It is called Cholula," Gabriel replied. "We will have to make the journey on foot as I do not want to draw too much attention to us. The forces of evil are ranged against us and I want to be able to keep the element of surprise on our side."

"I can hunt for food on the journey as I have done before," said the Woodchopper.

"We will leave in the morning," said the little old man as they both walked into the hut.

RETURN TO THE CITY

The journey to Cholula was uneventful; the two companions made their way through the jungle and climbed the ridge onto the plateau. There were more settlements than the Woodchopper remembered on the first journey. This time they walked freely among the people they met, greeted as travellers by them and given hospitality by the different tribes on the way.

It took them three weeks to get to Cholula, each night on the journey Gabriel taught Graeme the Woodchopper the language of the Conquistadors.

"So it is the Spanish that I will have to deal with," the Woodchopper said when he was first told he would need to learn a new language. "I remember learning when I was a boy that parts of Spain were under Muslim control."

"They have been removed now and Spain is at the head of the Holy Roman Empire. You speak the language of the Aztecs, if you learn Spanish as well you will be of use to them as a translator."

Gabriel and the Woodchopper walked over to the temple on their first morning in the city. There were no sacrifices that day.

"Do not dwell on the death of your wife and child. Death is only a door and I led them to a place beyond. It is that place that you have to fight for."

✻

It was midsummer and the days in the city were unbearably hot. The Angel and the Woodchopper were staying in a small dwelling arranged for them by a man Gabriel spoke to in one of the plazas.

"There have been rumours of the Spanish moving toward the city," said the Woodchopper.

"Yes, they have made alliances with the local tribes. The conquistadors defeated one of the tribes in battle and they too have now joined the Spanish."

The little old man looked out into the sweltering heat of early afternoon. "It is a formidable force they have amassed."

The following day the little old man left. The Woodchopper was on his own for a few weeks and by the time Gabriel returned the evenings had become a little cooler. He was sitting at the table eating tortillas when the Archangel entered.

"At least it is a little cooler here now."

"I didn't think the heat or the weather would bother you," said the Woodchopper.

"It does not, I was thinking of you," Gabriel replied.

"Did you find out anything when you were away?"

"They are moving closer and will arrive here by the middle of autumn."

"Only a few weeks left," mused the Woodchopper.

✳

Each day brought news of the approaching army. Eventually, impatience overcame the Woodchopper and he decided to go and look for himself.

"They will arrive here soon enough," said Gabriel.

"I know, but I cannot just sit around here and wait," replied the Woodchopper.

Gabriel acquiesced. "You should be able to reach them in a day or two."

"I will gather some things together and leave shortly."

He collected some arrows and a bow and slung them over his shoulder, he filled a leather pouch with water and set off eastward to look for the Spanish. Gabriel stood at the door and watched him walk down the street. Another form appeared by his side, this figure was tall with long hair and golden wings hanging relaxed behind him.

"You must look out for him," said the little old man.

"He will have my protection."

✻

The Woodchopper made good time across the grasslands of the plateau. He did not stop to hunt, but chose to eat the seeds and nuts that he brought with him.

Presently he saw the advance guards in the distance. He turned north to avoid contact and settled on a raised piece of rocky outcrop. The rocks offered some cover while, at the same time, affording a vantage point from which he could view the advancing army.

While he watched them pass due south of his position he estimated the total force to be between three and four thousand men. He also noticed horses, something he hadn't seen since he crossed the ocean.

The animals were pulling long large iron barrels positioned on wheels. He had never seen anything like them before and wondered what they were for.

The Woodchopper waited until all of the army had passed and then made his way further north so he could pass by unnoticed and get to the city before them.

✻

It was in the half-light just before nightfall when he first noticed the dark, menacing shapes following him. They were barely in sight, but he noticed they were moving quickly.

The two shapes were too far behind to be stragglers from the Spanish army he thought and besides he had pushed quite a way north. He decided to hide in the long grass until they came closer.

The Woodchopper took out an arrow and placed it in the bow, then lay down on his stomach and waited silently for the two figures to approach.

He could not see the two figures, but he knew they were close. A familiar smell hit his nostrils that left him feeling a little sick and very afraid.

The Woodchopper remembered the grey winged creature that attacked him in the forest and how that creature too had smelt of sulphur. He peered intently through the grass and could just make out the grey muscular shapes. One of the creatures began to unfurl his wings while the other watched silently.

With a loud whoosh the demon took to the air. The Woodchopper knew that he would be spotted as soon as the creature flew overhead. He rolled over onto his back and pulled the drawstring of the bow back ready to release the arrow.

Suddenly the second demon broke through the grass to where he was lying. The Woodchopper spun around aiming the arrow, but the demon was too quick. With one swing of his arm he knocked the bow from the Woodchopper's grasp.

The Woodchopper heard an unearthly scream as he saw the angel's blade slice through the demon's wings. The demon nearest to him spread his wings and took off toward his companion's assailant. All that was left of the first demon was a burning mass engulfed in flame plummeting toward the ground.

Hovering alone in the sky was a figure with long light hair that appeared to have a radiance all of its own and golden wings gently oscillating as he held his position in the darkening night.

He held a shield in one hand and a sword in the other and as the demon approached he swung the sword, but the grey figure dropped down beneath the thrust and flew around behind the angel. Without turning around the angel brought the sword around and placed it, point facing backward, underneath his armpit. He thrust its tip into the demon just as the demon prepared to pounce on his back. The demon burst into flames and then disappeared altogether.

The Woodchopper stood up. The angel flew toward him sheathing his sword at the same time.

"Quickly," the angel said pulling the Woodchopper into his arms. "More are coming."

He was protected by the angel's shield as five other demons came screeching down at them from the night sky. Three demons came upon them before they could leave the ground. The angel's sword cut an arc through the air, striking one of the demons. The grotesque creature let out a shriek and pulled away from the attack blood dripping from a wound in his side. Two others lashed out with their claws, the blows parried with the shield.

The angel stood up and threw the shield to the Woodchopper, at the same time lunging at one of the advancing demons with the sword. The blade drove straight through his breastbone.

Without pausing the angel withdrew the sword and swung it around his head; two demons retreated to avoid the blade, but the other one attacked the Woodchopper; who was now on his knees and being forced further down by the force of the attack. Only the shield was protecting him from certain death.

The angel pivoted as he swung the blade around and down striking the demon across the back of the skull and carrying it down his back amputating his left wing. It screamed in agony and then burst into flames.

The air was filled with screeches as the wounded demon joined the other two; they rallied for an attack. The Woodchopper dropped the shield and ran toward his bow and arrows; the wounded demon gave chase.

He loosed off two arrows into the torso of the creature; the creature dropped to his knees. Meanwhile the angel picked up the shield and charged at the other two. He flew up into the air and descended upon them quicker than a thunderbolt from Heaven. The two demons fell under the attack. One lost an arm under the ferocious swing of the sword and the other one was clubbed to the ground by the shield.

The Woodchopper loosed another arrow at the third demon, piercing his eye. The demon fell back with his elbows and wings resting on the ground. The Woodchopper dropped his bow and ran toward the stricken demon pulling out his obsidian knife from his breechcloth; he rammed the knife into the demon's neck and twisted the blade. The red orb of the demon's good eye grew dimmer as the Woodchopper kept on twisting the blade, until finally the demon rolled over onto his side and the stench of sulphur diminished.

"You fought well," said the angel.

The Woodchopper looked around and saw six dead or dying demons lying around. The angel walked among them looking to finish off the wounded.

"Let us return to the city," the angel said once he had made sure all the demons were dead.

✣

They flew quickly through the now dark night and were soon standing at the door to the dwelling.

Gabriel greeted them.

"The enemy are getting stronger," said the angel with golden wings.

"It will soon be time for us to take the fight to the very gates of Hell itself," said Gabriel.

The Woodchopper slumped in a chair exhausted.

"He must be tired, he is usually full of questions," said Gabriel looking over fondly at the man on the chair.

"I only have the strength for one," said the Woodchopper. He looked over at the angel standing next to the little old man on the other side of the table. "What is your name?"

"My name is Michael," replied the angel.

"Ego mandos vos ut tutela sanctus Michael protego vos," said the Woodchopper.

He felt a gentle hand on his shoulder and looked around to see Raphael smiling at him.

"You are tired let me put you to bed," said Raphael.

"You will need all of your strength for the days ahead."

Michael walked over to the doorway and stood looking down the street.

✣

Seven days later the Conquistadors and their native allies were at the gates of the city.

"The nobles are gathering to meet the newcomers," said Gabriel.

"I will go to the city walls and talk with the Spanish," said the Woodchopper. He walked down the street with Michael at his side.

"Tell me Michael, you don't look like a native and that shield and sword is most impressive, why don't people challenge you or stare at you?"

Michael looked at the Woodchopper with amused patience.

"I am an archangel, only the people who need to see me actually get to see me."

The two men strolled at pace past the central plaza.

"Look at all the people gathering," said the Woodchopper.

"The wealthiest and most influential people are all there," said a passing nobleman thinking that the Woodchopper was addressing him.

Before long they were at the main gates.

"Look," said the Archangel pointing through the gates.

The Spanish were approaching a small group of city elders standing at about two hundred yards outside the gates. The main force of the approaching army was about half a mile further back.

"I shall go and talk to them," said the Woodchopper as he hurried through the gates toward the group of dignitaries.

"Two men raised spears as the he approached the group.

"I come to offer my services," the Woodchopper shouted. "I can speak their language," he said.

146

One of the elders signalled for the men to drop their weapons.

"Come," he said. "You may be of use here."

The Woodchopper watched as a small group of about twenty Spanish approached them on horseback. They all wore metal breastplates and, while the three officers who approached at the front were unarmed, all the others carried long metal tubes that the Woodchopper knew to be muskets from the tutoring he received from Gabriel.

The commander of the group was a tall, bearded man with angular features. The Woodchopper thought to himself how much the conquistador reminded him of Hesper; although his features were not quite so sharply defined. The man and two companions dismounted.

"My name is Cortez," the man stated.

The Woodchopper began to translate, but was interrupted by one of Cortez's companions. Although wearing armour like the others it was obvious that the person who spoke was a woman. As the Woodchopper looked over toward her he noticed that she was a native.

"So you can understand Spanish." Cortez addressed the Woodchopper directly.

"I am from across the sea," he answered in Spanish.

The woman translator looked on with a puzzled expression on her face.

"Now how did you get here before me? I was led to believe that not many of our kind had made it here."

An elder spoke and the native woman in armour translated. "I want to welcome you to our city."

Cortez turned away from the Woodchopper, but his final glance said, "We will talk again."

"Our nobles are gathered in the main plaza and it would please us if your leaders would come to meet with us."

The elders held their arms out in greeting and turned toward the open gates.

"Come walk with me," said Cortez grabbing the Woodchopper by the arm and leading him through the gate.

The other soldiers gestured for the rest of the army to advance into the city.

"Do you think they are leading me into a trap?" asked Cortez.

"I did not see any preparation for battle when I walked past the plaza earlier," said the Woodchopper.

"And it is the nobility who I am to meet?"

"Yes"

Cortez signalled to his third companion, a large man who bore the scars of many battles.

"This may be our chance to impose our authority on these people," Cortez said to his captain.

The captain nodded and dropped back toward the body of soldiers.

"What do you intend to do?" asked the Woodchopper.

"Let me ask you a question," said the Conquistador. "What do you make of these people?"

A world of pain surfaced in the Woodchopper's face from a depth of sorrow that he hadn't experienced for some time.

"They killed my wife and child."

"You are indeed an enigma," said Cortez. "Not only are you out here on your own, but you had a family here as well."

They were now only a few hundred yards from the main plaza.

"Were they natives?"

"Not from this city, but they did die here."

"But from this locality?" Cortez asked.

"From a village near the coast."

The elders walked into the plaza and Cortez held his arm out in front of the Woodchopper to stop him following.

The captain and his men surged through the entrance to the plaza and began to attack the unarmed natives gathered before them.

"What are you doing?" screamed the Woodchopper.

"You said yourself they are capable of much bloodshed. How am I to know they would not slit open my chest and rip my heart out?"

The Woodchopper looked on at the scene of unfolding carnage before him.

"That is how they kill people isn't it?" asked Cortez as the woman translator approached them.

People were running in all directions, their screams filling the air and instilling terror in the hearts of the city dwellers not in the plaza. Soldiers were scything their way through the stampeding crowd wielding their swords around them.

The Woodchopper saw limbs being hacked off and heads parted from shoulders. He heard the roar of the muskets and saw flames erupting from the barrels; each musket shot heralded another body fallen. He thought he saw Gabriel in his angelic form at the other side of the plaza, but his presence there did not make sense to him.

He broke away from Cortez and his companion and ran blindly into the plaza. A native nobleman grabbed him and the Woodchopper saw the terror in his eyes. Blood spouted from the man and onto the Woodchopper's face as a musket ball entered the side of the nobleman's neck.

The Woodchopper vomited as the unfamiliar stench of gunpowder filled his nostrils; he turned to leave, stumbling in a daze toward one of the streets leading off the plaza.

He saw a familiar shield parry a sword swinging through the air toward his left arm and he noticed a look of amazement on his attacker's face as Michael the Archangel stood between them. The soldier dropped to his knees before Michael begging for God's forgiveness.

"We have to leave," Michael said as he carried the Woodchopper up and away from the slaughter.

"Is this God's work?" The Woodchopper was screaming at the angel as they flew over the city. "Why did you not stop it?

"It was not God's will for it to end."

"Why?" Graeme the Woodchopper's question flew off into the sky searching for a response.

The angel arrived at the entrance to the temple.

"What are we doing here?" asked the Woodchopper bemusedly.

"It is the portal."

"Portal! Portal to what?" The Woodchopper looked back to the city. "Is all this in Christ's name?" He was becoming hysterical now at the thought of all the slaughter; the temple's memories were rushing in on him, his wife's blood spurted once more into his mind and mixed with the blood being shed in the plaza.

"Centehua," he screamed. "Centehua!"

He began to run toward s the temple steps.

"Quickly," said Raphael opening the temple door. "Bring him in here before he looses his mind."

Michael grabbed him and led him through the doorway. The archangels carried the writhing figure of the Woodchopper between them. His body first went still, then limp as the two angels carried him down the corridor.

"Here," said Gabriel standing at the top of a flight of stairs leading down into an impenetrable darkness. The little old man assumed his angelic form and followed the three figures as they began to descend the stairway.

Down and down they went into the darkness. The Woodchopper, lost in his own mental anguish and carried safely between the two angels, had no perception of time or space. He was hardly aware of the blackness surrounding him and only had a vague sense of descent.

"We are nearly there." Gabriel's voice startled him into awareness.

"Everything is alright, we will explain when we stop." Raphael's reassuring words gave him some comfort.

Soon the four companions were in a large, square room.

"Come let us sit." Gabriel was pointing toward a large round table at the centre of the room with four chairs around it.

Gabriel and Michael sat down, but Raphael stood behind the Woodchopper's chair with his hand resting reassuringly on Graeme's shoulder.

"I don't recall this place the last time I was in the temple," said the Woodchopper.

"We are no longer in the temple," said Gabriel. "This is the threshold between the seen and the unseen."

"Of course it is all seen for us, and now for you too, but most human beings do not get to see beyond this place." It was Michael who spoke.

The Woodchopper could feel the healing power of the angel standing behind him as Raphael said, "Not many people ever get this far, not while they still live anyway."

"Why am my here?"

"Your quest lies just beyond here," said Gabriel.

"Is my family there? Centehua? Eztli?"

"They are in the unseen, but not in the place where you have to go first." Michael spoke again.

The Woodchopper looked at Gabriel. "You said I had work to do in the city before I came here."

"The Spanish needed no convincing to engage with the Indians and that is how they will end the sacrifices."

Michael spoke. "It is obvious that Cortez will not be tempted as Hesper was."

"But he was prepared to kill in cold blood as easily as any priest at the high altar."

"As are most men," said Gabriel. "It is easy for them to embrace the darkness at the centre of their souls."

Raphael sat down on the lip of the table facing the Woodchopper with one leg resting on the floor. "And that is why you have been picked," he said. "Even though the people of that city killed your wife and child you were still appalled at the bloodshed inflicted upon them."

The angel looked compassionately at the man. "You have not given in to the evil dormant in you and that is why you were picked for this quest."

"But why does God allow all this to happen? The centuries of sacrifice, the killing done in the name of Christ, Why?"

Raphael continued. "Do not think that Christ is not hurt by what is done in His name, but man was given free will. He was given free will to choose, to choose what he wants his god to be and how to worship him, to decide what he thinks is evil and what he thinks is good."

Gabriel spoke. "We too have free will so that we can choose to worship Him."

"And some chose not to." There was anger in Michael's voice as he spoke and his fingers tightened imperceptibly around the handle of his sword.

"So he allows us to choose?"

"Yes," said Gabriel. "The angels and archangels too."

"So you were right to be appalled at the destruction of the people in the city, and it is not their fault that your wife and child were killed," said Michael. "They were seduced by the idea of the Morning Star and Hesper was possessed by the instigator of that myth."

"Lucifer," said the Woodchopper.

"Thank you for the introduction."

Raphael jumped away from the table and pulled the Woodchopper in close; Gabriel and Michael took up defensive positions in front of him.

"You really must take more care this close to the gates of my home, especially you Michael. You should be especially watchful against the snares of the Devil."

The Woodchopper looked across to the far end of the room and saw, walking out of the darkness, an angel so beautiful not even Raphael could compare. Indeed his beauty outshone that of the three archangels combined.

"Do not look so surprised my human friend. Were you expecting cloven hooves? An overwhelming stench of sulphur perhaps?"

The Woodchopper could feel the bile rise up in his throat as the room began to stink.

"I'll show you the cloven hooves later."

Michael began to slowly advance toward the intruder.

"Come now Michael, all that talk of free will shouldn't I be allowed to present my case to your friend? Or are you afraid he will chose me?" Lucifer walked toward the table and sat at one of the vacated chairs. "God knows many have before."

"Speak your piece," said Michael then we start this.

"Well my little wood chopping friend, haven't you been wondering how these creatures of God, defenders of Christ are so quick to resort to violence?" Lucifer stared at the Woodchopper with a fierce intensity. "How many times have you seen them turn the other cheek?"

"They have protected me from your hordes."

"Oh but you have seen nothing of my hordes yet." A smile played gently across his lips. "Your friends here spend all their spare time with the Creator, but what does He ask them to do? Kill. Destroy all the Egyptian first born? Get an angel to do it. Didn't you think you saw Gabriel in the plaza?"

"I was mistaken."

"Oh no you weren't my friend. He may be a source of strength to you, but to others he is the Angel of Death."

Lucifer sighed and leaned back in the chair. "Your friends here may sit at the feet of God, but their wing tips dangle down into the fire and blood of Hell itself."

The Woodchopper looked closely at his three companions.

Lucifer continued. "And He had the audacity to throw me out of Heaven."

Gabriel spoke. "We are given free will to love God of our own volition."

"But I sought to rise above that. What makes Him so good? Look what he puts people through; death, suffering, disease."

"All of that came after the Fall," said Raphael.

"I gave man knowledge. It was me who showed them the light."

"Once given the knowledge of good and evil you made sure many chose evil," said Michael angrily.

"Only through using the free will He gave them," said Lucifer. "Not until the Light of Heaven is extinguished can we have a universe built on the truth of knowledge, a universe without God in it."

The room abruptly filled with light, a light so powerful the Woodchopper was forced to shut his eyes, but just before he did he thought he could make out the shape of a man as the light's source. The three archangels turned toward its source and kneeled.

"You have given only the offer of the knowledge of eternal death. To turn from you is to gain everlasting life."

"By accepting you I suppose," said Lucifer mockingly.

He was retreating away from the light with each word spoken. "Come with me Woodchopper or remain forever blinded by His light." With that the Fallen Angel was gone.

The light dimmed and the Woodchopper was alone once again with the three archangels.

"You may go with him if you wish," said Gabriel. "Each of us, man and angel, must make choices and we must live and die by those choices."

"Why are you forced to kill in His name?" asked the Woodchopper.

"Man's time on earth is his quest. It is there that he wanders through the wasteland of life looking for some truth to guide him. We attempt to offer some assistance in God's name and through His direction, but we can only do it if man asks," explained Gabriel.

"Did I ask?"

"Your prayers were heard and you were chosen," said Michael.

Gabriel spoke again. "If you find the Way in life it will serve you well in death. Indeed you will overcome death and have everlasting life through realising the Truth."

Raphael spoke. "Lucifer wishes to rule with God's absolute power and thus subjugate the universe to his will and we have to oppose him and those who accept him. God wishes to rule the universe with love and so wants men and angels alike to choose, not to be coerced into accepting his will."

"So once everyone chooses God, Heaven and Earth will be one?" enquired the Woodchopper.

"God is love," continued Raphael, "and, as such He will only allow suffering so that a greater good can come from it."

"That is the message of Christ's Passion, death and Resurrection," said Michael. "That is the true story of the Cross."

The three archangels walked toward the darkest part of the room, the part where Lucifer had first appeared. The Woodchopper noticed a door there.

"You have to go through there," said Gabriel. "You may stay there forever or find your way back."

"What is through there?" asked the Woodchopper.

"Your destiny," said Gabriel. "But you will need to find your way back to find God."

THROUGH THE GATES OF HELL

Michael opened the door and Graeme the Woodchopper walked through. He was suddenly engulfed in a dusty, choking blackness. The air felt thick and he panicked as he realised he could not breathe. The Woodchopper looked behind through the dust and saw three lights in the distance. Confusion and disorientation fogged his mind.

In a few moments he realised that the air was no longer heavy with dust, but his nostrils were filled with a noxious odour.

"Welcome to my home."

A huge wall of flame appeared and, standing in front of it was a gargantuan figure with a horned, ugly red head. It had a massive, red muscular torso and the lower body of a goat, complete with cloven hooves.

The Woodchopper's whole being was filled with terror; he knew he had to do battle with the monster in front of him, but how?

"Follow me," ordered Lucifer as he stepped through the flames.

The Woodchopper walked forward and the flames parted as he approached. The first thing he noticed was the unbearable noise. In front of him was a giant furnace stretching back as far as he could see and running near to this ocean of flame were forges where children worked at shaping the armour and weapons to be used in the final battle.

"Come." Lucifer gestured for the Woodchopper to walk beside him.

The fires flared orange and the sparks and fireballs rained down as the children poured molten metal into the casts; the banging of hammers and the hissing and spitting of the forges was nearly too much for Graeme's human ears. He noticed that all of the children had gaping wounds at their chests, empty cavities where their hearts should have been.

"I am here to free them," he thought to himself. "Here to make them whole again."

"Armour and weapons forged by the hands of the innocents are powerful indeed," said Lucifer. "They will bring Heaven crashing down around the ears of those pitiful angels and their three in one master."

The Woodchopper felt a powerful red arm around his shoulders.

"Come sit beside me," Lucifer said as he led his guest up to a stone throne that seemed to hang over the whole boiling, heaving, deafening inferno.

The furnace and the young figures labouring at the forges appeared to reach out to infinity.

"This is Hell indeed," said the Woodchopper.

"No, not at all, these children here have done little to deserve this." Lucifer waved his arm out in front of him. "But their protectors were good enough to sacrifice them to me."

"Then they are not damned?"

"Of course not." Lucifer fixed the Woodchopper with a malevolent and evil gaze. "Have you not come to free them?"

He saw the look of terror on the Woodchopper's face.

"Fear not," said Lucifer, "I have not given up on you yet." He smiled. "If you are here though God has."

The Evil One stood up. "I will show you Hell."

Another solid wall of bright red flame appeared to the side of the throne and the two of them walked through.

They stood on what the Woodchopper thought was a stone balcony and before them spread out a scene of indescribable anguish. He felt hope draining from him as the screams of the damned filled his ears.

Looking down into Hell he saw demons herding souls into flames even hotter than the furnaces he had just witnessed. His gaze moved on as brimstone rained down on the lustful and the lecherous.

The Devil pointed to demons tearing the arms and legs away from torsos and the Woodchopper looked on in despair as the arms and legs grew again only for the dismembering to continue forever, the cries of hopelessness reverberating eternally.

He saw demons casting souls into huge cauldrons of boiling oil and others immersed in freezing water; elsewhere he saw demons feeding rats, mice and other vermin to souls shackled to posts; he saw those souls vomit and be forced to eat again.

There were souls running from all these scenes, from the burning oil, from the fires of Hell, running and running; but there was nowhere to run to. Still they ran unable to stop, eternally at the point of breathless collapse; but no respite could be gained.

Graeme the Woodchopper looked at these scenes and listened to the cacophony of cries as the horrors repeated on and on into the distance as far as he could see in all directions. He looked at the monster by his side. He was marooned in a sea of suffering with the king of this odious ocean.

"Let me show you what we can achieve if we can capture Heaven itself," said the Devil.

He placed his arm on the Woodchopper's shoulder and turned him around. There was darkness now where previously there had been chaos. In the silent darkness the Woodchopper felt the stillness.

"This is what all the damned could experience, an eternal peace."

The emptiness reached down into the Woodchopper's soul.

"You are showing me an eternity without God. This is truly Hell and you know it, you have sat in the presence of God."

He saw the anguish on the monstrous red face and continued. "Hell is wherever God is not."

"What of mankind then?" the Devil asked angrily. "They have never been in his presence so that means that the whole world must be Hell."

"Mankind is aware of God. He has a god-space inside him and the world can bring him nearer to this space sometimes."

The Devil turned and everywhere was once again filled with the sound of metal being hammered and forges spitting fire.

"These children here will lead me to my rightful place." Eons of anger resounded in the Devil's voice. "As king of Heaven."

"What are you waiting for? If you are going to make your move it should be now," taunted the Woodchopper.

"There are still not enough souls here to win."

"I think there will never be enough for you to win and you know it."

"More will come."

"Not for much longer, the sacrifices will stop at the altars shortly. There will be churches built on the sites of the temples and there will only be the perpetual sacrifice of the Mass. No, if you are to win they must go now."

The Devil let out a roar and two demons appeared.

"Enough, it is time for you to feel the pain of your punishment."

"I may well have to suffer for my sins, but God sees all that is, was and shall be and he's expecting you to wait. Surprise is your only chance."

The wall of flame appeared again and the two demons dragged the Woodchopper toward it. He looked back to see the children donning armour and picking up swords as a portal opened behind the Devil.

✻

The heat was unbearable as Graeme the Woodchopper passed through the flames. He heard screams and felt a furnace in his lungs as he tried to breath. He found himself in a world of darkness and his last thought was, "God is not here."

THE RETURN

New York, September 11th 2001:

"Are you alright?" He knew the voice was speaking English, but he didn't recognise the accent.

"We've got to get out of here." The voice grew louder when Graeme did not move. "Quickly! It looks like it's all going to come down!"

The fire fighter grabbed Graeme by the arm and led him quickly into the lobby.

Through the dust he could barely make out three silhouettes, the beams of light from their torches reached out bravely through the dark grey gloom.

"What happened?" shouted one of the shadows.

"I think the South Tower has collapsed," shouted another. "We need to get out of here quickly."

"Is the Plaza clear?" The four beams of light gathered in a circle. Graeme stood amongst them, a fifth unlit silhouette.

"I can't tell," said the fire fighter standing next to Graeme.

"Where is this?" asked Graeme. The thick dust irritated his throat and he coughed to clear the feeling of choking. There was a smell he did not recognise, but he knew it to be an evil smell.

"This is as close to Hell as you're going to get without dying buddy," said a fire fighter with a thick Brooklyn accent, "and dying is still a strong possibility at the moment."

Graeme looked around as the dust began to clear a little. There was rubble everywhere and fallen masonry was strewn across the floor. Stepping over the debris he followed the fire fighters as they quickly picked their way out of the lobby.

"This way! Head toward West Street!" shouted the leading fire fighter.

The five men made their way toward an emergency exit and out into the open. Even outside there was dust and paper floating through the sky. The visibility was poor on what should have been a beautiful cloudless September morning.

"Here! Here!" they all ran under a bridge and out onto the street.

"Head away from the Trade Centre!" shouted one of the fire fighters.

Up the street they ran, through the grey dust slowly covering the floor and settling on nearby buildings. Five grey ghostly apparitions fleeing from Hell.

From the corner of West Street and Vesey they met other people emerging as the dust cloud began to dissipate. A willowy young lady stood staring at the spot where the South Tower should have been, the dust gently settling on her expensive hairdo and stylish skirt and jacket. "It's gone," she said in disbelief. "The whole tower has disappeared."

A policeman walked up to her and placed his arm around her shoulder. "Come on lady we need to move back from here."

The woman turned and began to make her way up West Street. Several emergency service personnel began shepherding people away from the wreckage of the South Tower and the smoking edifice of the North Tower.

Graeme looked back and began to see the remaining tower start to fall in on itself. Others in the crowd also noticed.

"Oh my God!" shouted a woman.

"The other tower's going!" shouted someone else.

People began to run north up West Street others along Vesey, all fleeing the descent of the North Tower.

Dust began to billow up and out from the crashing tower, following the fleeing people up the streets. The air was filled with bangs and crashes as pieces of the collapsed North Tower fell onto the street behind.

Graeme also fled away from the World Trade Centre site. He heard explosions behind as cars and emergency vehicles were hit and wondered if there were demons and gargoyles hidden in the cloud; punishing the damned caught within.

He ran along the unfamiliar concrete canyon of Vesey Street. The swirling, rumbling grey fog was gaining on him and the others fleeing for their lives. He saw one man dive under what looked to Graeme like a square metal box with wheels and windows.

The dust cloud was closing in, about to engulf him. In an attempt to escape he stepped into a doorway; the door opened and a strong pair of hands grabbed hold of him and pulled him in, another pair slammed the door shut.

"Over here!" A woman beckoned from behind the coffee shop counter.

Graeme leapt over and crouched down beside the woman, the two men followed.

"The second tower's gone hasn't it?"

Graeme looked over toward the man, and saw someone of similar build and age as Cardinal Caronni. He had ruffled grey hair and was dressed casually in blue Levi jeans and a check shirt. The man shifted uneasily under Graeme's intense gaze.

The roar and crashing of the passing debris burst into the moment causing the four of them to huddle further against the counter for protection. The woman screamed when rubble rolled through the window smashing glass and letting in the choking dark mass of dust particles. Before his vision became restricted Graeme saw the younger man put his arm around the woman to protect her.

"Here, put this over your mouth." The older man handed him a small towel. He put it to his mouth and waited.

"This must still be Hell," Graeme thought; and he wondered if he would ever get out of it alive.

"Maybe I'm dead already," he said to himself.

"Don't worry son, we'll get out of this alive," said the older man reassuringly. "I've been in tighter spots."

❋

As the dark cloud settled and the rumbling receded, the younger man stood up. Graeme noticed that he wore similar clothing to the woman, although they were both now covered in a thin layer of ash and dust.

"It's going to take forever to get this place ready for business again," he said. The woman rose and walked over to his side.

"Why would two planes fly into these towers?" the woman wondered incredulously.

"It must have been an attack," said the older man. "Can we get a radio signal? We might hear something on the news."

Graeme walked around from behind the counter and toward the opening in the front of the shop. Dust and debris were still settling in the street and pieces of paper floated innocuously through the air. He looked out in amazement at the sight before him.

People were emerging from the bottom of huge towering buildings the like of which Graeme had never seen before. Their faces haunted by the morning massacre. People dressed in crumpled suits and dirty jackets; some held items of clothing or towels over their mouths.

A tall, slight middle-aged man walked close to where Graeme was standing. He carried a brief case in one hand and the other hand held a handkerchief to his mouth. He looked straight at Graeme with red-rimmed eyes: bewilderment written in the pale dust coating his face.

Graeme could not understand what had happened and had no knowledge of where he was, but he read the question in the man's glance and responded silently in his soul. "I do not know why God would allow this."

A wailing that had Graeme running back toward the coffee shop shattered the stunned smoky silence. The older man in the check shirt stopped him. "It's the emergency services responding."

A large white vehicle came hurtling down Vesey with lights flashing and sirens screaming. Graeme too let out a yell and the man by his side put an arm around his shoulder and led him back into the coffee shop.

"You really are in bad shape," said the man, concern evident in his voice. "What's your name son?"

"Graeme."

"You sound as though you're from England."

"I am." Graeme suddenly felt very tired. "Where are we?"

"It's a coffee shop on Vesey Street. Did you work in the World Trade Centre?"

"I do not know this place." Graeme's confusion hung over each syllable.

"What's the last thing you can remember before the towers fell?"

"Before I was here I was in Hell?" There was a certainty to Graeme's reply that startled the older man.

"I think we all feel that son."

"No." Graeme's voice began to rise. "No! I really was in Hell. I spoke to the Devil."

The coffee shop employees overheard Graeme's statement. The man spoke. "I think he needs some medical attention."

"Come on, we'll get you some help," said the man in the check shirt guiding Graeme toward the door.

The two men walked back out into Vesey. People were walking away from the site where the towers had collapsed and Graeme noticed that men in blue shirts and black helmets were directing them down the street.

"My name's Tony," said Graeme's companion, "Tony Altredo."

"You remind me of someone I met once. He was a Cardinal."

"We'll talk later," said Tony as he spotted a police officer.

"My friend here needs some medical help."

The officer pointed toward an intersection. "There's a medical post down there."

A clear blue sky contrasted with the black and grey covering the city streets. Graeme stared unknowingly at his surroundings. The scale of the buildings dwarfed him and the despair and sorrow etched in the dust-covered faces shuffling past him made him think of the temple.

"There!"

Tony Altredo's voice startled Graeme. He looked over to see his companion pointing toward a large white mobile medical unit. There were six people waiting by the steps at the side of the truck. Graeme and Tony waited for their turn to enter.

∗

"He doesn't seem to have any physical injuries," said the female medic after conducting a cursory examination. "Where are you from?" the petite middle-aged woman asked Graeme.

"I have no home here," Graeme replied.

"He's from England," said Tony.

"What's the last thing you remember before the towers fell?"

Graeme looked at the nurse as she spoke. She placed a stethoscope to his chest as he answered.

"I was in Hell." The nurse let the instrument drop around her neck and stood back.

"He says he was talking to the Devil." The nurse glanced over at Tony.

"And before Hell?" she looked directly into Graeme's eyes.

"I saw the massacre at Cholula."

The nurse looked at Tony. "He's too young to have been in Vietnam, perhaps he was in the Gulf War."

"Cholula was a city in the Aztec empire," Tony said. "Cortez massacred thousands of the local nobility there."

"Is it there now?"

"Yes, but the massacre took place in the sixteenth century."

The nurse gave a puzzled glance toward Graeme and then turned to address Tony. "I can't do any more for him and there are more people outside. Can you take him to a hospital? I think he needs to talk to a psychiatrist."

Tony led Graeme out of the unit. "Do you have any family or friends you can stay with?"

Graeme shook his head.

"Okay then you can stay with me tonight if you like, we'll try to get you some help tomorrow."

Graeme nodded in agreement and the two men headed off toward Tony's apartment.

A NEW WORLD

They walked toward Brooklyn Bridge joining an ever-growing army of people fleeing the choking grey mist. The bridge itself was congested along the walkways. Graeme stepped out into the open space of the road and was pulled back by Tony as an ambulance sped across the bridge toward the desolate grey-black cloud hanging heavily over Manhattan.

The two men turned and looked back. Graeme stared in awesome wonder at huge rectangular glass and concrete structures rising into the sky.

Smoke and dust rose into the air above the skyscrapers and Tony thought of burning cities in other wars in other places. He remembered looking back down lush green valleys with the smoke rising through the trees after the Zippo attacks on the villages. He glanced sideways at Graeme and decided to offer the confused young man his support for as long as he needed it. They both tuned back into the moving throng of people and headed into Brooklyn.

After walking for about half an hour they turned down a street and approached a tenement block.

"Here we are," said Tony.

Graeme looked up at a dirty, red brick six-story building. He followed the older man up half a dozen steps and through a doorway into a small hallway with a staircase at its centre. They walked up to the third floor and down a narrow, dimly lit corridor. Tony stopped at one of the doors, took a key out of his pocket and placed it in the lock; turning the key sideways he pushed the door open. Graeme followed him inside.

"Shut the door."

Graeme closed the door behind him. He stood and looked at a room with a couch, an easy chair and a small table with a square object on it. Beyond a small breakfast bar at the back of the room there was a kitchen area. At the other end of the room and to his right he could see a door.

"Turn the television on. They may know who is responsible for the attacks by now."

Graeme looked around bewildered.

Tony walked over to the small square object and pressed a button. The glass front of the box burst into action with vivid colour images of the day's events blazing out into the room.

Graeme jumped back in surprise and then slowly moved toward the television.

"You mean to say you've never seen a TV set before?"

Graeme felt the hard glass of the screen against his hand and looked at the image of the plane flying toward the South Tower. He traced the smoke trail billowing from the North Tower with the index finger of his right hand. The flames erupted onto the screen as the second plane hit and Graeme pulled his hand away quickly.

Tony watched his guest with a puzzled look on his face.

"You really don't remember what a TV is do you?" He stated.

The noise and images of the burning towers was suddenly replaced by a man's face.

"We have Mayor Giuliani," said the voice of an unseen reporter.

A lean looking man with a receding hairline and spectacles appeared on the screen.

"Today is obviously one of the most difficult days in the history of the city."

Tony picked up the remote control and turned up the volume. He gestured for Graeme to move away from the television. Graeme sat on the chair while Tony leaned forward on the couch.

"The tragedy that we are undergoing right now is something that we've had nightmares about. My heart goes out to all the innocent victims of this horrible and vicious act…" continued Mayor Guliani.

A tear of remembrance fell slowly and silently down Graeme's cheek. The faces of Centehua and Eztli loomed large in his consciousness.

Tony noticed Graeme's sadness and recognised a personal aspect to it to be shared by many in New York in the days, months and years to come.

They sat in silence for a long time. The events of the day weighed heavily on them both, but for different reasons. Tony shared the hurt and anger of the western world at the atrocity committed in the name of religion. Graeme's confusion and despair drove him into the arms of Morpheus, where he dreamt of his family, of the archangels and then of Hell and the city of fallen towers where the Devil had left him.

*

It was dark when he awoke and one aspect of his dream came back to him vividly. He saw the gates of Hell flung open and the army of slaughtered innocents marching into Heaven; each one welcomed by Raphael. St Michael and an army of angels engaged the demon hordes that followed.

Graeme saw fallen gargoyles and defeated demons lying at their feet and a routed army running back to Hell.

He smiled as he sat up on the chair.

Tony had placed a blanket over him and he pulled this around his shoulders as he looked around the room. He was alone in the darkness. There was a crucifix attached to the wall in a small alcove to the side of the chair and Graeme took a few steps toward it. He knelt down, crossed himself and began to pray.

The lone figure praying in the dark called upon the archangels to reveal themselves. He became aware of a figure kneeling at his side.

"I haven't done this for many years."

Graeme recognised Tony's voice in the darkness.

"But you're right, it's only God we can turn to in a time like this."

Graeme felt the loneliness of centuries engulf him in the darkness; he looked at the figure on the crucifix and remembered His words at Calvary.

"Eloi, Eloi, lama sabachthani"

The two men knelt there in silent prayer for a long while.

Presently the cold grey light of dawn began to filter weakly through the small window in the kitchen area. Tony stood up slowly, firstly rubbing his knees and then putting his hands to the small of his back as he raised himself to his full height and gently leaned back letting out a little grunt. He stretched his arms toward the ceiling, turned and walked through the opening into the kitchen area. Graeme began to stir as the sound of running water reached his ears.

"Do you want some coffee?" asked Tony.

Graeme joined him in the kitchen area. He sat at the rectangular table running across the width of the room and watched Tony switch on the coffee percolator.

"We need to get you out of those dusty clothes and showered," said Tony who had showered after Graeme fell asleep the previous night.

He watched Graeme stare at the coffee pot as it began to bubble. The smell of coffee filled Graeme's nostrils and he felt the warmth of the cup as he lifted it two-handed to his mouth. The bitter taste of coffee felt good and he smiled at his host.

Tony smiled back. "I was a seminarian once," he said as he looked off in the distance thoughtfully.

"You were a priest?" enquired Graeme.

"No, I never made it." He looked back at his guest and smiled again. "A crisis of faith. I delayed my entry into the seminary because there was a war on; and I did not wait to be called up. I could probably have been exempted from the draft any way, but I volunteered. Some of the things I saw there tested my belief in a benevolent god. I could not reconcile what I was being taught by the Jesuit Fathers with my actions in Vietnam. Christ and Charlie were uneasy bedfellows."

Tony stood up. "Anyway, let's get you cleaned up. You're a bit taller and certainly leaner than me, but I'm sure we can find something for you to change into."

The two men drank their coffees, and then Tony showed Graeme how to operate the shower. The force of the water startled Graeme, but he soon began to relax as the grime and grit of the previous day ran off him and his muscles began to loosen.

There was a dry towel, some underwear and a pair of old jeans and a sweatshirt left on the bed. He left his old cotton trousers and loose linen top on the floor of the shower room. The smell of bacon grilling and bagels toasting wafted into the room and reminded Graeme of how hungry he was.

"Here we are," said Tony piling strips of bacon into some bagels and stacking them on two plates. A fresh pot of coffee sat at the centre of the table. "Do you want some eggs with that?"

Graeme nodded and Tony cracked some eggs into the pan.

"You mentioned Cholula and a massacre yesterday. You were there?"

"Yes," said Graeme between mouthfuls of bagel. "I walked into the plaza with Cortez. I was with him when the killing started."

Tony stared intently at Graeme. "That was over four hundred and eighty years ago," he whispered, the disbelief evident in his voice.

"Everything exists in an eternal present and God sees it all. I have had some experience of this before."

"But what about your family, your friends?" asked the older man incredulously.

"They are long gone." A shadow of sadness crossed Graeme's face. "Gone before I experienced God's time, and yet not that long ago for me."

Graeme told his host about the friar's visit to his cabin and his meeting with the Cardinal; he told him of his journey across the sea and his life with Centehua. He spoke with anger and regret at the needless death of his family; and he spoke fondly of his time with the angels. There was sweat on his brow when he spoke of his visit to Hell.

"And then you found yourself in the Twin Towers." Confusion and disbelief jostled for position in Tony's thoughts. "Your story is very hard to believe."

"I know, but it is the truth."

"If you came from fifteenth century Mexico then why were you not wearing a loin cloth or something like that?"

"Breeches and linen jerkins were also worn."

"But yours look so modern?"

"Modern? I do not know this word," said Graeme.

"They look as if they are from this time," replied Tony.

"That I cannot explain." Graeme smiled gently at the confused expression on Tony's face. "God perhaps? I have seen enough to know that anything is possible with God."

"Boy, if I had met you when I was in seminary my life might well have turned out differently." Tony poured himself another cup of coffee. "What of the archangels now? Have you seen them here in this time?"

He pointed the pot toward Graeme who shook his head. "When you were praying last night," said Tony with anticipation in his voice, "did they come?"

"I called upon them, but when I looked it was you who appeared at my side."

"The Legend of the Eternal Night that you speak of," said Tony. "It reminds me of some things I have read concerning the Mayan calendar. I believe it ends at about the time you speak of in the legend."

Tony walked into the bedroom and came out a few minutes later with some books in his hands.

"Here we are." He walked into the kitchen and put the books down on the table. Graeme followed.

"The Mayan's used a series of calendars each marking different periods of time. These calendars can all be linked, or synchronised to form greater cycles and are astronomically linked through lunar cycles, cycles of the orbit of Venus, solar cycles, and so on."

Graeme interrupted, "the Morning Star is linked in the Aztec calendar to Quetzalcoatl and I believe him to be another name for Lucifer."

"Venus is the Morning Star," added Tony placing a strong emphasis on the second word of the sentence.

"An old soothsayer I once knew told me that the interlinking cycles of calendars all culminated in a long calendar that ended on a winter solstice many hundreds of years in the future."

"And that future is now?" asked Tony.

"Not far away. Let us examine these writings and see where they lead."

"There is more than just books available," added Tony. "We can check out the Internet or watch the Discovery Channel, there's information everywhere. It's knowing what to accept and what to ignore, that's the difficult bit."

Graeme reached out across the table toward Tony. The older man stopped flicking through the books and looked up at his guest.

"Do you believe my story?" asked Graeme.

"I believe that you believe it and because of that I'm going to help you." Tony looked earnestly at the younger man. "But I'm going to ask you to talk to a psychiatrist to see if we cannot link you to the present."

"A psychiatrist?"

"Someone for you to talk to who may be able to help you remember."

"I remember everything," said Graeme with conviction.

"Maybe," responded Tony, "but humour me on this?"

"I will talk to whoever you wish."

"Good. In the meantime we can check out missing person lists. People have started to put photographs on walls and streetlamps we could check them out too."

Graeme nodded in agreement to reassure his host.

SEARCHING

"Hello Graeme, my name is Dr Stein. I'm a psychiatrist." Stein was sitting behind a large mahogany desk, a small man with wiry grey hair. "I am here to try and help you remember."

"Oh, but I remember everything."

"Not from a long time ago, but the events that led to you being in the World Trade Centre when the planes hit."

"I was in Hell and then I was in the dust and darkness, the men with lights shouting to me," Graeme insisted.

"It may have seemed like Hell, and God knows not many got out of there alive, but…"

"No!" interrupted Graeme agitatedly. "I really was in Hell, I bargained with the Devil for the souls of the sacrificed innocents."

"Who are the innocents?" asked the doctor.

"The children sacrificed to Quetzalcoatl."

"If they are innocent how is it that they are in Hell?"

"They were sacrificed by others."

Dr Stein hurriedly scribbled some notes.

"Do you have children?"

"I had a son he died over seven hundred years ago. So did his mother," said Graeme sadly.

The doctor continued. "Tell me a bit about Hell. What was it like there?"

And so Graeme told the doctor all that he had seen, the dismembering, the burning, all the ways to die and die again.

Tony interrupted. "Those are the classic accepted methods of death for the seven deadly sins. Well six of them anyway."

"What do you mean?" asked Dr Stein.

"Being cast into the flames is punishment for lust. Dismemberment for wrath and so on," he replied.

"So which one is missing?" asked Doctor Stein.

"Pride," said Graeme quietly. "Lucifer was cast out of Heaven because of pride," he explained.

"Hell itself is the result of pride," added Tony.

❋

Graeme went through his story for an hour, the voyage, his time in the village and his time with the angels until finally it was time to bring the session to an end.

"I'll see you the same time next week," said the psychiatrist.

Graeme walked through the door and Tony went to follow, but stopped when Dr Stein grabbed his arm.

"Wait out by there I'll be with you in a minute," said Tony.

"He's very convincing," said Dr Stein closing the door.

"Yes, he is. He's also very knowledgeable about theology and Amerindian culture," added Tony.

"I know someone who is an expert on the history of the Aztecs, I think he should talk to him," said Dr Stein quietly.

"I'll tell Graeme."

❋

The two men left the hospital and caught a taxi back to Brooklyn. It had been two weeks since the attack on the World Trade Centre, but Graeme still found the noise and the congestion of New York overwhelming. He was sweating profusely and breathing heavily when they finally made it back to the tenement block.

"It's hard work for you here isn't it?" said Tony concernedly.

Graeme nodded, then grabbed at the handrail as they walked up the stairs to Tony's apartment.

Tony pushed the door open and Graeme rushed past him, sighing with relief as he entered the relative quiet and familiarity of the room. He slumped down onto the couch while Tony walked into the bedroom, only to emerge two minutes later with a towel in his left hand and a photo frame in his right. He passed the towel to Graeme and cleaned the glass of the frame with his left sleeve as he sat down next to him.

"This is my wife." Tony held the photo up for Graeme to see.

The younger man wiped his face then looked at the photograph and let the towel drop to the floor. He took the frame in both hands and examined the image closely.

"She is very beautiful," commented Graeme.

"Was," Tony corrected him. "She died twenty three years ago."

"I'm sorry." He looked again at the photo before passing it back. "Did you leave the Church for her?"

"No. I met her a couple of years after I left the seminary." Tony held the frame gently in his left hand and run the fingers of his right tenderly over the glass covering the image. "She took sick two years after we met. There's never been anyone else."

"You could have gone back to the Church."

"That wasn't an option. Her death destroyed any remnant of faith I had." Tony walked over to the breakfast bar and stood the frame upon it. "Until now," he said looking over toward the crucifix.

The two men had some lunch then Tony went into the bedroom to log on to his computer. Graeme read a book about the history of the Twentieth Century.

After a while Graeme shouted in to him. "Cardinal Caronni had a vision of this century, the century before the Eternal Night."

"Dr Stein would say it is your knowledge of history surfacing in a way that allows you to deal with it," Tony shouted back.

Graeme carried on, keeping his mild annoyance at the interruption hidden.

"He saw aeroplanes, like the one that hit the towers and he saw nuclear weapons. He also said that he saw many millions snuffed out before they are born. What could he have meant by that?"

Tony tapped a few keys on the computer keyboard. "Come in here a second, I want to show you something."

Graeme walked in to the bedroom and stood looking over Tony's shoulder at a Priest's for Life website. On the screen he could see a counter rolling and the numbers were counting; counting over forty million. "That is the number of babies that have been aborted before birth in the United States," said Tony.

"What do you mean?" asked Graeme.

"The parents have chosen not to give birth to them and so have terminated the pregnancy."

Graeme sat down on the bed. He sat there thinking for a long while. Tony logged out of the computer.

"The Holocaust, the huge loss of life in two world wars and now this. If I did free those sacrificed by the Aztecs it was just a drop in the ocean compared to what's gone on since."

"The Devil must have collected enough souls by now," mused Tony with a wry smile on his face.

"Another thing the Cardinal said was Satan himself must be surprised at how evil man has become."

✳

For the next week the two men researched the history of the twentieth century, the atrocities, the genocides and the development of weapons of mass destruction. Graeme did not travel far from the apartment and so Tony visited the rows of missing people photographs alone. He checked news reports and Internet sights, but there was no one searching for a man like Graeme.

"You will have to go outside tomorrow, we have to visit Dr Stein."

"I know, I think I'll get an early night."

"You have the bed tonight and I'll sleep on the couch."

Graeme nodded his appreciation and Tony closed the door behind him as he walked out of the bedroom. Left alone the younger man undressed and climbed between the sheets. Before long he was sleeping soundly.

"Graeme! Graeme!" A woman's voice called his name. "Graeme!"

He recognised Centehua's voice and he strained to see where it was coming from.

"Where are you?" The air was filled with choking fumes; he could not see through the darkness. "What are you doing here?" he shouted. The familiar taste of the grey dust filled his mouth and choked his nostrils.

"Graeme!"

He saw the silhouette of a woman through the grimy gloom and tried to make his way toward her.

"No!" he screamed as he saw the woman's chin drop to her chest. The more Graeme tried to move toward the fallen figure the thicker the dust became until it formed a black impenetrable wall between him and his wife.

"Over here!" There were three beams of light penetrating the darkness and slowly making their way toward him. He did not know if they were calling to him or directing each other.

"Here! Here I am!" Graeme shouted desperately. "Look for my wife! She's here too!"

The lights grew bigger and bigger as they came closer until they merged into one brilliant light dispelling the dark cloud. He thought he heard music playing.

"Gabriel are you there!" His voice betrayed the desperation in his soul. "Michael! Raphael! Show yourselves!" Suddenly he was alone in the deep, dark silence.

Someone else was calling his name.

"Your appointment is at ten. We have to leave in an hour."

Graeme opened his eyes and looked at the ceiling of the bedroom. He lay there for a few moments remembering his dream.

"What do you want for breakfast?" The sound of Tony's voice dragged him out of bed; he began to run a shower.

*

The cab ride to Dr Stein's office was not pleasant for Graeme and beads of perspiration formed on his forehead despite the cold chill of a New York autumn morning. His stomach churned as he stepped out of the cab and onto the concrete walkway. He rushed through the hospital entrance into the lobby. Even here the large number of people milling around made him nervous.

"The panic attacks are not improving?" asked the doctor.

"I only get them when I am in traffic or large crowds," answered Graeme.

"That's pretty much all the time in New York" said Doctor Stein picking up his notebook. "Today I'm going to ask you to tell me more about your time living with the Aztecs in the village."

Dr Stein leaned back in his chair and waited for Graeme to speak.

"I should have been happy there, but I was continually haunted by my call to prevent the Eternal Night from happening." Graeme sat up straight and placed his hands in his lap.

"I found myself a wife and we had a child." Graeme reached up with his left hand and gently massaged his temples with his thumb and two fingers. "I wish I was there now."

"How did you communicate?" asked the doctor.

"I learnt the language of the villagers," came the reply. "Nahuatlatoa."

"What does that mean?"

"They speak Nahuatl."

Dr Stein noticed a brief look of despair crossing his face before the younger man glanced down at the floor.

"Spoke Nahuatl." Graeme corrected himself.

For the rest of the hour Graeme described village life in detail, the crops, the daily rhythms, the seasonal cycles. The doctor did not ask about his wedding or about his family and Graeme did not discuss it.

"The session is nearly over," the doctor said standing up. "Given your current unease in the city I think it would be a good idea for you to go to the country for a few days." He walked to the door and opening it he gestured to Tony, sitting in the corridor.

Graeme and Tony stood either side of the doorway with Dr Stein in the middle. He reached out and put an arm around each man's shoulders.

"There is a Roger Pendleton I would like you both to meet. He is a history professor with a special interest in Mesoamerican culture. I have spoken to him and he can see you on Thursday."

"Where is Professor Pendleton?" asked Tony.

"He's in New Hampshire, I'll write down the address and ring him to tell him you're coming."

"I'll hire an automobile," said Tony. "We'll leave in the morning."

WALKING IN WOODS

The further Tony drove the Chevrolet out of the city the more relaxed Graeme became. After three hours of driving through the New England countryside both men were feeling hungry so Tony pulled into a small diner.

"Coffee?" asked the plump middle-aged waitress in the lemon dress and white apron.

"Yes please," said Graeme. Both men ordered a burger; Tony had fries as well.

"We're about half way there," said Tony between mouthfuls of burger.

The door opened and a little old man in a raincoat and woollen hat walked past them and sat at a nearby table. Graeme looked at him intently.

"What's the matter?" said Tony.

Graeme ignored his friend and walked over to the old man's table.

"Do I know you son?" asked the stranger.

"Gabriel?"

"Sorry fella, my name's Archie."

"Gabriel." Graeme repeated as he grabbed the man by the arm.

"Hey! Let go!" shouted the old man as he tried to pull himself away.

"Come on now fellas." The waitress said, trying to calm the situation down.

Graeme began to shake the old man. "Don't you recognize me?"

"That's it. If you don't take your friend out of here I'm calling the cops." The waitress walked toward the phone hanging on the wall.

"Come on Graeme, let's get out of here," said Tony as he walked over to the two men.

"Gabriel! Gabriel!" the younger man shouted, almost dragging the little old man from the seat.

Tony took a hold of Graeme with both hands and began to pull. "That's enough!" he said sternly.

Graeme turned swiftly and swung his right fist at Tony. The blow caught him on the side of the head and sent him reeling. Graeme stood rigid with regret as he looked down at Tony lying on the floor between the table and the counter.

The older man leaned up on his right elbow and rubbed the side of his head with his left hand.

The little old man stood up and walked over to Graeme. "I don't know who this Gabriel is, but it sure ain't me fella." He looked over to the waitress. "Forget about the waffles Angela, I'll call back tomorrow."

Angela held the receiver in her left hand. "If you're not out of here in three seconds flat I'm calling the police."

Graeme bent over Tony and offered him his right hand. Tony grabbed it with two hands and the younger man lifted him upright.

"Not a bad right hook for a guy who's supposed to be nearly eight hundred years old," said Tony as the two men walked toward the automobile.

"Angels are not quite so much in evidence nowadays." Tony pulled back onto the highway. "If you have indeed seen angels and spoken with them then it might be wise to keep that information to yourself."

Graeme nodded. "I am sorry I struck you."

"That's okay, but you can't accost every little old man you come across."

"No." said Graeme flatly. Neither man spoke for the rest of the journey. It was in a stony silence that Tony pulled in to the small New Hampshire village four hours later.

✻

The automobile pulled in to the sidewalk and Tony reached in his pocket for the address. The autumn sky was beginning to turn red as the sun slowly slipped toward the distant tree line.

"I'm going to ask someone for directions," he said, stepping out of the vehicle. Moments later he returned. "It's just outside of town on the outskirts of those woods." He pointed in the direction of the setting red ball.

They drove along for about half an hour until they came to a fork in the road.

"It's down here." Tony turned the wheel as he spoke. They cornered a bend and before them was a large, ranch-style house with whitewashed walls, a low profile and three large windows at the front. A medium built man about the same age as Tony, but with a bit of a belly hanging over his jeans, waited in the doorway. His hair was thinning slightly and very grey.

"I saw you turn the corner up there," he said pointing back up the road.

Graeme walked toward him while Tony reached the two bags from the trunk. "You must be Graeme," said the man in the doorway holding out his hand in greeting. "I'm Roger Pendleton. Come in the two of you."

The three men walked into a spacious living area simply decorated. There was a wood burner in the corner and two large settees and two chairs evenly spaced around the centre of the room.

"Sit down, make yourself at home." A woman came into the room and the Professor gestured for her to take the two bags. "The maid will take them to your rooms. Would you like a drink?"

"I'll have a scotch if that's ok," said Tony.

Graeme shook his head. "No Thanks."

"My wife has just started supper. It'll be ready in about three quarters of an hour."

Roger Pendleton turned to Graeme. "So, Doctor Stein tells me you speak Nahuatl."

"That's right," replied Graeme.

"Do you mind if Graeme and myself converse in that language?" Roger asked Tony.

"No, that's fine. I'll leave you to it. I could do with some air anyway. I'll take a walk outside?"

"Be careful. Don't stray too far, it will be dark soon and it is very easy to get lost out here if you don't know your way around."

Tony downed the whisky in one and walked out the room.

"I've been told that you have an interesting story to tell."

"I learned this language when I lived in an Aztec village." Both men spoke in Nahuatl.

"Many years ago," added Professor Pendleton.

He watched Graeme closely, trying to read his facial expressions.

Graeme told the Professor about his life in the village until eventually Tony returned from his walk.

"It's getting quite chilly." Tony was rubbing his hands together vigorously. He walked over to the stove in the corner.

"It won't be long before the autumnal ochre will give way to the ice and the snow," said the host.

Just then a short woman walked in wearing slacks and a loose jumper. She was of a wiry disposition and announced that supper was ready in a slightly breathless fashion.

"This is my wife Linda," announced the Professor. "Come and meet our guests darling."

※

After supper the four of them got better acquainted. Roger and Linda Pendleton had been married for thirty-two years. Linda was also an academic; her field was astronomy. They had no children.

Tony explained how he had become a failed seminarian and why he had never remarried. He told them how he had become a toolmaker. He decided that when he turned fifty, provided he was not too extravagant, he could afford to retire. "Not in luxury you understand, but comfortably enough," he explained.

Graeme limited his life story to his post-Nine/Eleven experiences.

"What happened before is what we hope to shed some light on." The anticipation in Professor Pendleton's voice was apparent. "And we will begin tomorrow. I think it will be best if you stay here at least until next week. From what you tell me neither of you have got anything pressing in New York."

"No, we haven't," agreed Tony.

Graeme was happily looking forward to a few days away from the city.

Linda stood up and looked at her husband. "Come on darling let's show our guests to their rooms they must be exhausted."

The three men got up and followed her out of the room.

✳

Graeme arose just after dawn. There was a light rain outside, but it did not deter him. He put on an overcoat and set out into the woods.

The path was a faint one, but Graeme followed it for a while. He pulled the hood of the coat down from his head and felt the fine rain on his face and in his hair; he considered whether he should cut it short like Tony and the Professor.

Relishing the peace and solitude of the woods he decided to leave the path and walk where the trees were growing closer together. For the first time since he found himself in the World Trade Centre lobby he felt at peace. He walked slowly treading gently on a carpet of fallen leaves.

Memories of demonic encounters in other forests, of fleeing through other trees came suddenly back to haunt him. His feeling of peace was replaced by anxiety and fear. He began to look over his shoulder, his awareness heightening. He reacted to every woodland sound. The dawn chorus, previously just background noise to his thoughts, filled his hearing and he began to separate each individual bird song in his mind.

Graeme sat under a mature northern red oak tree. It had begun to shed its dark red leaves and a carpet of them lay on the ground around its base. He looked around watchfully, but saw only the trees, the leaves and the grass.

"Gabriel! Show yourself to me!" He shouted desperately out into the emptiness of the forest.

"Michael! Raphael!" Only the sounds of the forest came back to him. A squirrel ran up a nearby tree and disappeared into a hole in the trunk.

Graeme sat there for a long time. There was no connection with this forest and he now no longer felt the fear at its gloom and darkness. The trees were unfamiliar to him and he did not know if their fruits could sustain him. His sense of the supernatural was fading. At that moment he appreciated how Tony could lose his faith. He rose and began to walk slowly to the house.

"Where have you been?" "We were getting worried about you." Mrs Pendleton was looking through the kitchen window.

"I was up early so I thought I'd take a walk in the woods."

"Go and get out of those wet clothes. I'll get you some breakfast. The other two have just finished theirs."

Graeme took his boots off outside the kitchen door then made his way up to the room. Professor Pendleton shouted from the lounge as he walked past. "I'll see you in my study in an hour." He spoke in Nahuatl.

❊

An hour later, showered and fed, Graeme walked into the Professor's study. The older man pointed to a red leather armchair.

"Make yourself comfortable." He sat in another identical chair a few yards from the other.

The room was lined with bookshelves, groaning under the weight of the books filling them. Across the room from the two chairs was a matching red leather settee.

"How did you come to be in the Americas when Hernan Cortez arrived there?"

"I sailed there over two hundred years before."

Looking at Graeme with an impassive expression he asked, "With whom?"

"I joined a crew following the legend of an expedition that found a land far off to the West and never returned. Hesper, the master of the vessel, his grandfather had led the original party and never returned."

"Do you remember the name of the grandfather?"

"No, I did not really care as I had my own quest to follow."

Professor Pendleton walked toward one of the stacks of shelves. "Does the name Madog ring any bells?"

"Yes!" Exclaimed Graeme. "He was a Welsh prince."

The Professor turned the pages of a book he brought down from a shelf. "Here we are." He walked over to Graeme and pointed to a page as he handed him the book. Graeme looked at the words on the page before him.

"The Lord Madoc, sonne of Owen Gwyndd prince of NorthWales, leaving his brothers in contention, and warre for their inheritance sought, by sea (westerlie from Irland), for some forein Region to plant hymselfe in with soveranity: wch Region when he had found, he returned to Wales againe and hym selfe wth Shipps, vituals, and men and women sufficient for the coloniy, wth spedely he leed into the peninsula; then named Farquara; but of late Florida or into some of the Provinces, and territories neere therabouts: and in

Apalchen, Mocosa, or Norombera: then of these 4 beinge notable portions of the ancient Atlantis, no longer, nowe named America"

As Graeme read Professor Pendelton continued. "The extract you're looking at comes from the Brytannici Imperii Limites written by one of Queen Elizabeth's more notorious advisors John Dee in 1576.

"Hesper was Lord Madoc's grandson. It was Lord Madoc we were chasing on the Harbinger."

"The name of the ship in which you crossed the Atlantic?"

"Yes." The two men looked closely at each other in silence for a few moments.

"Graeme spoke first. "This must prove that my story is true."

"Or that you have a deep knowledge of the history of the colonization of the Americas."

Graeme sighed.

"The legend of the Welsh prince who settled in the southern states is quite well-known. There is even a commemorative plaque in Mobile down in Alabama." The Professor pointed at the book in Graeme's hand. "Its inscription is quoted in there."

Graeme thumbed through the book until he found the page.

"In memory of Prince Madog," the inscription read, "a Welsh explorer who landed on the shores of Mobile Bay in 1170 and left behind, with the Indians, the Welsh language."

He handed the book back to Professor Pendleton and walked over to the window.

"I can see how my story must look to you." Graeme spoke in an unemotional monotone.

"I think you believe your story." He too walked over to the window. "I don't doubt your sincerity, and I am not a psychiatrist, but I can show you alternative sources for your knowledge." He put his hand on Graeme's shoulder and held his other arm out offering a path back to the armchairs.

The two men continued their discussion of the Madog legend; the Professor spoke of the alleged eighteenth century discovery of the Mandan tribe of Indians commemorated in the Alabama plaque.

"Can we visit them?" asked Graeme eagerly.

With regret in his voice the Professor answered. "I'm afraid not. They were practically wiped out by a smallpox epidemic in 1837."

The discussion continued. Graeme spoke of Hesper and the other sailors on the Harbinger, and of the adventures and incidents on the voyage.

"It sounds like it was an eventful trip," commented Pendleton. Standing up he said. "I think that's enough for this morning. Come on, let's see if lunch is ready."

✻

Tony wasn't at the table for lunch and Graeme wondered where he was.

"He ate earlier and decided to get some fresh air," replied Linda briskly as she placed the tureen of vegetables on the table. "He was complaining of a headache."

Graeme stood up. "Actually, I'm not that hungry at the moment, I'll eat mine later." He too walked out into the garden.

Tony was leaning against a tree looking out toward the woods.

2012: THE ETERNAL NIGHT

"Are you alright?"

The older man turned with a start at the unexpected sound of Graeme's voice. "You took me by surprise."

"Sorry," said Graeme standing next to him and looking in the same direction. "Linda said you weren't feeling well."

"I'll live."

"Look, I'm sorry about the incident in the diner yesterday, I hope I didn't hurt you."

"You've already apologized once. Think no more of it."

Although the rain had stopped the air felt cold and damp; Graeme wished he'd put a coat on. A thin mist lay along the ground and wove its way weakly among the trees.

"I feel my memories slipping away. It's as if they don't belong in this time."

Tony looked at Graeme and patted his back. "That little old man didn't look much like an archangel to me," he said with a smile on his face.

Graeme smiled back. "No, he very rarely did."

After a long silence, Graeme spoke again. "Do you think I really did imagine it all?"

"It's an incredible story and I have to admit commonsense would have to dictate that it is all a figment of your imagination. But my belief in God has never been greater than when I knelt with you in prayer before that crucifix." Tony turned toward the house. "Come on let's go back."

✻

That afternoon Graeme and Professor Pendleton discussed the story of Quetzalcoatl. Graeme told him of the Soothsayer's explanation and of Hesper being mistaken for Quetzalcoatl in the city.

The Professor interrupted. "There is a historical aspect to the Quetzalcoatl myth, as well as Quetzalcoatl as deity. The historical Quetzalcoatl is attributed with abolishing human sacrifice for example and yet it's true that the temple at Cholula was dedicated to him, but even Quetzalcoatl the God is considered to be a beneficent God compared to others, what you say about the mass sacrifices of Hesper's time do not ring true."

"The sacrifices increased under Hesper because he was acting as Lucifer's agent."

The Professor made some notes. Then leaned forward and looked at Graeme over the top of his glasses.

"I want to talk a little more about Lucifer's role in your version of events and I would like Tony to sit in. Is that okay with you?"

Graeme nodded in agreement.

"I think his knowledge as a past seminarian may be of some use," continued the Professor. He stretched to his full height lifting his hands above his head as he stood up. "Let's take a break. I'll get the maid to make some coffee while I find your friend."

Graeme browsed through the shelves of books lining the walls until Professor Pendleton returned with Tony following him.

"Did you see anything that might be of interest to you?" he asked.

"You certainly have an eclectic collection," replied the younger man.

"The section you should find interesting is over there." He pointed toward the wall behind the settee.

"That's the Mesoamerican section." Graeme glanced to where the Professor was pointing.

Tony sat on the settee while the other two returned to the chairs they had previously occupied.

The Professor spoke first. "Your link between Lucifer and Quetzalcoatl, it is the references to both in terms of the Morning Star, yes?"

"That's right the biblical reference is in the Old Testament," confirmed Graeme.

"How art thou fallen from heaven, O Lucifer, son of the morning! How art thou cut down to the ground, which didst weaken the nations!" quoted Tony. "Isaiah Chapter 14."

"quomodo cecidisti de caelo lucifer qui mane oriebaris corruisti in terram qui vulnerabas gentes," said Graeme in a voice barely louder than a whisper.

The Professor looked at both men in turn.

"Lucifer is Latin for morning star," explained Tony.

"And in Aztec culture there is a further link as both are depicted as serpents, Lucifer in the Garden of Eden and as a feathered serpent according to Aztec representations of Quetzalcoatl," added Professor Pendleton. "My wife will also confirm an astronomical link with Venus, which is also sometimes known as the Morning Star.

"I am sure there is a psychological link here," said Tony thoughtfully. "No doubt Dr Stein could comment on all three as representations of a universal archetype."

Professor Pendleton began to pace slowly back and forth in the area behind the leather chairs.

Tony spoke again. "But the reference in Isaiah is descriptive, it does not refer to some demon of the underworld, it refers to the downfall of Babylon after its rulers took Israel into exile. The reference to the Morning Star should be seen in the context of the astrological references made earlier in chapter thirteen."

Professor Pendleton put his forearms on the back of the vacant chair and leaned forward. "I think we are in danger of going around in circles here. The crucial point was made earlier by you Tony when you spoke of collective archetypes. If these things are metaphorical references then how could Graeme here have lived and experienced them?"

Graeme slumped back into his chair, a distracted look on his face.

"You're saying that it could all have been a psychotic episode," remarked Tony.

"Yes, no doubt brought on by the trauma of the World Trade Centre attack."

"But that would mean that all religious experiences, all the lives of the saints for instance, are based on no more than some sort of mental imbalance," said Tony incredulously.

The Professor shrugged. "Let's call it a day, we can come back to it fresh tomorrow." He walked out muttering. "That maid never did bring the coffee."

*

Tony and Graeme stepped outside for some air.

"Let's take a short walk in the woods," said Graeme "It's peaceful there."

"I think we really have entered the forest now," said Tony scratching his head. "It's getting difficult to see the wood from the trees." He let out a loud guttural laugh.

ACCEPTANCE

"You said you were a woodchopper in your life in England." Only Graeme and the Professor were in the study, Tony had decided to do some research of his own that morning.

"That is what I recall," answered Graeme. "I certainly seem to have an affinity with the woods here. I find it very peaceful."

"Tell me about your memories of England."

For the rest of the morning they discussed Graeme's recollections of his time as a servant and his time in the forest.

Finally the Professor brought the conversation to a close. "There isn't much I can help you with here. I think you need to explore your memories as activations of the archetypes we discussed yesterday and Doctor Stein is the best person for that."

Tony unceremoniously entered the room. "I have had a response," he said excitedly.

"A response to what?" asked the Professor.

"I put Graeme's picture on the Internet." He looked over toward Graeme. "I got an email this morning from someone who says she knows him."

Graeme was a melting pot of confusion, trepidation and anticipation. "Who is she?" he asked.

"It was from an archaeologist and guess where she's currently working?" Tony paused for dramatic effect.

"Where?" Graeme asked impatiently.

"Cholula."

The word hung in the air like an eagle waiting to pounce.

"We must go there." It was the Professor's turn to get excited.

Graeme began to pace the study nervously. Tony walked up to him and said, "I have a picture of her. She sent it through as an attachment, but I can't get the Professor's printer to work."

"Sorry, it's out of ink."

The three men made their way hurriedly to the room the Professor used as an office.

The untidiness of the room was in stark contrast to the clean orderliness of the study. Papers and scribbled notes lay on the desk and there were books and journals littered around the floor.

Tony weaved his way to the computer on the desk and moved the mouse along the mat. The arrow rested on the email attachment and Tony left-clicked.

Graeme felt the colour drain from his face and his hands become cold and clammy. He saw the ceiling recede into the distance. All went black.

✻

"He's coming around."

It was Tony's voice he could hear cutting through the cotton wool inside his head. He opened his eyes and tried to get up, but the ceiling and the wall swapped places and he stumbled back onto the floor.

"Get him a glass of water." It was the Professor who spoke this time.

Graeme could hear a woman's voice say, "Out of the way."

The pungent aroma of smelling salts wafted into his nostrils. He shook his head to escape the smell and felt the fog lift at the same time. Graeme sat up, his head clearing; he accepted the glass of water offered by Tony.

"Are you okay?" said Tony, earnestly expressing his concern. He bent down to give his friend a helping hand. "Her name is Centehua," he whispered helping Graeme into a chair.

Graeme pointed at the young woman's face staring out from the monitor. "It is my wife." He seemed almost afraid to utter the words.

"Let's wait until you're in full control of your senses and then we'll email her." Linda too was looking at the image on the computer screen as she spoke. "She's a pretty young thing."

Linda sent an email asking the girl how she knew Graeme. There was no immediate response and the Pendletons left the room after a little while.

"Call us when you get an answer."

Tony and Graeme sat by the desk, but no reply came for over an hour.

✳

When the reply came it explained that Graeme was a researcher from an English university. He'd taken a leave of absence from his post to work on a book about Aztec village life before the arrival of the Spanish. They were both involved in the excavation and study of the remains of an Aztec village just past the mountain range between Cholula and the coast and that is where they met.

Graeme had left the dig to check out possible publishers for his book. He was due back now the rainy season was coming to an end.

Linda leaned between the two men seated at the computer and began to type.

"What is Graeme's surname?"

She clicked on send.

Another email arrived with hardly a pause.

Linda looked at Graeme. "Hello Mr Woodland."

Graeme looked back at her with a bemused gaze.

Tony began to type a response.

"Graeme was caught up in the collapse of the World Trade Centre, but he's alright. However, he has suffered some memory loss," typed Tony.

Professor Pendleton tapped his wife on the shoulder and she stood back. He moved into the space and asked Tony to add that Graeme would return as soon as possible.

"I am so happy that he is unharmed physically," came the response. "What's your number? Can I ring you?"

Tony turned to speak to Graeme, but was silenced by a shake of the head from the Professor. He indicated with a nod for Graeme and Tony to leave, then began to type.

"I think it unwise for him to speak to you at the moment due to his memory loss, but we will come down as soon as we can. If you can send us a contact number we will inform you of our schedule as soon as something can be arranged."

"Please hurry up, I'm very fond of Graeme. I've been very worried about him."

There was a cell phone number added at the end of the email.

✷

Tony and Graeme had gone to sit in the lounge, the Pendletons followed after sending the email. Linda sat down next to Graeme on the sofa, but Roger Pendleton remained standing.

"I have no doubt regarding her sincerity, but while you were waiting for a response I took the liberty of ringing Doctor Stein." The Professor made eye contact with Graeme. "He would like to talk to you before you meet her."

"I want to see her," demanded Graeme.

"Let's leave for New York tonight," suggested Tony. "We can be there by the morning. Graeme can see Doctor Stein first thing and we can get the first available flight to Mexico."

Linda put her hand on Graeme's knee. "I'll make some sandwiches or something for the journey and we can get underway."

"We can take my Jeep," said Roger. He looked at Tony and then his wife. "The three of us can take turns in driving."

Graeme shrugged his shoulders and reluctantly nodded his agreement to the plan.

✷

They got to New York by dawn and Graeme was in Dr Stein's office an hour later. The journey through the city had left him on edge; there was sweat on his brow and a slight tremor was visible in his hands.

"I can give you something for that," said Doctor Stein. "It'll help you relax. You're going to need it if you intend to fly to Mexico."

"Thanks."

Doctor Stein walked over to a locked cabinet in the corner. He opened it and took out a bottle of pills. "Take one as soon as you feel yourself getting anxious, but don't take another one for at least four hours."

Graeme took the bottle from the doctor and placed it in his jacket pocket.

Doctor Stein walked back to his desk and sat with one foot on the floor and one dangling free on its edge. "How do you feel about this development?" he asked.

"I don't know." Graeme leaned forward on the chair. "The picture looked like my wife. She even has the same name, but how can it be her?" He ran his fingers through his hair nervously.

"It's the wrong time, the wrong place," suggested the doctor.

The bewildered young man shook his head slowly from side to side. "I saw her die." He looked off into the distance with a thousand yard gaze that cut through the boundaries of the doctor's office and reached back into the centuries. "A long time ago."

The minutes ticked by and neither man spoke. Finally the doctor broke the silence.

"You must be beginning to realize that your memories of the Aztec village, of the angels and of Hell itself are based on experiences you have somehow repressed from your life here. Now."

"I know. I do not feel any sense of the supernatural at all here. No angels, no demons and no call to a path."

"Now that is where I disagree with you," said the doctor firmly. "You are on a great adventure. Your quest is not to save the world or free the damned, but to find yourself. To find your own place in this world."

Doctor Stein walked to the door. Graeme got up and followed him.

"Go and begin the search for your real identity in Cholula," said the doctor as he opened the door. "We'll talk again when you get back."

*

Tony met him outside. Graeme took a tablet from the dark brown bottle and swallowed it with a sip of water from a nearby font.

"Everything okay?" asked the older man.

"Let us go and find out who I really am," said Graeme with conviction.

A NEW BEGINNING

Graeme heard the voice on the public address announcing that it was time for boarding.

"That's us," said Professor Pendleton cheerfully; and the gang of four made their way to the boarding gate.

"How long does it take for those tranquillisers to kick in?" Tony asked Graeme.

"Not long. My trip from the doctor's office was really rather pleasant."

"Even so you may want to take one before we take off."

*

In no time at all they were seated on the aircraft. Tony had a window seat with Graeme sat next to him and the Pendletons seated behind.

Professor Pendleton leaned forward. "I don't know how things are going to pan out for you down in Mexico, but I'd like to make you an offer."

Graeme turned around to look at the Professor. "What offer?"

"Well I know you have a vast knowledge of Aztec culture and I am thinking of writing a book on the massacre at Cholula, we'll see what has been happening at the dig, then maybe you can come and work with me on the book."

"I may want to stay there," said Graeme firmly.

The call came through to fasten seat belts and prepare for take-off. Tony leaned forward adjusting Graeme's seat belt.

"How much will you be paying him?" asked Tony.

"The story of Cholula can begin at the dig. Anyway we'll see how it goes." The Professor shot a glance at Tony. "And don't worry, he will be paid well."

The plane began to taxi down the runway. Graeme wriggled slightly in his seat. The pilot opened out the engines and the roar resonated through the cabin. Graeme grabbed the armrests his knuckles turning white as the plane left the ground.

Tony spoke reassuringly. "It will level off soon and we can settle down and enjoy the flight."

It was early evening when they finally landed at Puebla airport. The temperature was noticeably warmer than New York and Graeme felt reassured somehow by this. He had enjoyed the trip and found it exciting rather than terrifying. There had been no need to take the tablets Doctor Stein had prescribed him. Even the crowds at the baggage carousel did not bother him too much.

"I'll get your bag," offered Tony.

Tony retrieved their luggage and the two men sat on plastic chairs while the Pendletons attempted to retrieve theirs.

Graeme looked at Tony with a serious expression. "I want to thank you for all you've done for me."

"Don't mention it," replied Tony his face reddening slightly.

"You've looked after me from the time I walked out of that collapsing tower block. If it hadn't been for you

God knows what would have happened to me. And now here you are, thousands of miles from home, helping me try to make sense of it all."

Tony shifted uneasily on the uncomfortable yellow chair. "It's me who should be thanking you. I think most New Yorkers changed the day the Twin Towers collapsed. Everyone's a little more considerate than they used to be, but you have changed my life. My days were spent in coffee shops, reading, watching television and occasional trips to the park. Look at me now, I'm in Mexico looking for Aztec villages and rubbing shoulders with professors and their scientist wives."

The Pendletons were walking toward them dragging their bags behind. The two men stood ready to leave.

Tony spoke again. "To tell you the truth I was turning into a lonely old man and you've saved me from that."

The Pendletons walked over to them. "Come on let's get a taxi. We'll find a hotel for tonight," said the Professor. "Centehua will be in town sometime tomorrow. Linda rang her a few minutes ago and she is on her way from the dig."

*

Graeme could not sleep. The air conditioning was noisy and the late night sounds of the town drifted up to the second floor room where he lay on the bed looking at the ceiling. On the other bed Tony snored softly. Graeme smiled as he glanced over at the peaceful form of his friend, the blankets rising in time with the older man's breathing.

The picture of the woman on the computer screen materialized in his mind's eye. She looked exactly like his wife and yet... "She is different." He spoke those words quietly to himself. Tony stirred and turned to face the door at the other side of the room. Graeme got out of bed and walked toward the window.

As he looked through the curtain down onto the street it reminded him of the streets in the city where he and his family had been taken. Although these streets and the streets of New York were like no streets he could ever remember seeing before, the people were the same. Each one hurrying through their lives trying to make some sense of it all. And every now and then death came shattering the frail facade of their existence, forcing them to re-evaluate the often-trivial things that seemed so important to them.

Graeme sat down in an armchair at the side of the window and looked up at the starry sky. He felt no urge or need to call for divine assistance any more. All that was now may be all that he could ask for. Presently he drifted off to sleep.

"Time for breakfast buddy." Tony shook the sleeping form gently by the shoulder as he spoke.

"What? Yes, I must have dozed off." Graeme reached his arms out and then up, stretching and yawning at the same time.

"This may be the most important day of your life," shouted Tony from the bathroom. "You don't want to be late for that now do you."

∗

Roger Pendleton had already made a start on his coffee and pancakes when Graeme and Tony arrived.

"The lady will be with us shortly," he announced.

"She arrived about twenty minutes ago after driving through the night to get here."

Graeme stood up knocking Tony's coffee cup to the floor. The other guests and a waiter looked over at the sound of splintering china.

"Take it easy." Roger tried to sound as reassuring as he could. "She wanted to freshen up so my wife took her to our room."

The waiter arrived with a mop and pan to clear up the crockery.

"Sorry," said Graeme to the waiter. "Let me help."

"It's okay signor."

Graeme played nervously with his knife. A croissant lay untouched on his plate and he shot frequent glances toward the entrance. After a while two women appeared. They stood framed in the arched entrance; the younger one was wearing three quarter length jeans reaching down to just above her ankles and a loose white cotton blouse that covered her slim frame.

Linda scanned the room looking for the three men, but before she could find them she saw Graeme walking rapidly toward them. Tony stood up to follow, but thought better of it and sat back down.

The girl saw Graeme approaching and smiled. She held her arms out and he fell into them; he pulled her tightly to him.

"Hey steady," she said jokingly. "Careful or we'll be asked to leave." Centehua pulled back from his grasp just far enough to be able to look at Graeme's face.

"You've had a hard time of it huh?" She noticed a tear running down one of Graeme's cheeks. "Come on, let's take a walk, we can tell each other what we've been up to since we saw each other last."

Tony watched the two figures leave the room. "Do you think he'll be alright?"

It was Linda who answered. "The girl seems genuinely fond of him. But I don't know if they were as close in this life as the life Graeme remembers for them." Her voice was edged with some concern.

Tony stared thoughtfully into his half-empty coffee cup.

✳

Graeme and Centehua walked along the streets of Cholula until they came to a small bar.

"Here we are," said the girl.

"Hey amigos how are you two doing?" asked the barman.

"We're fine," Cenetehua answered. Graeme stood just inside the door with a troubled look on his face.

"Are you okay?" Centehua asked. She spoke perfect English, but with a slight Mexican accent.

"I have been here before?"

The barman looked surprised as he asked, "Don't you remember me? I'm Pedro. I've been serving you with tequilas for months. Where have you been anyway?"

Centehua led Graeme to a barstool. "I think we'll try two tequilas now, Pedro." She looked fondly into Graeme's eyes, her focus moving from one eye to the other and then back. "You really have lost your memory, haven't you?"

"I have memories, but they are not of this time or this life."

"Come on." Centehua got up from the stool and grabbed the tequilas. "Let's find a quiet table and you can tell me all about it."

Graeme told her everything; he told her of his time as a woodchopper, the visit from the friar, the voyage and his life in the village.

Centehua made no comment on the tale only interrupting to ask Pedro for some tapas and the occasional refill of the tequila glasses.

He told her of the sacrifices at the temple and how she had died and at this point she did comment. "No wonder you were so pleased to see me this morning." She reached over the small round table and rested her hand on his forearm.

"Your hair is shorter than I remember it," Graeme said reaching to touch it.

"It's always been about this length." She said grabbing his arm. Her hair was black and straight, the ends brushed gently against her breast as she pulled his hand away. "You know I don't like people touching my hair."

Graeme looked down at the table disconcertedly.

Centehua leaned close to his ear. "Not in public anyway." She kissed him gently on the side of the head before she relaxed back in her seat.

"Pedro leave the bottle this time."

"I don't have any money on me," said Graeme concernedly.

"Don't worry we're good for it here."

They sat there talking and drinking. Centehua told him of the Graeme she knew. He turned up just after the dig in the village had started. All she knew about him was that he had been a lecturer at an English University - but she did not know which one - and had taken a year off. He never mentioned a wife or family.

"Did you find a publisher for your book?"

"I do not know. After my recollection of your death I went to Hell and spoke with the Devil."

"Well now you're freaking me out," interrupted the girl with a slightly mocking tone.

Graeme carried on with mild annoyance in his voice at the interruption. "And the next thing I knew I was being led out of the Twin Towers. I have no memories of this time before those towers collapsed."

"Well, let's drink to your survival and to the hope that your memory will come back." The girl raised her glass tilted it toward Graeme and downed its contents.

The sun went down and Graeme hardly noticed. He found it increasingly difficult to take in what the girl was saying about the time they shared together, but he was certain this was not the same Centehua that he had a son with in the village. He could also tell that she liked him, but he did not sense any deep feelings of commitment to him and he suddenly grew very sad as he realized he had none for her.

"What's the matter?" Centehua asked, a slight slur made her Mexican accent more pronounced.

Graeme mumbled an unintelligible reply and reached for the tequila bottle.

"Hey amigo!" shouted Pedro. Graeme had thrown the empty bottle across the room. He tried to stand, but fell back onto his stool.

"I think you two had better go home. I'll call a taxi."

Centehua nodded her thanks and rose unsteadily to her feet. Graeme crashed to the floor pulling the table with him.

✳

Graeme was woken by the musical tones of a cell phone. He opened his eyes; the wall beyond the dressing table seemed to move slightly as he tried to focus on it and he felt a throbbing behind the eyeballs. The rest of his head pounded persistently.

He sat up slowly, the room gave the impression of swaying slightly and the bed appeared to float in the sea of his hangover.

"Hello." Centehua sounded as if she was gargling grit as she spoke down the phone. Handing it to Graeme she said, "It's for you."

Graeme turned to his left to see Centehua lying next to him with a blanket covering her from the waist down. She held the phone out toward him.

"Where the hell have you been?" barked Tony down the phone. "I've been ringing this number for ages."

Graeme pulled the phone away from his ear and grimaced. He began to feel sick.

"I had a few drinks with Centehua. I'm not sure where we are, but…"

Centehua sat up and leaned toward the cell phone. "He's in my apartment," she rasped loudly.

"I'll see you later," Graeme added quickly.

Centehua kissed him on his shoulder, but the vomit rising in his throat stopped him from turning toward her.

"Where's the bathroom," he said urgently.

She pointed to a door on her side of the bed. He brushed against bare skin as he rolled over her and ran toward the door. Graeme could hear the girl laughing when he began to wretch into the toilet.

His hurting eased after he finished being sick. He was left with a slight headache and a dull pain behind the eyes. He brushed his teeth to get rid of the taste in his mouth and splashed some water over his face to clear his head further. With the alcoholic fog now more or less cleared he put a towel around his lower half and walked back into the bedroom.

Graeme could see his clothes spread loosely over a chair by the window; Centehua's were spread on the floor between the door and the foot of the bed. She lay uncovered on the top of the bed.

"Did we," Graeme paused shyly.

"Oh yes. You haven't forgotten anything in that department," she answered with a grin.

He began to pick up his clothes.

"What's your hurry?"

Graeme felt a muddled mixture of emotions as he looked at the girl on the bed. His body wanted to climb back into bed with the girl and he recognized her as the same one he recalled having a child with; her smiling face was as beautiful as ever, but he knew he did not love this Centehua. She was a child of this age and he loved the less complicated Centehua of the village.

"The book you say I was writing, do you know if I had any other copies?" asked Graeme.

"Yes, of course." Centehua sat up and wrapped the blanket around herself. "It's on your laptop."

"Where is this laptop?" He sat on the bed with his back toward her and put his shoes on, his shirt was unbuttoned. She leaned over him as he sat back up and pulled his shirt off his shoulders.

"It's here somewhere." Centehua kissed his neck. "We could look for it later," she said huskily.

Graeme turned and kissed her quickly on the cheek. "Can we look now?" he said urgently. "It's very important to me."

"Are you sure you've forgotten everything?" she asked, the disappointment tinged her voice. "You always were rushing off, or finding other things to do once you'd had enough."

Graeme shot her a puzzled glance.

The two of them searched through the mess that was Centehua's small apartment.

"Here it is." She was rummaging through a small set of drawers in a cabinet, on which stood a small television.

They were in a small room off the bathroom that doubled as a living area and study. There was no discernable place to sit and work, with barely enough room for the television and the large sofa that inhabited the room. Scattered around the sofa and on the floor were papers, scrap pads and textbooks obviously used by Centehua in her archaeological work. They both cleared a space on the sofa and opened up the laptop.

"It'll need charging," said the girl. She got up and wrestled a long lead and adaptor from a pile of paperwork in the corner. The machine whirred and Centehua scanned the icons and menu for the document. "Here it is."

Graeme leaned forward to look.

"Do you remember how to use one of these?" the girl asked.

He shook his head.

She positioned the laptop between them and showed him how to navigate the Word document.

Graeme stared incredulously at the title page.

'THE LEGEND OF THE ETERNAL NIGHT'

"This is my book?"

"Yes."

He began to read about a lonely woodchopper receiving a visit from an old Franciscan monk.

Centehua's phone rang. "It's your friend again," she said and handed him the cell phone.

"Are you coming back to the hotel?" asked Tony.

"I've found something," replied Graeme.

"What," said Tony. He sensed the anticipation in Graeme's voice.

"It's the book Centehua said I went to New York for."

"To find a publisher," added Tony.

"Yes, and it's not a history book." His voice rose in volatile mix of excitement and apprehension. "It's a novel."

Centehua interrupted the conversation. "Give me the phone," she said to Graeme. Holding it to her ear she said, "If I give you my address you can come and pick us up. The manuscript is on his laptop."

*

When they were all back at the hotel Linda printed off a copy each of the manuscript and they all settled down to read Graeme's book.

It was well into the evening before they all finished. Each one sat in silence as they waited for the others to come to the end.

Finally, just before midnight, Graeme himself finished reading the story. All eyes looked at him. He said nothing. They all sat there in an uneasy silence until finally Centehua walked over to the telephone, picked it up and asked for room service.

"Who wants tortillas?"

"I wouldn't mind some salami sandwiches," answered Tony.

Roger Pendleton walked over to Graeme. "It's your story; every last detail."

"I seem to have been living out my own novel in my memories."

"I'm flattered that you considered me as an inspiration for your wife," said Centehua from the other side of the room.

Tony walked over to the young woman. "You appear to be the only link between the two worlds."

"We can only guess at what it must have been like for you in the lobby of the World Trade Centre when the South Tower collapsed," Roger said sympathetically. "I think Doctor Stein should know about this development."

Graeme shook his head. "Not yet. I need to think this through."

"Of course," responded the Professor.

Graeme spoke to Centehua "I will need to talk to you further."

"Yes, of course." She paused and then added, "But what about the dig? Will you be going back there? I know I have to."

Linda spoke just as room service knocked the door. "Let's leave it for now. We all need some sleep. We can talk some more in the morning." She turned to Centehua. "I'll see if I can book you a room here for tonight."

∗

Graeme sat looking out the window of the hotel room. In the distance he could see the illuminated form of the Church of Our Lady of Remedies and beyond that was the great shadow of the Popocatepetl Volcano. He muttered a silent prayer toward the Church, and gave a resigned sigh when he finished. The Church lay on the site of the temple where, according to his memories, his wife and child had died; but looking at it now none of that seemed real to him.

He thought of the people here with him, the Professor and his wife in the room down the hall, Tony sleeping in the room next door and Centehua on the floor above. He decided he would need to visit the site of the dig with Centehua and the Professor. Probably even take up the offer of working with him.

"It's obvious that I am here to stay," he whispered quietly to himself. "There's no chance of an archangel descending from Heaven and whisking me away from this time and place."

Graeme turned the down air conditioning, he preferred the heat of the Mexican night to its clanking, and climbed into bed.

✳

Sleep engulfed him, but before long he felt the scorching heat of Hell on his lungs again and demons reaching for his limbs. The children poured through the portal in his peripheral vision; but the light of an angel welcomed them. He recognized Raphael greeting the formerly vanquished souls; Michael and Gabriel attacked the demons following behind them.

The two archangels fought ferociously and demon forms lay piled upon the floor at their feet. They quickly arrived at Graeme's side. He felt two angelic arms lift him and he was carried at speed between the two winged figures, over the flames of the combusting corpses.

✳

"Are you alright?" This time he did recognize the accent. He was coughing and retching with the memory of the dust and smoke of the Twin Towers. Tony handed a glass of water to Graeme as he came around. "I heard you crying out from the other room." Graeme put the glass down on the bedside table and Tony handed him a towel. "Here, you're sweating like a pig."

"Thanks." Graeme wiped his face. "I was having a nightmare."

Tony sat on the armchair across the room from the bed. "I'll stay here for the rest of the night."

"There's no need," said Graeme turning his face back down into the pillow. "It was just a dream."

*

Graeme got up just after dawn. He tiptoed past Tony's sleeping form and into the bathroom. By the end of the shower the dream was little more than a faint memory. He woke Tony and they made their way down for breakfast.

"I intend to take up the Professor's offer of a job," he told his friend.

"That's great," Tony replied. "Your novel is actually quite good too. I'm sure you'll get a publisher for it." His face opened up as a thought occurred to him. "The Professor will know publishers, you shouldn't have a problem."

The two men continued with their breakfast for a while, then Tony spoke again. "What about Centehua? I'm guessing your feelings for her as not as strong as you were expecting."

"She's a lovely girl," said Graeme. "But you're right I'm not in love with her. I intend to spend some time with her though. I'm going to go back to the dig." He smiled at his friend, then he picked up his coffee. "As you said last night she is my only link, the one constant."

"Well, you seem to be a lot more accepting of it all now. What about her claim that you took a leave of absence from an English university?"

"I'm still relatively young, I know I'm not over eight hundred years old anyway." Both men laughed. "I'll explore that avenue in good time."

THE REAL WORLD

Graeme went back to the dig with Centehua to find it was in the same area where the novel was set. He and Centehua re-established their friendship and they stayed together until the work on the excavations came to an end. They kept in touch while Graeme collaborated on a book about the Cholula massacre with Professor Pendleton. Tony went back to the tenement in Brooklyn. He was right about the Professor's literary contacts and Graeme's novel became a runaway bestseller.

The English University link was not pursued and, as the months turned into first one year and then two, Graeme moved back to New York. He pursued the theme of the Eternal Night through an academic examination of the cross-cultural links associated with the Mayan Prophecy and the significance of 2012.

Tony became Graeme's chauffeur and assistant, and he too became something of an authority on Mesoamerican culture. His work explored the link between its mythic symbols and those of Christianity.

*

"And, as I have shown tonight, the similarities between the myths found by the Spanish when they colonized Central America and their own

Christian beliefs were such that they believed the Devil had spread them there as some sort of grotesque parody."

Tony was giving a lecture to a group of young academics in Boston.

"They encountered tales of virgin births, resurrections even flood myths." He looked up at the audience. "It is generally accepted that there was no contact between the Christian west and the Amerindians before Columbus."

Graeme smiled when he heard his friend say this and he thought of the Prince Madog legend (which he now considered to be no more than a fabricated story to validate Elizabethan Britain's claim to the New World). He stood by the exit at the rear of the auditorium listening intently to Tony's lecture.

"Therefore these myths must have developed separately and through a common subconscious human need for their expression," continued Tony.

The audience began to clap and Graeme joined in, smiling as Tony stepped down from the podium and walked toward him.

"Or perhaps they are all true," said Graeme as his friend drew near.

"I hope you're kidding me." Tony looked at his friend seriously.

They both began to laugh.

"Come on," the younger man said. "I'll drive you back to the hotel for a change."

"Hey, seeing as how we're in New England, why don't we scoot over to New Hampshire and call on the Pendleton's?" asked Tony. "I hear the Professor hasn't been very well of late."

"We'll give them a ring in the morning," Graeme replied.

*

Arriving back at the hotel they decided to go to the bar for a drink.

"I've been working recently on the hexagrams of the Chinese book of divination, the I Ching," said Graeme rotating a bottle of Michelob back and forth between his hands.

"Well that's a change of direction for sure," said Tony.

"It's your constant talk of Yungian archetypes and the collective unconscious that made me think of it. Carl Yung suggested the use of material such as the I Ching to prove his idea of synchronicity."

"Temporally coincident occurrences of acausal events," quoted Tony.

Graeme shook his head slowly from side to side and smiled. "More easily explained as meaningful coincidence."

"If you like." Tony chuckled and took a sip of his bourbon. "But where does an ancient Chinese book of divination come into it all?"

"Synchronous events need an underlying pattern that justifies them, but are at the same time part of something bigger, possibly the collective unconscious." Graeme put his bottle down on the bar. "The I Ching gives a link to this. A method of linking what may be considered to be unrelated events through the hexagrams and so to the ground of being."

"Man and universe together through the tossing of the coins or yarrow stalks."

"Put simply, yes."

Tony signalled to the bartender for another two drinks. "Wouldn't it be easier to just read your horoscope?"

"Too many variables. Anyway, I think I'm on to something."

Tony nodded his thanks to the bartender. "This weeks lottery numbers?"

Graeme looked up at the ceiling and sighed dramatically. "I believe that the hexagrams can be linked to a chronological sequence."

"That is a change of direction," said Tony interestedly.

"It's early days yet, but I'll keep you posted," said Graeme.

"The bottom seems to have fallen out of the Mesoamerican myth market at the moment so my calendar's free for a while if you need me."

"Then maybe you can devote some time to your day job," teased Graeme. "I'm fed up with driving myself around."

"Don't lie, the novelty hasn't worn off yet. Anyway you need the practice."

The two men lifted their glasses and downed their drinks.

"It's your turn," said Tony nodding toward the bartender.

Graeme smiled in agreement and tried to catch the bartender's eye.

✶

The following afternoon the two men were on their way to the Pendleton's home.

"You're just in time for supper," said Linda greeting the two men on the drive.

"How's Roger?" asked Tony.

"He's sleeping at the moment," Linda replied with an undercurrent of concern in her voice. "I'll tell him you're here as soon as he wakes up."

They made their way to the guest rooms to freshen up before supper.

"Your usual rooms," Linda shouted after them before turning to speak to the maid.

✻

An hour later the three of them sat around the table in the kitchen eating supper.

"He has had difficulty breathing of late and the least bit of exertion tires him." Linda looked unusually tired herself.

"Have they said what it could be?" said Graeme concernedly.

"He's got a shadow on his lung, so they want to follow up the tests with a CT scan."

The maid entered and spoke softly to Linda.

"He's awake," Linda said. "I'll go and see if he's well enough to come see you."

Linda walked out of the room.

"It's not looking good for the Professor," Tony said.

"We don't know that yet." Graeme helped himself to a cup of coffee and the two men sat in silence until Linda returned.

"Well, look at you two."

Both men turned to see Professor Pendleton walking slowly into the room.

"It's good to see you Roger," said Graeme.

Tony got up and walked quickly over to the Professor.
"It's okay Tony I can make it on my own."

Tony walked back to the table; Professor Pendleton sat in a rocking chair nearer the fireplace.

"My wife has some information you might find interesting." Roger turned toward his wife. "You haven't mentioned anything to them yet?"

"No dear."

"Well, spit it out," said Graeme impatiently.

"For the last eleven years scientists from the Max-Planck Institute in Germany have been attempting to prove that there is a super massive black hole at the centre of the Milky Way. I cross-referenced this with some of your work on Mayan myth and believe that this black hole, still only a theoretical possibility at the moment, is situated within the Dark Rift."

"Also known as the Black Road to the Mayans," interrupted Graeme.

Tony leaned forward, his forearms on the table and his hands clasped together. "There is the symbol of the sacred tree that runs through both Mayan and Judeo-Christian sacred tradition..."

Graeme interrupted again. "The Mayans believed their sacred tree to be a gateway." He too leaned forward over the kitchen table. "And given the right astrological alignment it is supposed to allow access to the underworld."

Tony continued, "The Mayan sacred tree can be positioned at the beginning of the Dark Rift."

"The Mayans calculated an alignment with the earth and the Dark Rift to take place in Two Thousand and Twelve," added Linda.

"Yes, but what is its significance to us?" pondered Tony.

"Sounds like a direction for our research to follow." Graeme looked toward Linda. "How close is the Institute to proving the black hole's existence?"

"They are gathering evidence of star movements in that area. It will be another few years yet."

"The Legend of the Eternal Night links Two Thousand and Twelve with the End Time," said Tony. "I'll pursue current Christian thought on an imminent apocalypse and see if there's any correlation."

"I'll continue with my study of the I Ching, I think there's a link there with that date as well."

Roger got up to leave. "Walk with me," he said to Graeme.

Graeme realized how frail the Professor looked as they walked toward the bedroom.

"You need to be very careful pursuing this line of research," the Professor said after Graeme had helped him into bed. "Christians of one kind or another have been believing that apocalypse is imminent since the very beginning of their religion." He paused to catch his breath. "Do not let your own fears that you have buried so well over the last couple of years surface again."

"Don't worry Roger," Graeme said reassuringly. "The Eternal Night of Two Thousand and Twelve is little more than an academic curiosity to me now. The cross-cultural references no more than another example of a collective unconscious."

"It makes great reading though," Roger said, smiling.

"Yes it's about time we collaborated on another book together," added Graeme. There's certainly money to be made writing about 2012."

❊

Professor Pendleton's condition did not improve over the next year and he was not able to work with Graeme. Tony diligently pursued the differing apocalyptic viewpoints of Christian thought and Graeme hammered away at the hidden timeline of the I Ching hexagrams.

It was at approximately eight thirty in the evening on Christmas Eve when Linda Pendleton rang them to say her husband had taken a turn for the worse.

"He was admitted into hospital this morning," she said over the phone. "His breathing was very shallow and he was in some distress so I called for an ambulance."

"We'll come down right away," said Tony.

"It's okay. He's sleeping now and they've stabilized him. Enjoy your Christmas and we'll see you in a few days."

Graeme leaned over toward the receiver. "We'll see you on Boxing Day."

❊

The radio was giving constant updates on a natural disaster somewhere in Asia as the two men drove up to the Pendleton's New Hampshire home.

"It sounds serious, that tidal wave," said Graeme.

"The death count estimate is rising with every report," added Tony.

As soon as they arrived Graeme rang Linda on his cell phone from the hospital car park.

"I'll meet you in the lobby," she said.

Roger lay motionless in the bed with several wires and tubes trailing from him. His chest rose almost imperceptibly. Both Graeme and Tony were shocked at the emaciated state of their friend.

Linda sat down on the chair next to the bed and held his right hand sandwiched between hers. The three friends sat in silence.

"Hey, I'm not dead yet." The voice was weak, barely above a whisper.

"Graeme and Tony are here, dear."

He tried to lift his head up to look, but it fell back onto the pillow; he began to cough.

Linda reached for a glass of water and put it to his lips.

"Thanks. Can you raise me up on these pillows a little?"

Tony jumped up. "I'll do it," he volunteered.

Roger smiled weakly at him as he gently lifted the skeletal frame. Linda positioned a pillow higher up against the back of the bed.

"That's better, now I can see you all."

"I'm still waiting for your go ahead on a book collaboration," said Graeme.

"I have an idea for a book," replied Roger. "But I think you may have to write it yourself." Roger began to cough again.

"Careful dear you'll wear yourself out."

"Better still," continued the Professor between weak gasps of breath, "you could write it with Tony."

He pointed toward the oxygen mask hanging by the side of the bed. Linda carefully placed it over his mouth.

Tony and Graeme watched until Linda removed the mask and replaced the two tubes previously clipped to his nostrils.

"Write a book that denounces all these tenuous cross-cultural references to Two Thousand and Twelve." He paused for breath. "It's no more than an astronomical event..." another breath, "...of little importance to the human race."

"I'm convinced of its psychological importance," said Tony. "But I do not think any great physical event will spring out of it."

"Enough of this nonsense for now," said Linda firmly. "Tell us about your Christmas."

"Nothing to tell really," said Tony. "I've turned into a sad old bachelor and, if Graeme's not careful he's going to go the same way."

"What happened to that girl?" gasped Roger.

"We used to email each other now and again, but I haven't heard from her for a while," Graeme said thoughtfully. "I guess she's moved on. Probably got a regular boyfriend or something."

The small talk continued for half an hour. Roger began to doze off.

"It's time for us to go," said Tony. "We'll find a hotel nearby. So if you need us."

THE GOLDEN FEATHER

Roger passed away the night before New Year's Eve and was buried a few days later.

It was a bitterly cold winter's day and the cemetery was whitewashed with a thick layer of snow. Graeme and Tony walked into the crematorium chapel and took seats near the front.

There was a humanist ceremony, "to celebrate Roger Pendleton's disregard for religion," Linda had said.

Graeme gave a eulogy based on the Professor's life work and written by Linda. Tony read a poem:

"Our thoughts do not recall a time
When angels walked this Earth
The life we have is the heaven we get
And not planned before our birth
The dreams we have are the only plans
Considered any worth
The paths we walk doth soon expire
And life's roads lead us to the pyre"

The funeral party returned to the Pendleton's home. Graeme and Tony stayed a while to pay their respects. Both offered their condolences to Linda and mixed with the other mourners, family and friends.

"We'd better be going," Graeme said to Linda. "It's getting dark and it's a long drive back to the hotel. I think there is more snow on the way."

"Yes, of course. Thank you for your support."

"We'll ring you tomorrow before we head back to New York," said Tony putting on his coat.

Graeme looked back at Linda waving as the automobile pulled away. Her small frame stood sadly in the doorway.

"What's that!" he shouted.

Tony pulled the car up sharply. "Where?"

"On the roof of the house."

"I don't see anything."

Linda began to hurry toward the automobile as Graeme got out and began walking toward the house.

"Graeme!" shouted Tony. "Where are you going?"

Graeme stopped walking and stood staring at the roof. He shook his head in disbelief.

Linda and Tony reached him at the same time.

"I saw something."

"What did you see?" asked Linda.

All three were now looking up at the roof.

"A very bright glow."

"It's not there now," said Tony matter-of-factly.

"It went down behind the house," explained Graeme.

"Probably just a trick of the light," said Linda. "Come on. We'll check it out anyway."

The trio walked around to the back of the house. It was all in darkness except for the light shining out of the windows.

Linda opened the kitchen door. "It'll be quicker to walk back through the house," she said.

Tony walked in after her and Graeme took a last look around. He turned to walk through the kitchen door when something glistening on the snow caught his eye. There on the ground was a beautiful golden feather about twelve inches in length.

✳

Graeme sat silently lost in thought as Tony drove through the crisp, clear night. After a while he reached over onto the back seat and pulled the feather out from under his coat. He sat back down and stroked the feather thoughtfully.

"What have you got there?"

"It's a feather. I found it outside the kitchen door."

"Probably from an eagle, or some other bird of prey."

Graeme did not answer. He looked out into the darkness. The thumb and forefinger of his right hand travelled slowly up and down the outer edge of the feather.

✳

Back at the hotel Graeme still maintained his distracted silence.

"Do you fancy a drink in the bar before we turn in?" asked Tony.

Graeme didn't answer. He lay on his bed looking at the feather.

"What's bothering you buddy?" Tony spoke a little louder this time.

"I'm sorry," said Graeme looking up at his friend.

"What you saw was probably no more than something reflected off the snow," offered Tony.

"No. The light was very intense, and I couldn't make out the shape at its centre." He sat up quickly. "But it felt

236

as though I knew it, whatever it was." Graeme began to pace across the room. He stopped and stared intently at the feather; then looked at Tony.

"And it knew me."

Tony looked at his friend with a great deal of concern. "You're beginning to worry me, my friend." He walked out of the door leaving Graeme alone with his thoughts.

✻

The tsunami in Asia dominated the news for a number of weeks and both Graeme and Tony did not mention the feather or the circumstances surrounding its discovery.

Graeme continued his work on the hexagrams and Tony, with some reluctance began to delve into Christian expectations of the Rapture.

✻

"It's been over a year now since Roger's death," Tony was speaking into the telephone. "I think its time we came up to visit you."

"I tell you what. I could do with getting out of the house. What if I come down and visit you?"

"That would be great. Graeme and myself have been a bit busy researching the idea for the book Roger mentioned."

"How's it coming?" asked the voice at the other end of the line.

"We're just about ready to sit down and put our ideas together."

"Linda's voice lowered imperceptibly. "Has he mentioned anything else about what he saw the night of Roger's funeral?"

"No. He's still got the feather though. I've seen it in his bedroom." A hint of amazement entered Tony's voice. "And you know, it's the strangest thing. The feather is in as good a condition now as when he first showed it to me. You'd swear it had just been plucked from the bird, or whatever damn thing it came off."

"Now don't you start to turn medieval on me," teased Linda. "Will next weekend be alright for me to visit?"

"That'll be great we'll see you then."

*

Linda arrived the following Friday evening and the three friends sat down to a pasta dish for supper.

"You'll have to give me the recipe." Linda said to Tony.

"It's no real secret, you just have to use fresh ingredients and only the best beef."

They spent an hour or so catching up and making small talk. Linda was herself writing a book on super massive black holes and the likelihood of each galaxy having one at its centre.

"At least it'll show that we're not unique and these Two Thousand and Twelve apocalypse theories are based on no more than an astronomical alignment.

We need to give the Mayans and the Aztecs their due. They must have been bloody good cosmologists," she said.

"The Mayans developed a very sophisticated mathematical system," added Tony. "They used several bases for counting, often based on planetary movements."

"All is number. God is number. God is in all." Graeme stated quietly.

Tony and Linda looked toward him with mild concern in their eyes.

"Pacal Votan, a seventh century Mayan king," Graeme said with a smile.

Tony tried to lighten the mood. "You know I read a book the other day that says, due to some complex maths superimposed on the Old Testament the world is going to end this year."

"If that's the case then we had better start on the wine." Graeme walked over to the drinks cabinet and pulled out a bottle of Merlot.

"Don't worry it forecast the end of the world for last month," said Tony.

"You know I think you need to get away from all this and find yourself a girl," Linda said to Graeme. "Leave the book stew for a year or two and the both of you can crack on with it then. You never know you may even end up writing a completely different book."

Graeme opened the wine and poured three glasses. "I think that's a great idea. We can go to Europe or something, look at some Cathedrals, maybe even see the Pope."

"I was thinking more of lying on a beach somewhere and watching the girls go by," added Tony.

Linda chimed in. "In Europe you can do both."

✳

Three weeks later the two men were on a transatlantic flight. They spent some time in London and did some walking in the Lake District. One evening Tony decided to search for island monasteries on the Internet and came up with a website for Caldey Island.

"I think this is the island in your novel."

"That was where I first met Gabriel."

Tony was worried at the conviction in his friend's voice and Graeme read it in his face.

"Don't worry, I have no wish to go there. What I have seen of the churches we visited in London it's probably overrun with tourists."

"Tourists like us," added Tony with a grin.

Graeme sat down on the side of the bed. "I think I'll give the bar a miss tonight," he said.

"Okay then, I'll go and turn in too." The older man got up to leave.

"Wait." Graeme said firmly. Tony was surprised at the authority in his friend's voice.

"You have never asked me about what I saw on the night of Roger's funeral."

"I thought it best to let it go. Anyway you told me it was an intense light."

"I knew that light, and thinking of Gabriel now just reminded me."

Tony sat on the edge of the bed, worry written across his lined face.

"Lucifer said that Gabriel was the angel of death."

"But Roger didn't die that night, by that time he was already cremated," said Tony desperately.

"Maybe he wanted to leave me a message." He leaned over to the bedside table and pulled out the feather.

"No don't go down that road." Exasperated, Tony walked quickly toward the door. Before leaving he turned to Graeme. "You may not be able to find your way back."

Tony left.

*

"Ask him what he has unearthed in his research."

Graeme jumped up with a start. He saw the little old man at the foot of the bed and rubbed his eyes vigorously.

"Yes it's me. You can stop rubbing."

"It's a dream, I'm going back to sleep." Graeme put his head back down on the pillow and screwed his eyes shut.

"The time is approaching and you will be called upon again. But first ask your friend about his research."

✻

"You know you shouldn't leave your door open like that, even in England."

Graeme's head felt fuzzy and he struggled to get his bearings. "What? Where…"

"Did you have a drink after I left last night?"

Graeme recognized Tony's voice.

"Sorry, I'm still half asleep." He sat up in bed and squinted at his friend's silhouetted form against the light shining through the thin curtains.

"If you were drinking it sure smells nice." Tony sniffed the air. "What is that?" He sniffed again. "Roses?"

Graeme leapt out of bed, Tony's casual remark woke him more effectively than a bucket of iced water thrown over his face.

"Then he was here." He said to no one in particular.

"Who was here?" his friend asked.

Graeme hesitated before speaking. "Oh it's nothing. I was having a bad dream that's all." He walked into the bathroom.

Tony lifted the kettle, gave it a shake and, hearing the water slosh around inside, put it back down and plugged it in. It was just coming to the boil when Graeme came out of the bathroom.

"Our flight to Rome as been confirmed. We're flying tomorrow morning," said Tony.

Graeme didn't answer.

"Did you hear me?"

"Sorry," said Graeme. "Yes, we're leaving tomorrow."

Tony emptied some sachets of coffee into two cups.

"Did you unearth any revelations in your research?" Graeme shouted from the bathroom.

"I did come to realize how deeply fundamentalist we are in the United States," replied Tony.

"It's all that TV evangelism," quipped Graeme.

Tony handed him a cup of coffee then sat on the armchair by the window. "Did you know that fifty five percent of the American population believe in the Rapture?"

"That should ease the traffic around Manhattan."

"I can't see many New Yorkers being whisked away," replied Tony with a grin. His face darkened. "Some say the attack on the World Trade Centre was a punishment for our sins."

"I've heard the same thing said about the tsunami in Asia."

"Many think these signs are evidence of an imminent Armageddon," said Tony with a frown. "Four fifths of Americans believe in the Second Coming and a quarter of those think it will happen soon. Those who believe in the Rapture believe it will happen in their lifetime."

"Wars and rumours of wars," said Graeme. "Earthquakes and famines."

Tony stood up. "Enough of this, we're on vacation. Let's get some breakfast."

Graeme followed him out of the room deep in thought.

*

It was Easter and Rome was packed. Tony decided to go to the coast, but Graeme stayed for the Urbi et Orbi address. He joined the crowd in Saint Peter's Square.

"It's just too much theatre don't you think?" He turned to his left and saw a small woman, slightly over-weight and with curly shoulder-length dark hair. Her round open face was looking up at him and smiling.

"It's very full here," replied Graeme. "It reminds me of a baseball match I went to once with my friend, only without the action."

"No one could accuse the Pope of being very dynamic that's for sure."

The two of them stared up at the figures on the balcony in the distance. The Pope switched from Italian to Latin.

"Christus resurrexit, quia Deus caritas est! Alleluia!" echoed through the sound system.

The crowd broke into applause.

"I don't know very much Italian, and I know even less Latin, but that last bit seemed to strike a chord with everyone."

Graeme looked more closely at her this time and guessed she was about the same age as him.

"It was difficult to hear, but I think he said that Christ was resurrected because of God's love."

"Alleluia," the woman added. "So, you speak Latin," she mused.

"A little."

"How's about leaving this circus and grabbing a coffee somewhere?" She slipped her arm through his. "We can watch the rest of it in the comfort of a café. It's bound to be on the tele."

＊

They decided to sit at one of the café's outside tables. The street was relatively quiet and beside themselves there were no other customers. The café's solitary waiter leaned against the counter inside looking up at the Pope's image on the screen hanging from the wall.

She told Graeme that her name was Margaret and she was from Bury St Edmunds in England. "So what brings you to Rome?" she asked.

"I'm on vacation," Graeme replied.

The smell of the rich espresso assaulted his nostrils as he raised the small cup to his lips. He blew gently before taking a sip.

"Me too. My husband died about a year ago." She paused sadly. "And I've decided that now I'm ready for a bit of adventure." Her tone became more upbeat.

"I'm sorry,"

"That's okay I'm coming to terms with it." She slowly rolled her tongue around the tip of the vanilla ice cream perched on top of the cone.

"Are you traveling alone?" she asked Graeme.

"No, I'm travelling with my friend Tony."

She peered quizzically over the top of the ice cream. "Are you gay?"

Graeme feigned a hurt expression. "Do I look gay?"

Margaret laughed. "No, not really."

"Tony helped me once when I was lost and alone. He works for me now. Well that's not strictly true, we're going to write a book together once this vacation's over."

"Really?" she said, her interest aroused. "What's it about?"

"I don't know if you'll be interested. It will be a dry academic tome."

Her ice cream began to run down the cone and onto her hand. Graeme passed her a napkin.

"I'm sure I will," she said wiping her hand. She looked over expectantly at him as she began to lick the slowly melting ice cream off the cone.

"I've been looking for references to the date of the end time of the Mayan long calendar, which is December 21st 2012, and my friend has been researching Christian eschatological ideas and any possible links with this date."

"I'm more of your liberal, left-wing Church of England type of Christian," said Margaret. "No End Time or mystical magic for me."

"No wonder you weren't impressed by the Pope's address."

"Well, that's not the whole story," Margaret said thoughtfully. "I was left asking a lot of questions when my husband died and I think my trip here was to try and find some answers."

"You would probably be wise to give Tony and myself a wide berth then," he said half-humorously. "All we have is questions."

They talked on into the afternoon. Margaret spoke of her family and her husband's death and, eventually Graeme told her about his escape from the Twin Towers and his inability to remember anything of his life before. He told her of his friendship with Tony and the

Pendleton's, and he told her of his work, but not his memories of the Legend of the Eternal Night.

"I think its time we made our way back to our respective hotels," said Margaret.

The Italian sky had moved from pink to a richer crimson. It would be nightfall before very long.

"My hotel's just around the corner from here," she said.

"I'll walk you back," offered Graeme.

"There's no need."

"Don't be silly." Graeme stood and held his hand out to Margaret. "It's on the way to my hotel in any case," he lied.

*

"Well this is it," Margaret said stopping at the hotel entrance. "There's a taxi rank over there."

She leaned forward and gave Graeme a kiss on the cheek. "It's been a lovely afternoon."

"What are you doing tomorrow? Graeme asked quickly."

"I don't really have any plans, I'm leaving in two days," she let go of Graeme's hand. "So I don't really know."

"Come to the coast with me," said Graeme excitedly. "I'm supposed to meet Tony there. He's gone on ahead."

"I don't know." She looked pensive. "I should take a last look around I suppose."

"I'll bring you back tomorrow night we can have a look around together."

Margaret ran the fingers of her left hand through her hair. "Okay, pick me up in the morning."

TONY

Tony waited until evening, but had heard nothing from Graeme. He rung the night before to say he had met someone and would be bringing her down with him, but nothing since. His friend's mobile was switched off and the hotel confirmed he had left that morning. The receptionist said Mister Woodland had hired a car. Sometime just before midnight Tony rang the police.

No accidents had been reported on the route from Rome and no corpses had turned up matching Graeme Woodland's description. Tony decided to return to Rome.

*

"No." The hotel manager was adamant. "He did not check out. Signore Woodland said he would be gone for a day or so, but he wanted to keep the room."

Tony and the Italian detective searched the room. The only thing that Tony did not recognize was a card for automobile hire. The detective spoke to the company and the car had not been returned. He put a trace out for the vehicle.

*

Three hours later Tony and Detective Bianchi were talking to the manager of the hotel where Margaret had stayed. They had reported the car abandoned when no one returned to pick it up.

"Please give me a list of people who have checked out over the last three days." The detective pulled out a notebook from his jacket pocket.

The manager hit a few keys on the computer on the desk in his office. "There were quite a few yesterday. They were here for the Pope's Easter address."

"Were there any women, maybe travelling alone, probably in their thirties," asked Tony.

"Si signore. There was an English woman checked out yesterday."

"What was her name?" Tony asked quickly.

The manager glanced back at the computer monitor, "Margaret Baker."

The detective spoke in Italian. "I'll need contact details, address, credit card details, next of kin. Whatever you have on the hotel key memory."

The manager rang through to reception. "I am sorry Signore Bianchi, but the room has been taken. The card details have been wiped."

"Did she pre-book the room?" asked Tony. "You may have some contact details."

"No signore, she was lucky to get a room, she turned up at reception just after we received a cancellation."

*

Detective Bianchi drove Tony back to his hotel. "So all we know is that she is English and her name is Margaret Baker."

"I'll check flight records, train tickets purchased, things like that. She will have left some sort of trail. That is of course assuming that she is the woman that your friend actually met that day."

"No you're right," said Tony. "We don't know for sure if it was her."

✳

The search continued and Tony saw the detective every day. There was no sign of Graeme, and neither could the police find any trace of Margaret Baker.

"I tell you it is as though the two of them just vanished off the face of the earth." Tony was talking to Linda Pendleton over the phone.

"You can't stay over there indefinitely. It's been a month now since Graeme disappeared." Linda's voice became firmer. "It's time you came home."

"I know, but I don't feel that I can give up on him yet." Tony held the golden feather in his hand. It still looked as healthy and radiant as the day he first saw it.

"I tell you what," Linda said. "I'll fly over and we'll have a final look together. Then we can both come home."

Tony put the feather down on the bed. "There's no need, I'll…"

Linda interrupted. "I'm coming over as soon as I can. That's final."

✳

The two of them stayed in Rome for another three weeks. Tony gave a contact number to Detective Bianchi before they left.

"I know it's a long shot," said Tony, "but it's worth checking out the English connection."

"We have no links," replied Linda. "We don't even know where in England Margaret Baker is from."

"What about London." Tony suggested. "We spent some time there before coming to Italy, there's the Lake District as well."

"Why not it's worth a look."

Tony looked thoughtful. "We could also try Wales, an island of the coast of Tenby to be precise. I think it is the island mentioned in the Legend of The Eternal Night."

When they were in England Tony learnt about electoral registers and decided he would see if he could locate as many Margaret Bakers in England as he could. Linda returned home after another month in Britain, but Tony decided to stay.

"It's just as easy for me to write and research here as in New York. In fact it's easier. They have libraries and universities here that are older than the United States," he explained to Linda before she left.

And so Tony divided his week up into three sections. The first three days he worked on his research and writing and for three days he searched for Margaret Baker. He set up a website dedicated to the search for his friend, and asking for information on Margaret Baker. On Sundays Tony began going to Mass again. When he had time he occasionally went to confession on Saturday evenings.

✻

"This book is beginning to drag on. When are you going to publish?" It was Christmas Eve and Linda was ringing from her New Hampshire home.

"In the New Year. Anyway Linda, I thought you were going to come visit me before Christmas."

"I've been busy," she replied. "I'll come over the beginning of January. Don't publish your book before I see you. I'd like to read over the manuscript."

"Don't worry I'll email you a draft."

✣

Linda arrived at the beginning of the second week in January. Tony and Linda pulled up outside his cottage in Pembroke in the early evening. It had been six hours since Linda's flight had touched down at Heathrow and both of them were tired and hungry. Tony carried Linda's bags up to the spare bedroom, and set about cooking some supper while Linda freshened up.

"So," said Tony clearing the dishes off the table, "they have proved that there really is a black hole at the centre of our galaxy?" It was more of a question than a statement.

"The scientists are happy that they have gathered enough empirical evidence to confirm its existence," agreed Linda, shouting after him into the kitchen.

He returned carrying two cups of coffee.

"And on December 21st 2012 our planet and the Sun will come into alignment with the area where the Max Planck scientists confirm this black hole to be," Linda added.

Tony relaxed back into his chair. "I've found some interesting research on the I Ching."

"Really?"

"It confirms Graeme's hypothesis that the hexagrams can also be used for measuring time." He leaned forward. "And it also confirms that the time it is measuring ends in Two Thousand and Twelve, in December."

Linda took a sip of her coffee. "So, there is even more evidence of convergence on this point by separate cultures?"

"Yes, but the important point being, is it through separate development?" His tone became earnest. "Or are we using it as a link to find connections that aren't really there?"

"Starting with an hypothesis and making the evidence fit," suggested Linda.

Tony walked over to the fireplace and put two logs into the centre of the flames.

"I for one will be glad when we reach Two Thousand and Thirteen," Linda added.

"At least it will put paid to most of this speculation," said Tony. "I don't think it will have much of an effect on those Christians waiting for the Second Coming though. Most of them do not fix it to a specific date."

"The end of the world is nigh brigade have always been with us in that respect," added Linda flippantly. "What about your search for Graeme and the mysterious Margaret Baker? How's that going?"

Tony sighed. "I'm drawing a blank with Margaret Baker, and considering there wasn't any firm evidence linking her to Graeme in the first place, I've given up looking."

He walked over to a small writing bureau. On the top of the bureau was a small wooden chest about fifteen inches long. From the box Tony pulled out the long golden feather. "This is the only real lead I have to him."

Linda took the feather from his outstretched hand.

"It looks as good as new," she said scrutinizing the feather closely.

"The most interesting thing about it is its aroma," said Tony.

Linda lifted the feather to her nose. "Oh yes!" she exclaimed. "What Is that?"

"I think it is a very faint smell of roses."

"Have you tipped anything on it?"

"No." Tony leaned toward the feather. "I didn't notice it at first, but I smelt that aroma once in Graeme's hotel room here in England. I recognized it on the feather soon after he went missing."

"So, what does it mean?" Linda handed the feather back to him.

"Smells are associated with certain saints and are often taken as a sign that a saint has been in the room or near to the person who smells the odour."

Tony placed the feather carefully back into the box and closed the lid.

"Is that why you've started going back to Church?"

"There is some comfort in the familiar rituals, and after two thousand years of asking they must have found some answers."

"Anyway," said Linda. "Have you tried to trace any of Graeme's past before Nine Eleven?"

"Not really. Other than the trip to Cholulah I don't have much to go on. He never pursued it himself. And you'd think someone would have come forward to claim him once he started publishing."

Tony noticed Linda stifling a yawn. "You must be exhausted," he said. "Go to bed. We'll discuss it in the morning."

✻

Tony woke with a start. The clock on the bedside table showed 3:00am. He lay perfectly still, straining to hear again the noise that had awoken him. *'There!'* he thought to himself. *'A creaking floorboard.'* ...Again, another creak...

With his heart thumping so hard within his chest he thought it was going to escape he slowly, silently got out of bed.

The next groan of wood seemed to come from farther away. Tony very carefully opened the bedroom door and peered cautiously through the gap. The sound was clear now. He heard footfalls, someone running down the last few steps.

Tony ran to the top of the stairs. "Who's there!" he shouted.

From the corner of his eye he saw the ink black cavern of Linda's bedroom. The front door slammed. He flew down the stairs and wrenched open the door. The sound of a car engine grew faint in the distance as he stood out on the drive.

*

Linda's room exploded into brightness as Tony threw the switch. The cover had been pulled back revealing an empty bed. Linda was nowhere to be seen. He dialled 999 and shouted down the phone that someone had been kidnapped. He gave his name and address and waited for the screaming siren.

"Not again!" he shouted out into the night.

*

The police set up roadblocks and called in a helicopter. Linda's photograph was circulated. Tony paced the living room until dawn.

LUCIFER'S RETURN

Linda shivered; the marble was cold against her bare skin. Opening her eyes she tried to get up, but the ropes held her secure. Linda lifted her head as far as the bonds would allow; she saw an inverted cross on the wall behind where her naked form was laid out on what she now realized was an altar. By the light of the many candles positioned around the altar and beyond, she recognized the interior of a disused church. Three hooded figures dressed in black stood between the cross and the altar.

She turned her head to peer out into the body of the church and noticed a figure slumped on a chair. He too was tied securely. One of the cloaked figures walked over to the man and lifted his head.

Linda gasped as she stared into the emaciated features of her friend Graeme. His eyes stared back, full of infinite sadness and helpless despair.

Through her rising terror she attempted a smile of reassurance, but as it began to form it was cut short by a sudden sharp intense pain in her abdomen that became indescribable as the tallest of the hooded figures slammed the knife into her stomach and dragged it up to her throat.

"NO!!!" Graeme screamed as the hooded man ripped her heart out.

He walked around Linda's lifeless body carrying the still pulsing organ over to Graeme. He squeezed it and the blood dripped onto Graeme's head; the warm thick liquid ran slowly down onto his face.

"Why? Why?" Graeme whispered as his head fell back onto his chest.

"I'm afraid it's easier with atheists."

Graeme's blood ran cold at the sound of the voice. He lifted his head slowly, afraid to confirm his worse fears.

The grotesque diabolical form stood before him smiling. "Your friend Tony would have done, but he's started going to Mass again." The hatred rose in him as he spat out the last few words.

"I did consider Margaret here." The Devil pointed toward the smallest of the three hooded figures now lying prostrate on the floor before him. "But she would have given herself gladly and where's the fun in that."

He bent down and took the heart from the grasp of the tall hooded man. "This could have been your heart. You were my first choice." He squeezed the dripping organ thoughtfully. "But they had to give you that feather. Your doubt was nearly complete until then."

He threw the heart to one side. "It was the feather that sent your friend Tony scurrying back to the Church."

Graeme struggled against his bonds to no avail.

"It is of no account now, I've had my sacrifice." The Devil held up a hand and Graeme's bonds burst into flame. "You're coming with me!"

❋

Graeme recognized the familiar smell of sulfur. It grew stronger as the Devil dragged him down the large straight staircase. Soon he recognized the view from the stone balcony; the screams of the damned filled his ears once again.

"Welcome home," said the Devil mockingly. "We've missed you." His voice turned to anger. "They had no right to take you from me." He smiled. "I did force them to drop you off at the foot of those two beautiful towers though." This time the horned red face took on an expression of satisfaction. "The things men do in the name of God. If only they knew."

"But what about the Centehua of this time? Her memories of me at the dig?" Graeme could not bring himself to believe that this was happening and hoped beyond hope that he would soon wake up.

The Devil pointed toward one side of the balcony, at the figure of a woman walking toward them out of the flames. He let out a loud mocking laugh as the form of Centehua turned into a demon. Graeme watched the transformation through a mask of horror.

The Devil gestured toward the vast panorama of pain and suffering spread out before them. "Come, let's go mingle."

He led Graeme further down a spiral stone stairway. Flames fanned toward them from all sides, faces implored them for mercy and hands reached out in desperation.

"There are some old friends down here who I would like you to meet."

Graeme saw the red of a cardinal's hat disappear into a huge vat of boiling oil. The Devil nodded and a demon pulled the priest out of the cauldron. A look of immense relief crossed the man's face quickly to be replaced with shame when he saw Graeme the Woodchopper.

"He hungered for the power his position brought and he just could not get enough," said the Devil. He nodded to the demon and Cardinal Caronni was thrust back into the boiling oil.

The Woodchopper stared at the bubbling liquid in disbelief.

"There are others who would like to see you," said the Devil as he led him onward through the sea of tortured souls.

They came across a man tied to a wheel. His scream pierced through to Graeme's own ground of being every time a demon brought a bar down smashing a limb.

The Woodchopper watched horrified as the broken bones healed and the demon smashed them all over again. Two other demons lifted the wheel up to the vertical.

"My God!" Graeme exclaimed.

"Your God can't hear you here," said the Devil with annoyance.

Strapped to the wheel was Roger Pendleton.

"Pride I'm afraid, the mother of them all."

"The fool hath said in his heart, there is no God." Graeme quoted the Psalms; grief and sadness threatened to overwhelm him.

"Keep up!" The diabolical form strode on in front of him. "You have yet to meet one of my latest guests."

The Woodchopper couldn't take much more. His head swam in a sea of sorrow, threatening to drown him in the ocean of horrors he now found himself in.

"Here we are," the Devil said cheerfully.

Graeme the Woodchopper saw a horde of demons in a flaming inferno. One of the gruesome creatures reached down into the flames and pulled up the petite naked body of Linda Pendleton. She vomited at the brimstone breath of the gargoyle as he pulled her close and kissed her deeply on the lips. A forest of demon arms reached up out of the furnace and dragged Linda back down and out of the Woodchopper's sight.

Graeme let out a yell of anguish and hurled himself at the Devil. Two demons flew out of the inferno and held him firmly in their grasp.

"I'm afraid she was not always the devoted wife to her beloved Roger that you knew." The Devil let out a low lustful laugh. "Now, let me see. What did we have you down for last time?" He stroked his chin thoughtfully. "Ah yes I remember, your sin was anger." He stared deep into Graeme's soul. "You haven't changed much have you?"

The demons left as quickly as they appeared. Without their restraining clutches Graeme the Woodchopper surged forward, but there was no one there. He collapsed to the floor sobbing uncontrollably.

"I'll leave you alone for a while."

Graeme looked up through tear filled eyes, he was in a small dark room, but the Devil could not be seen.

"It will give you time to reflect." The Devil's disembodied voice resounded around him.

Time lost all meaning as Graeme lay on the floor in a foetal position. Images of the Cardinal and the Pendleton's enduring everlasting agonies haunted him until he could bear no more. His mind shut down and he became a catatonic corpse.

✳

"They found a body yesterday." Tony and the priest were sitting in the church vestry.

The priest looked at Tony with great affection and concern. "Linda?" He spoke the word gently.

"Yes," said Tony struggling to contain his emotions. "She was in a derelict church." His emotions overwhelmed him and Tony broke down.

The priest walked around to the back of his parishioner's chair and placed his hands on the distraught man's shoulders.

"Her heart had been ripped out in imitation of an Aztec sacrifice."

The priest crossed himself.

"There were inverted crosses on the walls."

"A satanic sacrifice." The Father had a grave expression on his face.

Tony nodded confirmation as he began to compose himself.

"Let us go before the altar and pray for her."

The priest helped Tony up off the chair and the two men walked into the altar area.

"And your friend Graeme too," he added.

They knelt either side of the aisle behind the first line of pews. The priest pulled out a rosary.

Three figures stood in silence at the back of the church, a bald old man, a tall man with long golden hair and another man in a hat. All three wore long black coats.

The two men knelt in prayer and meditation before the monstrance for over an hour. A smile played across the face of the little old man. He turned to the golden haired figure and nodded. The tall man turned and walked out of the Church.

*

"He is coming!" a demon shouted. The others turned to look at the figure in the red suit walking toward them.

"Put them down," he ordered.

Margaret and her two companions were thrown back onto the marble altar. She immediately pulled her cloak around her bruised body and fell into a ball behind the stone back piece.

An arm of one of her companions dropped lifelessly over the side. She let out a petrified yelp as it brushed against her hair.

The body of the tall man flew over her head and hit the wall behind the altar. There was a crash as the inverted cross fell to the floor beside his lacerated body. Margaret grimaced as she looked at the countless slashes crossing his naked form, his body glistening under a blood-red sheen.

The man in red walked around the altar. He grabbed the arm hanging down by Margaret and casually tossed the corpse against the wall next to the barely breathing, bloody pulp of the tall man.

"Don't worry I have other plans for you," he whispered leaning down and stroking her hair.

The old door of the church fell in with a bang.

"Come in," he said convivially to the tall winged figure at the entrance. "I have a welcoming committee for you."

With their screeches filling the air six demons hurled themselves headlong at the Archangel. He swung his sword and the first two fell, bisected by the blade. Raising his shield above his head he dropped down onto one knee. Talons lashed out and a gargoyle screamed as he made contact with the shield, retreating with a smouldering hand.

The Archangel stood up, his shield in front of him and the sword held above his head. The demons backed away slowly.

"Well, what are you waiting for?" the man in red said impatiently.

Forward they charged for a second time. In the blink of an eye the four of them were reduced to dust by the thrusting blade of the Archangel.

The Devil reached down and pulled up the trembling Margaret, throwing her onto the altar. "Shall we offer a sacrifice Michael?"

"She chose to follow you," answered the Archangel indifferently.

In a voice barely audible and quivering in stark terror Margaret said, "God help me."

As she spoke Michael flew onto the altar and stood above her. The Devil jumped back in fearful surprise. "She's mine!" he screamed at the Archangel.

"Not any more."

*

Graeme dreamt he was back in the subterranean temple tunnels. He walked aimlessly through the dark corridors until he saw a dimly lit stairway leading up. There was a very dim light far off at the top of the staircase and Graeme decided to make his way toward it.

Minutes turned into hours as he kept on ascending the staircase, but it seemed to get no closer. He sat down on one of the cold steps.

"He's here!"

"Is he alright?"

"He seems to be coming out of it."

Graeme heard the voices and wondered if he was still dreaming. He struggled to open his eyes.

"Where am I?" He felt himself being lifted onto a stretcher.

"You're in a derelict church," answered one of the paramedics.

The voices began to fade and he drifted back into unconsciousness.

✳

"Nurse! Nurse!" Graeme heard a familiar voice calling. "He's waking up."

Tony looked down in transparent relief and joy as his friend opened first one eye and then the other.

"Excuse me, Mr Altredo." The nurse stepped past and began recording readings from a monitor by the side of the bed. "The doctor is on his way."

Tony left the room while the doctor examined Graeme and paced the corridor nervously until the nurse opened the door. Smiling she gestured for him to enter.

"Mister Woodland here is a little malnourished, but considering his ordeal he is in fairly good shape. We want to keep him in for a day or so for observation, and for some counselling."

Tony turned to his friend. "What do you think?"

"That's fine."

The doctor spoke again. "As soon as you feel up to it, the police want to talk to you."

"It's good to see you again," said Tony emotionally.

"It would be better if we left him alone for a while," said the nurse. "Let him get some rest before the police interview him."

"I'll come back this evening," said Tony.

Although Graeme had many questions for his friend, he just nodded his agreement and put his head exhaustedly onto the pillow.

"You cannot stay here." Graeme saw a little bald man at the foot of the bed. He wore a long dark overcoat.

"Where in God's name have you been?" said Graeme furiously. He sat back up and leaned toward the little old man.

"I've witnessed another sacrifice and this time I've seen her and her husband suffering the torments of Hell. And there was no sign of you or your two friends." He slumped back against the pillow. "Do you expect me to listen to you now?"

"We forced Satan to release you the first time." The old man walked around to the side of the bed. "You did well to convince him to send his army when you did. They were no match for us. Unfortunately he was able to cast you down on September 11th 2001."

"Could you not have come to me then?"

"He chose well. This time we are in now is indeed God-forsaken and his plan worked. You began to doubt. The death and destruction man has reigned down on himself in the last hundred years has surprised even the Evil One. If those souls were added to the army of the sacrificed innocents, we could not have contained them."

"The Pendleton's, they were good people." Anger and sadness flavoured Graeme's words.

"They were Godless people, people of this time. But there is still hope. Your friend has regained some of his faith and it was his prayers that brought you back. He must continue to pray for Linda and Roger Pendleton, because all prayers are heard."

Graeme realized all he could see was the bed and the angel. A brilliant white light surrounded the scene. "This is another bloody dream, isn't it?"

"Do not doubt we need you to leave this place. Tell your friend you're going to go on a retreat. And tell him to keep on praying." The light began to fade and the Archangel moved slowly away from the bed.

"Wait, where shall I go?"

✳

He awoke some time later and was interviewed by the police. They explained that he had been discovered in the same church where Linda's mutilated body had been found over two years before. Two other bodies were in the building at the time he had been located. Those bodies too had been horribly disfigured.

"Why did you go back there after all this time?" Graeme asked the detective interviewing him.

"We found a near naked woman wandering around close by," he answered. "She was rambling incoherently, but she kept on pointing at the old church."

The police asked Graeme where he had been since his disappearance in Rome. He told them he had no recollection of his whereabouts. Presently a nurse entered and told the police it was enough for one day. Graeme agreed to speak to them the following morning.

✳

Tony arrived that evening. Graeme told his friend what the police had told him about him being found in the old church.

"Did they tell you about Linda?"

"I saw her being killed," Graeme explained.

"Where have you been since then?" asked Tony incredulously.

"I have been kept prisoner. I don't know where," Graeme lied.

"No idea at all?" asked Tony in a disbelieving voice.

"All I remember is a small, dark room without any windows."

"Did you see who was holding you there?"

"No," Graeme lied again.

Tony stared thoughtfully at the floor. "There's something you're not telling me here. The woman they found was Margaret Baker."

"I'll explain what I can to you when I'm ready." Graeme sounded irritated. "As soon as I'm well enough I want to take a retreat for a while. I want you to pray for me and for the Pendleton's."

"Of course, but…"

"I'll explain everything when I can." Graeme put his head down on the pillow and feigned tiredness. "Just remember to pray, your prayers are heard."

"But not very often answered," muttered Tony under his breath as he left the room.

*

The police returned the following morning.

"What happened the morning you went to pick up Margaret Baker at her hotel in Rome?" the stocky, overweight and slightly dishevelled detective asked.

"After driving to the hotel I asked the man on reception for her room number. He rang to say I was there and then told me to go up, she was expecting me. I knocked the door and Margaret shouted for me to come in. I turned the handle, opened the door and

2012: THE ETERNAL NIGHT

walked in. I saw Margaret sitting on the edge of the bed smiling and then I felt an explosion of pain at the back of my head and I lost consciousness."

"Do you remember anything after that?"

"Vague recollections of shadowy figures and confined spaces. I remember being injected occasionally, but the next, and last thing I remember fully is my friend Linda Pendleton being murdered on the altar chapel."

"Did you see who by?"

"No they wore long robes and hoods. There were three of them."

"And after that?"

"The next thing I remember was being lifted onto a stretcher and being brought here."

"You do realize that you have a memory gap of about two years?" the policeman asked suspiciously.

"Yes, it has happened to me before."

The detective asking the questions turned to a uniformed officer and said something Graeme could not hear. The detective stood up as the other officer left. "We will need to ask you further questions. If you are discharged from here is there an address where we can reach you."

"I can answer that," said Tony as he entered the room.

Tony and the detective swapped details and Graeme could hear his friend giving assurances that Graeme would not leave the country.

"I don't think they quite believe you," said Tony. "You receiving two periods of amnesia must look at the very least a little suspicious."

"Not really." Both men turned to look at the door.

The speaker was a tall young man with short dark hair in a white coat and, if he did not have a moustache his face would have exhibited an almost feminine beauty. It was a face that Graeme had seen before.

"An initial traumatic episode such as the events of Nine Eleven can often lead to Dissociative Amnesia. His subsequent kidnapping could well have resulted in a repeat of the original Fugue State. Granted Dissociative Fugue is a very rare condition, but it looks as though your friend here has been through a lot."

"Tony, meet my psychologist. I think they call them counsellors in this country," said Graeme.

Tony held out his hand and the doctor shook it warmly. "Graeme tells me you're a Catholic," the doctor said. "You should pray for his full recovery."

"Yes, yes. Of course," stammered Tony. "I will."

"There's a chapel on the ground floor."

"Oh. Sorry." Tony turned to leave.

"Come back in an hour," shouted the doctor.

"There is not much time. I will explain to the police that you need rest. I have signed you out of here. Go to your friend's home and tell him you must leave."

"But he will ask for an address and so will the police," said Graeme.

"Tell them you are going to the abbey on the island in Wales, the one you began your quest at. By the time they realise you have not arrived there you will be gone."

"Gone where?"

"We have much to do to prevent the darkness from engulfing the universe. We will speak again soon."

Immediately Graeme began packing the few belongings Tony had dropped at the hospital.

"Where are you going?" asked Tony on his return.

"Will you take me to your place?"

"Of course. Let me help you with that bag."

*

"That doctor," said Tony driving back to his cottage, "there was something about him."

"He's a good physician," said Graeme smiling. "Probably the yardstick by which all other healers are measured."

"What?"

"Never mind." Graeme paused for a moment. "I have to leave tomorrow, I'm booked into the retreat I told you about."

"Do you need to go so soon?"

"I'm sorry old friend, but I need to sort myself out. I'll only be gone for a week or two, we'll catch up when I come back."

"I'll drive you."

"There's no need. The doctor has a home out that way and he said he'd give me a lift."

"If that's what you want," said Tony dejectedly.

The two friends continued the journey in silence.

They said very little to each other that night at Tony's cottage. The Archangels came for Graeme before dawn. He wrote Tony a note before he left.

'Don't worry everything will be okay, pray for me and don't doubt no matter what happens.'

"AND, BEHOLD A DOOR WAS OPENED IN HEAVEN."

(Revelation 4:1)

Graeme and the three Archangels ascended among the stars. "How is this possible," he said incredulously. Gabriel smiled at him. On and on they travelled, Graeme held firmly in Gabriel's grasp. The angel was no longer an old man, but now in his angelic form. Past countless stars they flew, through yet unnamed solar systems, on and on.

There was no concept of time for Graeme as he was held within the circle of the Archangels and he had no idea how long he had been travelling when he noticed a great darkness ahead of them.

"It is what the Mayans call the Black Road," said Gabriel to Graeme's unspoken question.

Michael pointed to an area at the start of the darkness.

"That is our destination," Gabriel confirmed.

"The sacred tree," volunteered Graeme.

"Not quite," said Raphael. "It is supposed to be the point at which the Mayans ascend after death."

"But, as you know they and the Aztecs were deceived by Lucifer," Gabriel interjected.

"So what is it?" asked Graeme.

"It is the doorway to the underworld." Michael paused. "There is to be found the gates of Hell."

✳

Graeme found himself on a dark, barren rocky landscape; the only discernable light came from the heavenly glow of his three companions.

"So what do we do?" he asked. "Knock?"

A familiar voice answered from behind the huge metal gates. "You are always welcome here Woodchopper."

The gates slowly began to swing open.

"It is close to the time of the prophecies. My armies are strong now. Even I could not have imagined how evil mankind would become. They have exceeded my wildest dreams and filled my kingdom until now I have to expand.

The Woodchopper tried to peer through the darkness into the now fully opened gates. He saw nothing, but sensed an unimaginable evil waiting to charge out into the cosmos.

Behind his three companions he heard a rustling sound. It grew louder and louder. Behind him he could see the whole, flat inhospitable landscape fill up with luminous winged creatures; each one carried a spear and a shield and Michael stood at their head.

"Here is your axe." He turned to see Gabriel holding out a magnificent golden double-headed woodchopper's axe.

"Come take up your positions here by me," said Michael to his three companions.

"Your last chance Woodchopper, come with me, rule the universe by my side."

The massive red torso walked out on cloven hooves. The noise of impatient evil crackled out from the gates behind him.

The Devil looked out at the angelic army before him and sighed. "It is time."

The Woodchopper's fear began to ascend unbearably and his whole body trembled in terror as the hideous hordes of Hell came screaming through the gates. Raphael laid a reassuring hand on his shoulder before racing forward to meet the Demonic divisions flying headlong toward them.

Angels and demons fought hand to hand, none giving ground. Angelic spears pierced hard, muscular monstrous bodies, the stench of dying demons threatened to overpower Graeme's senses.

"It is the smell of victory!" shouted Michael to Graeme as another demon fell at his feet.

Graeme the Woodchopper advanced through the confusion and destruction of the battle. He swung his axe and a gargoyle-like head rolled to the ground at his feet. A talon caught him on the shoulder and sent him reeling. Raphael caught him before he could fall.

He lurched headlong back into the fray.

On and on they fought. Time had no meaning in this black soulless plain and the Woodchopper briefly wondered whether they had been fighting for hours, years or even centuries.

The fallen forms of both demons and angels lay across the battlefield, but there was no decrease in the ferocity of the fighting.

"They are falling back!" Gabriel's shout echoed across the vast wasteland.

"After them!" Michael cried.

The Woodchopper's axe fell across the back of a retreating demon. The foul odour was now familiar to his nostrils.

The gates of Hell closed and Michael and his heavenly army destroyed the demons left outside.

"Is that it?" asked the Woodchopper.

Michael peered around suspiciously. Graeme saw Gabriel approaching and in the distance he could see Raphael treating the injured.

"Fall back!" shouted Michael urgently. "Regroup, it isn't over!"

Gabriel and the Woodchopper took up positions around the injured. Michael turned back toward the gates, just in time to see them fling open and another army charge headlong toward the angels.

This army was different. Graeme recognized the hopelessness and despair surrounding the souls now pouring out of Hell.

This was the army of the damned, all driven insane by never ending torture and no hope of escape. They poured out of the gates in a tormented torrent.

Michael's voice carried above the crescendo. "We cannot destroy these! They must be driven back through the gates."

The angels moved out and began to surround the unfortunate souls pouring out of Hell. They turned away from the luminous angelic forms hiding their faces in shame.

Graeme the Woodchopper positioned himself close to the gates themselves in the hope of sighting one of the Pendleton's.

Gabriel moved up beside him. "There is nothing you can do for them. Their only hope now lies in the prayers of your friend."

"There!" Graeme pointed toward the small frame of a woman, her exposed flesh striated by the tearing of countless talons.

The Archangel looked to where the Woodchopper was pointing and saw the woman rush into the blistered arms of her husband.

Graeme the Woodchopper put down his axe and threw himself into the retreating crowd. Gabriel saw the soul of a young man fell him before he could reach his two friends.

Gabriel was about to go after him when he saw the winged outline of Michael swoop down and lift the Woodchopper out of the sea of lost souls heading back toward the gate.

He saw Graeme point toward Roger and Linda huddled together in the distance. Michael shouted and another winged figure swooped down over the Pendleton's. Gabriel smiled as he saw the two Archangels carrying their loads toward him.

Graeme rushed over to his two friends. Both looked bewildered and fearfully at the Woodchopper.

"Linda! Roger! It's me, Graeme!"

Roger was the first to recover. "G…Graeme," he stammered.

Raphael's wings encompassed them both. "Come with me everything will be well now."

The Archangel turned to Graeme. "You can tell your friend his prayers have been answered."

Graeme collapsed down onto the ground; exhaustion overwhelming him in an instant. He heard Gabriel's voice as he drifted into a deep sleep.

"Rest now Graeme the Woodchopper you have done well in the eyes of God." He opened his eyes one

last time and saw the majestic figure of Michael
hovering above him.

❊

"Graeme!" Tony called up the narrow staircase of the
cottage. He called again, but when there was no answer
he made his way quickly up to the guestroom.

The note lay on the bedside table. He read it with a
mixture of annoyance and sadness.

"What was so important he couldn't have woke me to
say goodbye," Tony muttered to himself.

❊

Tony continued with his work and went to Mass on
Sundays. Each day he expected a telephone call or email,
even a letter from his friend, but nothing came. He spoke
to Father McCreadie about his concerns and the Father
agreed to contact the Abbot at the retreat Graeme said
he was going to.

"He has never heard of your friend, and there has
certainly been no one of that name on retreat there," said
the Father concernedly.

Tony sighed and walked to the window of the priest's
house. He looked out onto the road.

"Where have you gone this time my friend," he
whispered to himself.

"Shall we call the police?" asked the priest.

Tony turned back to face Father McCreadie seated on
a leather armchair. "Wherever he's gone, he did not want
me to know about it."

Tony sat down on the chair a few yards to the left of
where the Father sat. "He asked me to pray for him and
not to doubt, so I guess I have to keep the faith and trust
that all will be well."

"Will you look for him again?"

"No Father. My book has received some critical acclaim and I have been offered a research post at Dr Pendleton's old university."

"You'll be returning to America then," said the priest in a lilting Irish brogue. "Don't forget to keep up your attendance at Mass. Academia can be the biggest challenge of all to faith."

"I promise I will Father."

The priest stood up. "Come." The two men knelt before a small shrine in the corner of the room. "Let's say a prayer for your future and for all the friends you've lost."

*

Tony settled into university life and his research and teaching went well.

He didn't keep his promise to Father McCreadie and, as his studies in comparative religion progressed so his attendance in Mass decreased.

He eventually settled into a comfortable intellectual agnosticism. There had been no contact with Graeme and he avoided thinking too much about Linda's death.

It was superstition and ignorance that had destroyed Linda the same way it had destroyed the countless numbers sacrificed on the Aztec altars. And it was the same foolish preoccupation with the supernatural that sent Graeme off to God knows where.

On a cold winter's morning in mid December 2012 he left his apartment and hailed a taxi to the PBS television studio.

*

It was hot under the study lights and Tony could feel a trickle of sweat trace its way down his spine.

"Are you ready to start?" Asked the man in the expensive suit sitting opposite him.

"Yes" Tony replied. He lifted up a glass of water from the small table between them and drank deeply.

"On tonight's program we have the well-known academic, Professor Altredo," the speaker paused as the studio audience clapped, "who is going to discuss the speculation concerning December 21st."

The speaker turned toward Tony. "Well Professor, is the world going to end next week?"

"It seems that many disparate cultures suggest this to be the case."

"Do you have some examples?"

"They are all quite well-known now."

"In no small part to your own work Professor."

Tony smiled, nodded shyly and continued. "The Mayan Long Calendar, the hexagrams of the I Ching, the end of the Kali Yuga, all these in some part or in some way see this year's Winter Solstice as an end. Some Christians have even given it as the date for the start of Armageddon."

"A compelling case for the end of the world then?" asked the interviewer.

Tony ignored the question and continued. "The Egyptians, the Aztecs, the Sumerians, they all busied themselves with the day to day minutiae of living. Yet they all constructed stories to enable them to come to terms with the transient nature of their existence. And their civilizations did indeed come to an end. Sometimes through their own fault, but also sometimes by natural disasters."

"Which they interpreted in religious terms," added the interviewer.

"Stories of floods, fire from the sky all the usual culprits, but somehow most of them prophesied some important event on this Winter Solstice. Even our rational scientists recognize that the astronomical alignment may have some effect."

"How so?" the interviewer asked.

"NASA has determined we are going to experience the next big solar cycle shortly. It is to take place sometime during 2012. They have labelled it Solar Cycle 24 and are expecting a massive increase in solar storms. This will have an effect on satellite communications, GPS, cell phone signals that sort of thing."

"But we've experienced these before," stated the interviewer.

"They expect these to be the most intense since records began. Also they expect an increase in meteor activity."

Tony poured himself another glass of water. "And now that we know there is a supermassive black hole at the centre of the galaxy, we can calculate the date for the alignment between the earth and the Sun and this galactic phenomenon as due to take place on December 21st. If we consider that this is likely to create an effect on the magnetization of our entire solar system and that solar storms also have a geomagnetic effect, then there may well be a physical effect on the Earth."

"Such as?"

"Earthquakes, tsunamis, volcanic eruptions, indeed many of the things mentioned in biblical apocalyptic texts."

"It could just be another false alarm, like the Y2K scenario when all computer programs were supposed to fail," suggested the interviewer.

"And I am inclined to agree with you on that. I think there may be an increase in natural disasters and some possible small-scale satellite interference, but we are in danger of transposing all our archetypal fears onto this one date.

Solar Cycle 24, as I have just said, hasn't been given a specific date and is likely to build up and decrease over time. Even the Mayan calendar can be interpreted as ending on a different date."

"We are all falling into the mindset of millennialism. Is that what you're saying?"

"Yes, fundamentalists and doomsday merchants the world over are having a field day."

The listener turned his chair around to face a camera in the distance. "I think you will all agree that Professor Altredo's critique of the 2012 doomsday prophecies is fascinating."

He swung back to face Tony. "Would you care to give us your version of the future beyond next week's Winter Solstice?"

Tony drew breath and began to speak again. "Since we have lived in caves humanity has feared what it doesn't understand and it has created elaborate myths to explain what has often seemed like the unexplainable. Now we can give explanations for the calamities that befall us from time to time, but we still persist in viewing these events through the looking glass of our own unconscious archetypal realities."

It was Tony's turn to engage the camera. "Each person, each passing culture or civilization attempts to integrate itself with the impermanence of existence and each create metaphors to link themselves back to something beyond this mortal coil, this veil of existence."

Tony paused for effect.

"I think we should all stop chasing metaphors and get on with living."

Applause rose up from the studio floor.

✳

Tony walked out of the television studio and down the New York street. In a coffee shop across the road two handsome young men in black coats sat at a window table watching him pass by. They saw Tony pull his collar up against the biting cold of the wind blowing across from the adjacent Avenue.

A bald-headed little old man walked to the table carrying a tray with three coffees. "He didn't keep his promise to Father McCreadie," he said in a matter of fact manner.

"To hide the Truth it is best to surround it with falsehoods," said the man with the long fair hair.

"And the Enemy knows this," said the other young man seated at the table. "Tony has been duped by the Devil."

EPILOGUE

21st December 2012,
Rome:

The young priest ran up the stairs, taking them two at a time. He grabbed the handrail at the top and pulled himself around to the left of the landing. Two nuns walking in front of him stepped quickly out of the way as he rushed past. He knocked the door in front of him loudly three times in rapid succession.

"Come in. It's open," echoed an authoritative voice from inside the spacious office.

"He has been found," said the priest breathlessly.

The Cardinal stood up to his full height of five foot eleven and ran his fingers thoughtfully through a head of silver hair before replacing his zucchetto.

"Bring him here."

The priest hurried back down the wide straight staircase.

The Cardinal stood before the crucifix on the wall behind his desk; he crossed himself solemnly and made his way toward the papal apartments.

✳

Los Angeles:

"It's a boy," the midwife exclaimed joyfully.

The cries of the infant filled the small room of the downtown Los Angeles apartment. The plump old nurse wrapped the baby tightly in a blanket and handed it to its mother. She looked at her watch to record the time of the birth. It was eleven minutes past three in the morning. The streetlights outside flickered, briefly throwing the room into darkness.

"That's odd," commented the midwife as she looked at the street lamp outside. "Must be a power surge or something."

She turned back toward the mother and child. "I noticed some marks on the back of his head."

Margaret lay the baby down carefully and looked malevolently up at the woman.

Lightning Source UK Ltd.
Milton Keynes UK
12 October 2010

161113UK00001B/2/P